# THE REST

## GHOST SQUADRON
## 3

AUDEAMUS

# ERIC THOMSON

# Die Like the Rest

Published in Canada
By Sanddiver Books Inc.
ISBN: 978-1-989314-43-2

Sanddiver
Books

# — One —

Some nights make everyone miserable. Many are even worse. In Major Curtis Delgado's opinion, this one belonged to the second category, but only because a third option didn't exist. For a moment, he considered inventing a new term that might adequately describe a night so dark, so damp, with the air so thick thanks to monsoon-like rain but found his imagination didn't quite stretch that far.

In short, it was the perfect night for a raid, the sort with weather his instructors in basic training, on the Pathfinder course, and the command sergeant course considered optimum in helping catch an enemy by surprise. Of course, if the opposition was blind, deaf, and miserable, the raiders couldn't be in a much different state. Both moved through the dense rain forest, low-lying swamps, and over rocky outcrops under a thick carpet of black clouds at oh-dark-thirty, their sensors rendered myopic by the raging downpours, gales of wind, and the chameleon armor worn by both friend and foe. Helmet visors struggled to give searching eyes a coherent picture in such conditions, and no one saw more than a few meters in any direction, less among the ancient trees.

Delgado, officer commanding Ghost Squadron's Erinye Company, and his winger, Sergeant Carl Kuzek, found the designated observation post on the heights surrounding a shallow, broad valley bisected by a narrow, albeit lazy, mud-bottomed river. As he crawled between boulders covered by moss that likely predated the arrival of the first humans, Delgado wondered why he was bothering. Even from this perch, he couldn't begin to spot the hundreds of troopers below. He might as well have stayed at the rendezvous position with his reserve troop and company first sergeant. The three troop leaders conducting the raid on a string of enemy hides would either succeed or not, and there was nothing he could do to change the outcome. Once they'd vanished into the forest an hour earlier, they were essentially on their own.

At best, if the plan to infiltrate the enemy positions, set explosive charges, and extract without being spotted succeeded, he'd see and hear those charges going off at the right time, which was in just under two hours. If they failed, he'd spot defensive gunfire much earlier. It depended on how good their opponents were by now and how well they'd learned the lessons inflicted by Ghost Squadron over the previous weeks.

Like many Special Forces officers, Delgado came up through the ranks and went from command sergeant leading a troop to captain in charge of a four-troop company. It meant he was older than most captains in a line regiment but vastly more experienced. Yet, the one thing he would never get used to was waiting while his troop leaders carried out their missions. He wished he could hand back his commission at times like these, put up the six stripes and crossed swords of a command sergeant again, and jump back into the middle of things. But Delgado's commanding officer, Colonel Zack Decker, another old mustang who started his career as a private, had plans for him, despite the fact he'd often confessed to feeling the same way. And Admiral Talyn, whose division within Naval Intelligence made liberal use of the 1st Special Forces Regiment to carry out black ops, nurtured plans for both.

At least, he reminded himself, the light combat armor they wore kept out the damp chill and the rain. And the smell of rotting vegetation, animal droppings, and mold. He could only imagine how his professional ancestors managed before technology made challenging environments more bearable.

Delgado composed himself, eyes on the valley, knowing that Kuzek was watching his back, and waited to see if his plan would succeed. If those were ordinary foes, he'd not even wonder, except about the unknown unknowns that derailed even the best schemes, but they represented something new.

As he settled into a quasi-meditative state, Delgado experienced the eerie sensation of sinking into an isolation tank, his senses dulled by the white noise of rain drumming on tree leaves and his helmet and the impenetrable darkness. The first click over the company frequency startled him, and he checked the time on his visor's heads-up display. It meant the first of the three troops had set its charges and exfiltrated from the enemy hide.

Five minutes or so later, Delgado picked up another click, signifying two out of three were on the way home, and he allowed himself to hope for a clean sweep. Alas, it was not to be. No sooner did the thought occur to him that the treetops to his right, almost at the valley's eastern end, were briefly outlined by gunfire.

Within moments, he heard three clicks in a row, the signal that Charlie Troop, whose objective it was, ran into enemy resistance and was withdrawing rather than engage in a firefight with three times their number. Delgado knew the enemy troops in that hide were even now rousing their comrades in the other locations via radio, which meant a change of plans. They would no longer blow their charges simultaneously since the element of surprise was gone.

Delgado flicked on his helmet radio. "Fire in the hole. I repeat, fire in the hole."

Seconds later, the first set of explosions lit up the valley to his left, then another in the center as Bravo and Delta Troops activated remote detonators. A third came several heartbeats later at some distance from the target, proving Charlie Troop was scattering its charges and using them to cover the withdrawal. But the enemy would not pursue the most highly trained Marines in the known universe through dense forest in total darkness anyhow. They'd learned Ghost Squadron laid hasty ambushes like no one else to cut down pursuers.

The valley fell silent just as quickly as it woke, all illumination gone as if the short, intense violence of a night raid moments earlier never happened.

Just before daybreak, Erinye Company's Marines, tired but satisfied, climbed aboard the dropships waiting for them at the rendezvous. After a short flight, they landed on Fort Arnhem's main parade square, climbed out, and formed in three ranks under First Sergeant Hak.

To Delgado's surprise, Colonel Decker and Lieutenant Colonel Josh Bayliss came through the regimental HQ's main doors and headed for him. Both were smiling contentedly.

"What say you, Curtis?" Decker asked in a booming voice when he came within earshot.

"That two out of three isn't bad?" Delgado grinned as he saluted his regimental commander. "They're getting better with every training cycle."

"Who's that?" Bayliss cocked an eyebrow at the younger man. "Your Erinyes or our new comrades from the 1st Battalion, Marine Light Infantry?"

"The latter, sir. I don't know that we can do much more to improve their capabilities as a Tier Two Special Forces unit. I am looking forward to Isaac Dyas' after-action report on how the MLI caught him before he laid his charges."

"Luck, most likely. But I agree. The 1st MLI is pretty much up to the standards set by General Martinson, and more importantly, by us. I'd be glad to have them at my back, covering us while we work black ops with them." Bayliss glanced at Decker. "Agreed, sir?"

The big man nodded. "Agreed. Well done, Curtis."

"Yes, well done." Bayliss studied the Marines standing patiently by the dropships, waiting for orders. "Sort yourself out, eat breakfast in the cafeteria, and once you've done your hot wash, you can send them off for the weekend a few hours early. I'll see you in my office for the after-action report at thirteen hundred."

"Yes, sir."

# — TWO —

The following Monday morning, a smiling Curtis Delgado stuck his head through Lieutenant Colonel Joshua Bayliss' open office door.

"You summoned me, sir?"

Tall, muscular, with short red hair framing a sharp, pale-skinned face, he didn't seem old enough to be a Special Forces major, certainly not compared to weathered warhorses like his squadron and regimental commanders.

When he noticed Colonel Decker in one of the chairs around the small conference table, he amended his question. "You summoned me, *sirs?*"

"We did." Ghost Squadron's commanding officer pointed at the chair next to Decker. "Close the door and sit."

As he complied, Delgado grimaced theatrically.

"Nothing good ever happens when both of you want to speak with me together."

Decker patted him on the shoulder.

"Then you'll love the mission we're about to lay on Erinye Company."

"I remember the last time you called me into this office for a new tasking. And based on that, my gut tells me I won't like what I'm about to hear, Colonel."

"I thought you enjoyed the little jaunt to Earth."

Delgado let out an amused snort.

"The trip had its moments, but Erinye Company isn't made for that sort of thing. Fortunately, we carried out a proper job on the way back. It cleansed the palate nicely. Dare I ask what this next one is, or should I put in my notice of resignation?"

Decker tilted his head to one side and gave him a disapproving look.

"Admiral Talyn would be crushed if you walk out on the regiment. She's become quite fond of the Erinyes and their talent for adjusting to any situation or mission."

"When you lay it on this thick, I really know I won't like what's coming, sir."

Decker winked at Delgado. "Want to bet?"

"I've learned betting with you, or Colonel Bayliss, is a losing proposition, sir. But please, go ahead and tell me about Erinye Company's fate."

As if a switch had been thrown, both Decker and Bayliss lost their amused expressions.

"What follows is top secret special access, codename *Phalarope*. As usual, nothing about this mission is to be discussed beyond the confines of Erinye Company."

Delgado, now equally serious, nodded. "Understood."

"Did you ever hear of an installation by the name Tyrell Station?"

The younger officer took on a thoughtful expression, then shook his head.

"No."

"It's a Fleet-owned mining operation on an airless planet in the Rim Sector, specifically in the otherwise uninhabited Keros system."

A frown creased Delgado's forehead.

"I didn't know the Fleet operated mines, sir."

"It's a relatively recent development to gain greater control over the extraction and refining of strategic metals and rare earths used in warship and weaponry manufacture. Tyrell is a former Assenari Mining installation that's been in operation for a long time. However, the only actual change is a naval officer overseeing the chief administrator and the security arrangements. Instead of private guards, a Marine company polices and protects the place. The folks operating the mine and smelter and most of the support staff are from Assenari under contract to the Fleet."

A look of dismay replaced Delgado's frown.

"No. Don't tell me we're going to Tyrell as overpaid and over-trained rent-a-cops."

The grin splitting Decker's square face could have lit up the darkest of nights.

"Tyrell is an interesting operation. Interconnected modules that can be detached from each other and airlifted by a small starship when ore veins play out. Remove the humans, seal the modules, detach them, move to a new location, reassemble, and off they go. The current location has been mined long enough that it's due for another move within eighteen to twenty-four months."

"With due respect, sir, you're not answering my question."

Decker's grin widened as Delgado let out a long groan.

"Must I? Really?"

"Why always us?"

"Because you're good at adapting to anything, Curtis. And right now, you're the best I have for the job."

"Give it to a company from the 42nd Marines. I'm sure they'd be glad to leave Caledonia for a bit."

Bayliss chuckled. "Funny you should mention the 42nd."

"Here it comes," Delgado said in a theatrical whisper while rolling his eyes. Then, in a louder voice. "May I know why we're going to Tyrell as a security detail from the 42nd instead of wearing the winged dagger?"

Decker raised a finger.

"Yes. So, listen closely."

"I'm all ears."

"The real reason why the Fleet forced Assenari to sell Tyrell isn't because our superiors desperately want control over raw material supplies, but that's a nice add-on. The same applies to other facilities and properties the Fleet bought in recent times. You've no doubt read somewhere in the intelligence briefs I circulate that countless ammunition and ordnance depots from the Second Migration War remain undiscovered because the records were lost."

Delgado nodded. "Sure. Apparently including a number with weapons of mass destruction that were banned on pain of death after the war."

"A while ago, intelligence came across incomplete data about several of the lost depots, and one of them is located on Keros, in the general vicinity of Tyrell, exact location unknown. Or at least it was when the records were uncovered. Assenari was persuaded to sell, and when we took over, the mining scout droids used to sniff out new ore veins quietly received an addition, a droid programmed to find the depot. Three days ago, it did, and immediately acted on its programming by sending an encrypted message directly to HQ with images of the depot's contents. Of course, it couldn't exactly operate without Tyrell's commanding officer knowing, but part of the programming was placing a top secret special access restriction on the find. However, while he knows about the depot's existence, no one on Keros is aware of its contents. We, on the other hand, are in the know because the images showed clear markings."

A faint smile crossed Delgado's lips. "Is this where I'm supposed to ask what the droid found?"

Decker nodded, smiling. "Yes, it is."

"So, what's in that ammo bunker?"

"Our worst nightmare. Biological and chemical warfare payloads. And it's in a spot near where Tyrell is likely to relocate during its next move."

"Oh, goodie." Delgado shook his head. "The sins of the past come to haunt us. I shudder at thinking what evil beings might do with such things. But why is the Admiral sending us there instead of making sure the current garrison keeps an eye on the depot until someone retrieves its contents and renders them harmless?"

"Because we suspect either Tyrell or, more likely, HQ has a leak, Curtis. We never found every last Black Sword traitor. Word came from our friend Miko in Geneva less than a day ago that the *Sécurité Spéciale* got wind of an exciting development in the Rim Sector. Considering what's happening these days, Intelligence decided the probability it's related to the ammo bunker was high enough we couldn't ignore the threat."

"Seen. Those bastards will want to retrieve the forbidden ordnance before we make it vanish. The Almighty knows what they may do with that nasty stuff, but it can't be good."

Josh Bayliss tapped his index finger against the side of his nose.

"And if worse comes to worst, the resident Marine company won't be capable of keeping them away until Fleet HQ organizes a retrieval operation, simply because they've not been exposed to the realities of our fallen galaxy. They neither know about the depot, nor can they be told, and they don't have experience dealing with the *Sécurité Spéciale* and its hired goons. You and the Erinyes, on the other hand…" Ghost Squadron's commanding officer left the rest of the sentence unspoken.

"When do we leave?"

"You're at twelve hours' notice to move from this moment on," Bayliss said. "The Admiral is organizing transport as we speak. It'll be whatever is in orbit now or will arrive within the next day. Prepare your Erinyes. You should receive the necessary insignia making you H Company, 3rd Battalion, 42nd Marine Regiment shortly. And yes, their CO knows the 1st SFR will re-badge a company to the 42nd for an unspecified operation of limited duration. That way, if questions land on his desk, he can at least back our story while making it clear H Company is on a classified task. Colonel Decker spoke with him personally just before we called you up."

Decker fished a data wafer from his black tunic's left breast pocket and placed it on the table in front of Delgado.

"Everything you need to know about Tyrell Station. Digest what's on the wafer, discuss the mission with your people and let Josh know when you're ready to back-brief us. Needless to say, this is another one which interests Grand Admiral Larsson personally."

"Story of my life, sir." Delgado stood. "It shouldn't take long."

"Dismissed."

Once back in the corridor, he pulled out his communicator and called First Sergeant Hak.

"What's up, Skipper?"

"Assemble the command team in the squadron conference room, stat."

"Wilco."

"Delgado, out."

By the time Delgado arrived, Hak and Command Sergeant Rolf Painter, who led Alpha Troop, were already there. In quick succession, the other troop leaders — Ejaz Bassam, Isaac Dyas, and Faruq Saxer of Bravo, Charlie, and Delta Troops, respectively — along with Sergeants First Class Metellus Testo and Enrique Bazhukov, Erinye Company's operations and quartermaster sergeants filed in.

When they were seated, Delgado looked around the table. "What follows next is top secret special access, codename *Phalarope*."

Everyone present was intimately acquainted with TSSA designations since Ghost Squadron never operated under any lesser classification, and they merely nodded.

As he retrieved the data wafer from his tunic pocket and placed it in one of the conference table's readers, he relayed what Decker and Bayliss told him.

When he fell silent, Hak grimaced. "I thought I'd heard it all, Skipper, but standing guard on an old, forgotten, weapons of mass destruction cache is a new one."

"Saves us from endlessly playing practice dummies for the divisional buildup, Top," Sergeant Painter said. "At this point, a mission, any mission, will be more interesting than handing the MLI their collective heads time after time."

"True. Although they've come a long way since their first lesson courtesy of Erinye Company."

"Right. Let's see what we're facing." Delgado's fingers tapped the reader, and the room's primary display came to life with the image of a planet labeled Keros.

"Airless, in a system with no habitable planets. The scientists say it once had an atmosphere and could probably support life. The crust is unusually rich in strategic minerals, especially around Tyrell Station. Tyrell gets its oxygen and water from underground ice veins."

A schematic of the mining and smelting installation appeared.

"Pretty primitive, on a par with most such operations in uninhabitable places. The actual work is done by Assenari Mining Corporation under contract with the Fleet. There are four-hundred and fifty civilians — miners, smelter operators, support personnel, and administrators — and one company of Marines to provide security. It's commanded by a Naval Engineering captain, a four-striper, but an Assenari chief administrator runs the place except for security."

As Delgado ran through the various views of the installation, Sergeant Testo let out a low whistle.

"That thing is huge. And it can be disassembled and moved? Impressive."

Delgado nodded. "Whenever they exhaust the ore veins within reach. It's already shifted several times over the decades. Let's see what it says here. Mining and smelting operations run twenty-four hours a day, seven days a week. Workers wear pressure suits in the mines because the shafts and galleries are airless. One ship visits every fourteen days to pick up refined product shot into orbit by a giant railgun. It also lands fresh workers and supplies and takes those whose tour is over back home."

"Sounds like real fun." Command Sergeant Saxer made a face. "Must drive the Marine garrison mad. How long do they stay?"

"It says three months at a time."

"By the Almighty, I hope we don't stay a full three months."

Delgado gave him a shrug. "We'll be there until everything is removed and spend our days carrying out the usual garrison duties. Which could mean knocking rowdy mine operators over the head if they don't calm down. And, oh. It'll be as H Company, 3rd of the 42nd, not as Erinye Company."

"Masquerading as line infantry. Excellent." Hak let out a soft groan and rolled his eyes.

A lazy grin crossed Delgado's features. "You may recall my favorite principle of war, Top. Can't use it if we show potential enemies right away that we're not ordinary troopers."

"I suppose so."

"Let's talk gear."

Delgado turned to Sergeant First Class Testo and his comrade, Bazhukov.

"Draw a tactical AI from regimental stores. I'd rather not rely on Tyrell Station's system, just in case it's been compromised. We'll set up our own parallel network and node constellation. See what ammo and supplies the garrison already has — it's supposed to be on the data chip." He tapped the reader. "We should bring two sets of small arms and munitions, non-lethal for policing and our regular ordnance for combat."

Bazhukov nodded. "So needlers and scatterguns, then."

"While the mine is probably well equipped with explosives, detonators, and the like, I also want us to bring our own demolition kits so we can fashion devices that suit combat needs, especially triggers and control mechanisms."

Another nod. "Got it."

"Alright, everyone. Go through the material we have. We'll reconvene right after lunch and go through questions, concerns, and comments. I plan on back-briefing Colonel Bayliss and Decker at sixteen hundred."

Delgado stood. "Dismissed."

# — Three —

Shortly after twenty-two-hundred hours that evening, four large personnel shuttles with Fleet Auxiliary markings, their position lights on and flashing, punched through the low cloud cover and slowly descended for a landing on Fort Arnhem's parade square. There, Erinye Company waited in three ranks, by troop, each Marine carrying a duffel bag and a heavy backpack and wearing pressurized battle armor.

All had their visors up, so they could enjoy a few more minutes of fresh air before spending the coming weeks or even months breathing the recycled sort.

Containers at the edge of the parade ground turned landing strip held ammunition, extra equipment, spare weapons and parts, and a dozen demolition kits. They, and what the Marines carried, would be the sum total of Erinye Company's holdings for this mission, along with whatever the garrison armory in Tyrell contained.

Moments before the shuttles from CFA *Carentan* landed, Lieutenant Colonel Bayliss appeared out of nowhere and headed for Curtis Delgado, standing to one side with First Sergeant Hak. Both stiffened when they noticed him.

"Good evening, sir." Delgado saluted.

"Ready and raring to go?"

"You know us, Colonel. Footloose, fancy-free, and always in the mood for a good fight."

"Colonel Decker and Admiral Talyn send their best wishes. She wanted to come up and see you off in person, but she was briefing the Grand Admiral on Tyrell Station at twenty-one hundred, with Colonel Decker joining in from his office. Apparently, they're still at it. Otherwise, he'd be here with me."

Delgado guffawed. "The Grand Admiral is still in the office this late?"

"You'd be surprised how many of the big shots in the Puzzle Palace routinely work longer hours than you and me."

"Good thing I'm not destined to become a general. Pushing paper after sunset isn't my idea of serving the Commonwealth."

"Nor mine, but unless you purposely screw up, there's nothing you can do if the Corps wants to pin a star on your collar. Other than refuse, that is. And refusing promotion generally means early retirement. Then what? Sitting on the dock, fishing?" Bayliss gave the younger man a smile that clearly said, not me.

"Didn't you buy a place south of here — waterfront property in the tropics, if I recall correctly?" Delgado asked, eyes on the shuttles now lowering aft ramps as their thrusters spooled down.

"Sure. And the operative word for that house is vacation, not retirement. At least not in the foreseeable future. The same goes for Colonel Decker and Admiral Talyn, who bought their own place nearby. She has her eyes on the CNI's job and won't let Zack go off by himself. And if he doesn't go, neither will I."

Bayliss paused when he heard Delgado's helmet speakers come to life.

"This is *Carentan* shuttle flight. Passengers and cargo may now board."

Bayliss rapped his knuckles on Delgado's armored shoulder. "Enjoy your mission, Curtis. If someone goes after the payload stash, give them hell."

"Sir." Delgado snapped off another salute. Then, he raised his hand over his head and made a wide, circling motion, the signal to mount up.

Well-practiced as they were, Erinye Company's Marines vanished into the shuttles along with their personal and collective gear, portable containers included, so quickly that Bayliss allowed himself a fatherly smile.

Moments later, the aft ramps rose while thrusters spooled up again. Bayliss watched them lift off and followed the flashing navigation lights until the low cloud cover swallowed the shuttles again.

As always, when seeing off one of his units, he felt a pang of regret that his time leading Marines on missions, combat or otherwise, was over for good. Squadron commanders rarely led from the front nowadays. Operations in the dirty little wars of peace cropping up with alarming frequency were for captains and majors. Of course, that might change if the centralists and their corporate masters upped the ante.

With Erinye Company gone, the entirety of Ghost Squadron was deployed, along with half of B, C, and D Squadrons. The other halves were busy helping the 1st and 2nd Battalions, Marine Light Infantry, and the 2nd Special Forces Regiment ramp up, leaving Bayliss with little to do.

He pulled out his communicator, and, unsure whether Zack Decker and Hera Talyn were still communing with the Grand Admiral, he sent her a brief text message confirming Erinye Company's departure.

**

First Sergeant Hak poked his head through the open cabin door.

"Everyone's settled in, Skipper, and thankfully we're the only passengers. The facilities are way better than what we normally enjoy aboard Savoyard class Q-ships, so it'll be a nice, relaxing cruise."

He pulled a data wafer from the breast pocket of his black battledress tunic.

"Here's the layout of the ship, listing the cabins and their occupants. The working compartments are off-limits, as is the bridge, but I expect the captain will invite you for a tour and at least one meal at his table. You can choose between the passenger's mess or the ship's wardroom. Noncoms and junior ranks will use the passengers' mess. Drinking rules are pretty strict, and they expect us to enforce them. The rest of the details are on there."

Delgado snorted. "Not that our Erinyes are in the habit of getting loaded, so I doubt it'll be a problem."

"One thing, though. The crew members I dealt with gave me the impression they were not overjoyed at this sudden change in plans, which might explain our rather abrupt reception by the hired help. If we're delaying shore leave, you could get an earful from the captain."

Civilians working for the Armed Forces crewed Commonwealth Fleet Auxiliaries such as *Carentan*, a mixed passenger, and freight transport. They weren't covered by the Code of Service Discipline, though they came under their own rules, stricter than those of the regular civil service.

"I'll handle our captain. Have no fear, Top. Make sure Metellus sets up a daily training schedule for us. We'll use the sim facilities this ship offers for more than just fun and games. Ditto for the gym."

"He already started on that, Skipper."

"Right then, First Sergeant, let's take a tour of our little kingdom and see how the peasants are living."

Delgado put away his personal tablet and stood. For a moment, he felt naked wearing battledress without his sidearm, but CFA personnel didn't like passengers carrying weapons aboard their ships. He couldn't really blame them.

Though armed, they were neither designed nor used as operational transports.

**

That evening — *Carentan*, like all Fleet vessels, Navy and CFA, operated on universal time, and they'd arrived in what was the middle of the ship's day — Captain Leung invited Delgado to dine at his table in the wardroom. After settling in, the latter had slept to adjust his internal clock, and he felt sufficiently refreshed for polite conversation.

As Delgado entered the wardroom at the appointed time, a stout spacer in his fifties with black hair and a gray beard stood and held out his hand to greet him. He wore a quasi-naval uniform with merchant rank insignia, the sort where the Navy's executive curl above the top stripe was replaced by a sharply angled lozenge.

"Major, welcome. I'm Yan Leung."

"Curtis Delgado, sir. Thank you for the invitation."

"Please sit." Leung indicated the chair across from his. "I always try to dine with the senior officers from among the passengers on our first night out. You felt us go FTL, I presume?"

"No, sir. I was sleeping. When we lifted off from Fort Arnhem, it was after twenty-two-hundred hours local time, and I'm one of the lucky few who isn't woken up by the transition."

"I understand you're from the 42$^{nd}$ Marines." Leung and Delgado sat back as a steward placed brimming soup bowls in front of them.

"Yes, sir. H Company, 3$^{rd}$ Battalion." Delgado picked up a spoon, intrigued by the soup's subtle aroma.

"First assignment to Tyrell Station?" Leung tasted his and nodded in approval.

"Yes. Is this your first time heading there?"

"Indeed. Any idea what precipitated this sudden assignment? *Carentan* was due for a few weeks in refit when Fleet HQ laid this trip on us — bring you there and take the current garrison home."

Delgado gave him a shrug. "Your guess is as good as mine, sir. Keeping those on the sharp end in the dark is SOP. This is excellent, by the way."

"Thank you. We keep high standards in the galley. Your troopers are enjoying the same food, by the way. And as for being kept in the dark, I've been a Fleet Auxiliary spacer for twenty-five years, and it's always the same. But other than that, I can't complain. How about you, Major?"

"Can't complain either." Delgado gave him a quick grin. "I'm a lifer. This is what I'll do until they put my sorry ass out to pasture once I hit my promotion ceiling, which might already have happened."

"Are you an Academy graduate?"

"Mustang, sir. Made command sergeant and took a direct commission to captain."

"Pardon me for saying so, but you look pretty young for a major who started as a private."

"You know how it is." He made a self-deprecating gesture. "Luck, hard work, and being in the right place at the right time. Mostly the latter."

"And no other officers in your company."

Another grin. "My CO figured I could handle three months of garrison duty by myself. The others are taking advantage of the situation and catching up on their career courses. I'll probably spend my downtime on distance learning. Us mustangs need to do things twice as well as Academy grads to be thought half as good. Fortunately, it's not difficult."

Leung let out a bark of amused laughter that attracted the attention of the wardroom's other occupants — a dozen Fleet Auxiliary officers enjoying quiet meals at four-person tables.

"A man after my own heart, Major. I started as an ordinary deckhand and made my way up as well."

"If it's not impolite to ask, why the Fleet Auxiliary, sir?" Delgado knew little to nothing about the civilian spacers serving aboard non-combat vessels, transporting people and supplies throughout the Commonwealth.

"And not the Navy, you mean?"

"Or the commercial shipping sector."

Leung put on a thoughtful expression as he picked up his fork, speared a chunk of meat, and popped it in his mouth. After swallowing, he took a swig of water.

"There are plenty of spacers in my family tree, some of whom served in the Navy during and after the Shrehari War, so you could say wanting to see the galaxy was in my blood. But I couldn't stomach the idea of boot camp, then trade school, and afterward a five-year hitch under naval discipline. So, once I graduated from high school, I attended one of the merchant spacer training institutes on my homeworld and learned the bosun's trade. When I received my apprentice ticket, I applied to the major shipping lines and the Fleet Auxiliary.

"They replied first and offered a decent billet, which I took right away. Over the years, I climbed up the ranks, earned my watchkeeping certification, went back to school, and earned my master's ticket — paid for by the Fleet, mind you. The rest is history. You could say I made a decent career for myself wearing a diamond rather than a loop, without spending my waking hours focused on cutting operational costs at the behest of a shipping line's head office."

He finished his plate, then said, with a wry smile, "I'm a lifer in the Fleet Auxiliary and glad of it. Even if the Navy can send me haring off in all directions at a moment's notice. But that's part of the game. We'll enjoy our time ashore once we've delivered you and the unit you're replacing."

"So not too many hard feelings aboard?"

"Oh, a fair bit of irritation at first — postponed leave plans will do that — but now that we're on our way, it's just another job for the Fleet. We'll be home with our feet up, watching the sunset, while you're not even a third of the way through your tour in Tyrell Station."

# — Four —

Tyrell Station was stacked along the slope of a sharp rise approximately a kilometer north of a deep canyon that sliced through Keros' surface for over a thousand kilometers from east to west. Mighty mountain ranges marched both north and south of the canyon for hundreds of kilometers before petering out.

The outpost was an extraordinary collection of large, standardized, rectangular modules supported and joined by fragile-looking, spidery struts and tubes. It seemed to sit so precariously on the rugged surface that an observer might think it could slide into the canyon at a moment's notice.

The top level of the installation rose a few stories above the crest and was home to hydroponics modules which ensured a constant supply of fresh air and food. Administrative offices and recreational facilities sat immediately below them. Those modules and the hydroponics were the only part of the installation that received a full twelve hours of sunlight.

Two modules, arranged alongside a flat space of slagged rock, were more prominent than the rest and held the hangar and smelter. A long, spindly, symmetrical construct emerged from the latter at an angle, facing northward — the railgun which sent refined product into orbit for harvesting by the regular supply ship.

As mentioned in the briefing package, four three-hundred millimeter plasma guns, powerful enough to make anything in orbit think twice — the sum total of Tyrell's outer defenses — sat on the heights surrounding the base. Remotely controlled by the operations center, they weren't part of the station proper and could only be accessed by personnel wearing pressure suits.

"You know, Skipper," Sergeant Testo said, staring at the passenger mess primary display along with every other Erinye, "the only sort of attack we can stop with those oversized peashooters is a head-on assault from space. Anyone planning an attack won't be stupid enough to do so, at least not without inside help."

"It'll be a bitch if we end up fighting." First Sergeant Hak grimaced. "Those structures look like they couldn't absorb even the lightest broadside from a sloop."

"Hence the big guns, Top."

Before Hak replied, the public address system came to life.

"Marines, prepare for departure. I say again, Marines, prepare for departure."

As one, Erinye Company's troopers stood and filed out of the mess, headed for their quarters where pressure suits and packed luggage waited.

"And so our pleasure cruise is over," Hak muttered as he followed hard on Delgado's heels. "Oo-rah!"

By the time Delgado entered the hangar, his company was formed in three ranks, suits buttoned up while the troop leaders checked their Marines to ensure those suits were pressurized and the rebreathers working correctly. Luggage and supply containers were already loaded, and as Delgado appeared, Sergeant Kuzek grabbed his bag and marched off toward one of the shuttles.

Delgado watched as, one by one, the troop leaders reported to First Sergeant Hak, confirming everyone was good to go. When all four, plus the company HQ section — first sergeant included — were ready, Delgado shut his visor and put his suit under pressure so Kuzek could run the usual buddy check.

Once the latter slapped his armored shoulder, Delgado raised his hand and made the mount-up signal. The hangar's inner airlocks swung shut at that moment while a red warning light began to strobe.

The last to board, Delgado climbed aboard his assigned shuttle and headed straight for the flight deck, where Hak was already settling into one of the spare jump seats. He felt the vibration of the aft ramp closing through the soles of his armored boots and took the other jump seat.

The pilot, also in a pressure suit, received terse commands over the ship's network from the hangar deck controller as the main space doors opened, leaving a shimmering force field curtain behind to keep the deck's air from escaping. One by one, the shuttles nosed through that curtain and out into space, initiating a lazy spiral downward.

As they lost altitude, Tyrell Station turned into a dazzling array of light, its metallic and transparent surfaces gleaming under the rays of a setting sun. It looked pretty, a bright jewel nestled in the dark, brooding, airless landscape. But that beauty was cold, uninviting, menacing, even, and Delgado felt a faint shiver go up his spine.

He was used to missions on habitable worlds, where he and his Marines need not worry about their air supply and a habitat's pressure integrity. Where they could battle the elements if need be. But a world without an atmosphere was one of the deadliest environments for humans. The slightest mistake might kill, never mind enemy fire.

\*\*

Heavy space doors closed as the last of *Carentan*'s shuttles settled down on the painted landing spot. On one side, a dozen ground vehicles with oversized wheels sat idle under the bright, industrial lighting, along with four tired, old administrative shuttles.

Pressure-suited figures equipped with backpacks, duffel bags, and small arms waited near the inner airlock beside a stack of collective equipment containers. One of them, a man with the three diamonds of a captain on his armored chest, stepped forward, helmet visor raised, and waited patiently for the new arrivals to disembark.

Delgado climbed out of his craft and headed for the man while lifting his own visor. The other officer noticed the oak leaf wreath around his single diamond and sketched a salute as he came near.

"Welcome to the hind-end of the universe, sir. I'm Dave Jerrold, Delta Company, 2nd Battalion, 18th Marines, formerly the CO of the Tyrell Station garrison. You can't imagine how glad I am you showed up before our time here was over. The hardship bonus we receive isn't worth it, as you'll find out in the next forty-eight hours or so."

"Curtis Delgado, H Company, 3rd of the 42nd."

"Caledonia, eh?" A knowing smile crossed Jerrold's tired features. "Can I assume we're handing this place over to you early and unexpectedly because something's afoot? I've heard rumors one of the recon droids found something classified. And if that's the case, might I venture you're not from the 42nd, but another, more secretive unit stationed on Caledonia?"

"You may well think so, but I certainly couldn't comment."

Jerrold winked at Delgado.

"Seen, sir. Mum's the word. Anyway, we've cleared out the barracks, and as you can see, my people are ready to load up the moment yours disembark. You'll find one of Tyrell's admin types standing by that door over there to guide you to your new digs." He offered Delgado a small plastic box. "These are our logs and all the info you'll need.

You'll find time crawls by around here, and nothing ever happens."

"If nothing happens during our tour, then I'll be happy."

"Understood, sir. I'm sure the station commander will fill you in on anything you need to know. A final word of caution. As the saying goes, keep your hand on your wallet, your back against a wall, and don't trust the locals. You'll understand soon enough. Goodbye."

"Enjoy the trip home."

Jerrold saluted, closed his helmet visor, turned on his heels, and headed for *Carentan*'s shuttles where his Marines were loading while Hak formed the Erinyes in three ranks by the inner airlock.

Delgado, who also buttoned his suit up again, watched him go. A few minutes later, a klaxon sounded, the space doors opened, and the shuttles filed out. Once they vanished from sight, Delgado walked over to where a slight, pressure-suited figure stood apart from his Marines, waiting patiently.

# — Five —

"What an ugly place. Sure, I've seen worse, but this has to be among the bottom three."

Hak shook his head in disgust. The Marine barracks were simply a module filled with wire-mesh cubicles stacked five high like the miners' quarters. Each cubicle measured a bare three meters square. It contained only a cot and a small shelf for personal items. Roll-up blinds provided what little privacy there was. Steel ladders welded to the horizontal beams supporting each level gave access to the upper levels.

At one end of the module, as stark as the rest, lay the showers and latrines. While the toilets provided the customary privacy, the showers and sinks were wide open for everyone to see. The command post, fully enclosed, occupied the other end, along with an armory for spare weapons, ammo, and demolition kits. Personal weapons were kept locked up in each trooper's cubicle when not carried. But, if nothing else, the place seemed clean, as befit proper Marine barracks.

Delgado nodded, eying his surroundings.

"No wonder Captain Jerrold wanted to leave this place so fast. Crowded living, no privacy, and no amenities for three months have to be a stretch. Even troopships on long passages offer more comfort. How the hell do civilian workers live like this without losing their minds?"

Hak shrugged. "They must get a much bigger hardship bonus than us. If so, three months in, one week travel, two and a half months at home, one week travel back and do it again until you can retire before the age of fifty. When you look at it that way, it's worth doing."

"Not where I come from, but I understand the attraction."

The first few cubicles on the ground level, close to the command post, were permanently screened off by scrounged sheets of polymer and steel. One was marked Commanding Officer and another First Sergeant. Delgado pushed aside the curtain of what would be his home and walked into what was effectively a suite of three adjoined cubicles, one for sleeping, the other two arranged as an office, complete with a workstation.

Leaving Hak and the troop leaders to sort out the accommodations and settle the company in, he stripped off his tin suit, carefully hung it on pegs set aside for that purpose, locked his weapons in the rack welded to the cubicle wall, and unpacked, which didn't take long.

Then he sat at the metal desk, switched on the workstation, and scanned the data dump Jerrold gave him. Breaking up fights, or preventing them in the first place, dealing with the odd narcotics smuggling case — most were never uncovered, in Delgado's experience — and generally showing the flag seemed to be ninety-nine percent of the garrison's work. Jerrold also ran a few combat scenarios of the repel boarders kind Marines in warships would practice. But that, in essence, was it.

Delgado found the garrison information node and uploaded Jerrold's files so everyone else in the company could read them. He saw that Sergeant Testo had already posted the first patrol assignments, which meant his people would be out and about within minutes.

Before he could think about paying the station commander a courtesy visit, Delgado received a summons to report as soon as possible. He checked his battledress uniform to make sure it was presentable and holstered the needler with non-lethal loads police patrols would carry. Then, he put on his sky blue beret with the silver insignia of the 42nd Marines, a stylized thistle surrounded by a band inscribed with the regimental motto *Nemo Me Impune Lacessit*, No One Provokes Me With Impunity. As mottoes went, Delgado considered it a good one, the sort applicable to their present situation even if it wasn't the Special Forces own *Audeamus* — We Dare.

He called up a three-dimensional holographic map of Tyrell showing his current position and Captain Engstrom's office with a blue line connecting them via several sets of stairs. He could have taken lifts instead but wanted a quick familiarization tour along the way. After memorizing the route, he ducked into First Sergeant Hak's quarters next door.

"I'm headed upstairs to make my manners with the station's CO."

"Roger that, Skipper. Enjoy."

The metal staircases seemed endless, but Delgado met few people since this was the middle of a shift. One-third of the complement would be working, one-third sleeping, and the other third enjoying what little recreational facilities there were.

Those he encountered barely acknowledged his existence. That the Marine garrison now wore a different badge on their berets wouldn't register right away with civilians anyhow. They saw the uniform and dismissed its wearer as just another part of the station's utilitarian tapestry.

The contrast between the lower levels and the administrative modules was striking. Gone were the unpainted steel beams, naked deck planking, and plastic pipes overhead. Carpets in a pleasant light blue shade covered the corridor floor while pastel-colored wall sheets hid the steel walls and ceilings. Delgado even saw potted plants placed at strategic intervals. He bet the brass around here didn't sleep in steel-mesh cubicles either.

Upon arriving in front of a door marked Commanding Officer, he touched the call panel, and it opened silently, revealing a small antechamber where a woman sat at a narrow desk, working. She looked up at him.

"Yes?"

"Major Curtis Delgado for Captain Engstrom."

The woman touched her desktop, and the inner door opened, revealing a large, well-appointed office dominated by a stylish black desk surrounded by soft, comfortable-looking chairs. Three were occupied — two men, one in uniform, and a woman.

"Please go in. The captain is expecting you."

When Delgado walked through the doorway, the large, bearded man wearing a captain's four stripes and executive curl on his tunic collar rose from behind the desk and held out an open hand.

"Welcome, Major Delgado. I'm Nero Engstrom."

Engstrom had a solid grip. However, Delgado thought his smile seemed somewhat forced.

"Pleasure, sir."

The naval officer gestured at a vacant chair.

"Please, take a seat, Major."

Neither of the other two stood. They merely examined Delgado with expressionless eyes, as if he were an inferior ore specimen mistakenly brought back by one of the mining recon drones.

Engstrom gestured at the thin, sallow-faced woman of indeterminate age clad in a severe business suit that seemed out of place. Frown lines and thin disapproving lips gave her a permanent look of supercilious disapproval.

"This is Romana Movane, Chief Administrator, under contract from Assenari Mining."

She nodded once but didn't offer her hand.

"And this is Edgar Limix, the Tyrell shop steward of the Assenari Miners and Smelters' Union."

Limix was a complete contrast to Movane. Delgado wondered how the two related. Broad, heavily muscled, clean-shaven, he wore a pair of used but freshly washed coveralls. His handshake was firm, testing, and Delgado returned the pressure. They locked eyes for a few seconds, and then Limix smiled broadly.

"Pleased to meet you, Major, I'm sure."

Where Engstrom's smile held a hint of uncertainty, even insincerity, Limix seemed like the hard-working, open, honest, and law-abiding miner he probably was. The calluses on his hands and neck proved he wasn't one of those professional unionists so common back on the industrialized planets. Most of them never worked on the shop floor or underground and were politicians rather than defenders of workers' rights. No, Limix showed the signs of doing his shifts at the ore face, alongside the men and women he represented.

"Can I offer you a coffee, Major? Or something stronger?"

"Thanks, sir, but I've ingested my dose of caffeine for the day."

"Did Captain Jerrold brief you before he left?" When Delgado nodded, Engstrom said, "Good. You'll find there's not much for you to do here. Tyrell Station isn't well known and pretty isolated, so it's unlikely we'll ever use those big guns out there." He jerked his thumb over his shoulder at the nearest ridge visible through the transparent aluminum window. "As for internal security, you know that you're the station's provost marshal?"

"Yes, sir."

"Edgar can tell you his people like to party rough when they're off shift, but it rarely gets out of hand. At least by Tyrell's standards. Removed as we are from civilization, things are bound to be different. I suggest you get a feel for the place and our tolerance levels before you knock any heads. In my view, if operations keep going without a hitch, I can tolerate roughhousing."

Limix nodded at Captain Engstrom's words. When the latter stopped for breath, he said, "Of course, your Marines are welcome to socialize with the rest of us. Can't avoid it since there's only one cafeteria and one bar, the *Miner's Reach*. We enjoyed a good relationship with the last batch of Marines, and I'm sure we'll manage just as well with you and yours."

Limix gave Delgado a friendly smile when he finished speaking. Engstrom took over again.

"Major, I expect you to keep me informed of everything you do. Conversely, don't hesitate to call on me if you need anything. As they say, my office door is always open. We three here often eat supper together, and I hope you'll join us. It's our way of keeping on top of things and ensuring the station works smoothly."

"Thank you, sir."

"Just one question, if I may," Movane said, speaking for the first time in a low, raspy voice.

Delgado turned to her. "Please go ahead."

"Why did Fleet HQ replace the garrison before Jerrold and his people finished their three-month tour?"

Delgado shrugged. "I don't know. My regiment received orders for a company to deploy here, and the CO picked mine."

"Aren't companies usually commanded by captains?"

He nodded. "Usually, but sometimes promotions come through before people are reassigned. For instance, in my case, I'll be moving to a major's position on the regimental staff when we're back home."

"I see."

For a moment, Delgado wondered whether Engstrom would broach the matter of the recon drone's classified discovery. He presumed that despite secrecy warnings, both Limix and Movane would be aware something was afoot. He could detect a faint hint of suspicion in the latter's eyes, suspicion he and his Marines relieved Jerrold's company before time because of the unusual event, and that they weren't just another normal, albeit early, rotation.

"Well," Engstrom tapped the desktop once with his fingertips, as if to punctuate the conversation, "I expect you face a lot of work right now, so I won't keep you any longer. We will speak again soon. It was a pleasure meeting you. Please pass our welcome along to your troops."

"Yes, sir. Thank you."

Delgado stood, although none of the others did, and saluted. Then he pivoted on his heels and walked out, feeling their eyes on his back until the office door closed behind him.

Moments after entering the Marine barracks, First Sergeant Hak intercepted Delgado.

"So?"

"It seems this place is being run by a sort of triumvirate." Delgado briefly described Engstrom, Limix, and Movane and recounted the gist of the conversation.

When he finished, Hak nodded knowingly. "Sounds like they might suspect why we're here, or at least this Movane character does. Will you speak with Engstrom privately and discuss the matter?"

Delgado thought about it for a moment, then shook his head. "We already know Tyrell might leak all the way back to Earth. Better if the opposition doesn't receive confirmation about us and our mission."

# — Six —

The *Miner's Reach*, a vast, low-ceilinged space wedged between the administrative levels above, the workers' living quarters below, and the cafeteria to one side, was in full swing as Delgado and his Marines finished unpacking and settling into their new roles. Workers from the beta shift, whose day ended an hour earlier, were enjoying their free time after a challenging eight hours overseeing excavation machinery deep in the bowels of the planet or the smelter as it processed ore.

A handful of Marines, equally off-duty, sat around a table in one of the corners from which they could watch the entire bar and slip out unnoticed if need be. Throbbing, overly loud music from unseen speakers filled every nook and cranny of the industrial-chic decor and made conversation difficult.

The aroma of spilled beer and whiskey fought with that of vat-grown food high in proteins. Gyrating men and women filled the small dance floor while others played various games at crowded tables or simply stared into the void while drinking the tipple of their choice.

Delgado's Marines, who could whoop it up with the best of them in the Pegasus Club back home, were among the latter, save for the empty stares. They considered themselves Erinye Company's recce party, getting a feel for the place where they'd likely be breaking up fights regularly and nursed their beers while studying everyone and everything.

The workers barely looked up when they entered, even though word of a fresh contingent must be making the rounds by now. Same uniforms as before, even if the faces were different. Nobody paid them any attention except for two miners in a corner booth not far from their table.

"Those aren't ordinary Marines like the last batch, Joey." The man who answered to the name Harry shook his head before taking a sip of his drink.

"What do you mean? Marines are Marines. The last batch didn't give us any trouble. Why would this lot?"

"Something about the way they move, the way they're scanning the room, and barely drinking tells me that this isn't the usual sort. I did a hitch in the Corps when I was younger. Guys like that, they're more likely to be something different from simple line infantry. The watchful eyes, Joey, they worry me."

"What does that mean, different from simple line infantry?"

"They remind me of the Pathfinders I once worked alongside. You know, special operations. The toughest, most dangerous fighters in the Commonwealth. The thing is, they spend their time hunting raiders, pirates, rebels, and every sort of scumbag there is. And they nab them too, without fail. The one thing special ops don't do is garrison duty, especially not in a damned mine at the hind-end of the galaxy."

"Doesn't that prove they're not special ops but simply new guys getting the lay of the land?"

Joey slammed back his drink and carefully placed the unbreakable plastic tumbler on the table before him.

"Maybe. Or not. The last batch left early. Never saw that happen since I started my rotations here. I heard this lot is under a major when the others are always run by captains." Harry rubbed his chin with a calloused hand. "You have to wonder, after the rumors that a recon droid found something funky the other day, the sort that made upstairs clamp down on any information coming out."

"So, you think the Fleet sent special operations guys for that?"

"That's what I wonder now that I've seen them up close. They might wear the insignia of the 42nd Marines, but I'll bet my next performance bonus that's not their usual badge. I think we should go see Lyle. If he doesn't know yet what Santa Claus brought us, he needs to find out."

"Who the hell is this Claus guy, Harry? Some sort of Fleet bigshot?"

Harry stared at his friend.

"Seriously? You never heard of him? Talk about missing out, old buddy. Anyway, if my gut feeling is on the money, these guys could be serious trouble."

"The last batch wasn't a problem. They minded their own business."

"And I keep telling you, these aren't regular Marines. They look way more dangerous. Have you ever studied how a predator hunts, like in nature documentaries? Well, that's what they remind me of. If I'm right, they could really bust our chops because they're good, the best in the Corps."

The two miners put on a nonchalant air as they left the bar. But Joey, who was drinking harder than his friend, kept glancing sideways at the Marines, looking for what made them so special. Sure, they came across as tough — muscular, steely gaze, emotionless features — and seemed as if they were eyeing the bar's patrons rather than enjoying themselves. But from there to worrying?

When they reached the main elevators, Harry punched the call button and thrust his hands in his pockets to keep from fidgeting. The chime announcing the arrival of a car caught him by surprise, and he instinctively stepped forward as the doors slid open. Then, he did a double-take and took two steps back.

A pair of Marines, clad in black battledress and tactical harness with holstered needlers, and wearing blue berets with the 42$^{nd}$ Marine Regiment's thistle, stepped out of the car. Both carried scatterguns slung over their right shoulders. Superficially, save for the insignia, they didn't differ from the previous Marines. But the way they moved, the way their eyes seemed to search everywhere, that was different.

Harry quickly recovered, hoping neither of the men noticed his reaction. The senior of the two, a corporal, politely nodded at the two miners as he and his partner walked by. Harry pulled Joey into the elevator car and savagely punched the 'door close' button. He was furious with himself.

When the doors slid shut, and the elevator slipped downwards, he wondered whether his imagination was spinning out of control. Still, he should tell Lyle, just in case he was right, and these weren't the regular brand of Marines rotating through Tyrell every three months.

\*\*

"I must say, Skipper, our temporary command post in the VIP block on Earth was light years ahead of this." Sergeant First Class Metellus Testo grimaced at Delgado as the latter surveyed his new, albeit temporary, domain. "By the way, I swept everything and found no listening devices, so at least there's that."

Three of the command post's four walls were plastered with displays above workstations, but Delgado had to admit that his operations sergeant wasn't indulging in hyperbole. The entire setup screamed cheap security guard station as if the Marines were nothing more than rent-a-cops.

Most of the equipment probably dated back to when Delgado was nothing more than a brand new private and bore plenty of signs it had been subjected to expedient field repairs. In comparison, the gear they'd drawn on Earth had been new and installed to Sergeant Testo's exacting specifications.

"The equipment isn't even the biggest problem," he continued. "Sure, we can watch any of the public spaces from here, and I programmed the tactical AI to alert us if it sees something that needs our attention. But we can't access Tyrell's systems, meaning we're blind to many potential threats and dependent on the station's operations center. And you know how much I enjoy depending on others for my information."

"Is there a way of tapping in with no one catching us doing so?"

A smile spread across Testo's face.

"I was hoping you'd ask, sir. What would you like me to concentrate on?"

"As Master Sun said, 'If you know heaven and know earth, you may make your victory complete.' Give me omniscience, Sergeant, which shouldn't be a problem since you're such a good hacker they sent you to Ghost Squadron. What was it again you did on Starbase 25 that saw you posted out of the 122nd Pathfinders with a boot-print on your backside?"

"Never mind, Major, sir, never mind. Omniscience is probably beyond even my considerable skills. If we want it kept quiet. So how about you list the essential elements of information you figure we need?"

"First thing I need is access to personnel files, logs, reports, and such. The Admiral's people figure the opposition might have at least one operative already in Tyrell, and I wouldn't mind finding out who that could be."

"Read-only access? I can hide that from just about anyone, but I can't hide data manipulation, at least not from an expert."

"Okay, read-only, but give me an out, in case we're stuck doing dirty work."

Testo nodded. "Check."

"Next, I want a copy of internal and external messages sent by anyone other than us. Think you can hide the diversion?"

"That'll be a lot easier than hiding the file access path, especially with the subspace radio messages. What else?"

"Every airlock, elevator, door, and maintenance access hatch on this base has a coded lock, which is monitored and controlled by the main computer. We're supposed to go through the ops center for access to any out-of-bounds section or to seal off any area. Now that's not the right way of running a defensive operation, is it?"

"No kidding, Skipper. It'll take a while, but I can program the main computer to accept a secret access code for every lock, one that won't register with the ops center."

"With one little modification, Sergeant. Have it register the use of our own code on our segregated node. Just an added precaution in case something happens. While you're doing that, the Top and I will modify our predecessors' patrol routes so everyone in the unit walks over every square centimeter of the base. And as the guys are doing their familiarization tours, they'll be updating the schematics. Things must change fast in a mining facility built so it can be moved, and we need to know every detail. It could mean the difference between success and failure if things go sideways."

"You'll send them into the mine shafts as well?"

"Yeah, there too."

"From what I read in the logs, our predecessors never went underground. I'd check with the head digger before barging in, sir."

"I plan on discussing that matter with Chief Administrator Movane shortly. While I'm up in the ivory tower, is there anything else we need?"

"Other than a brand new command post? No. But please don't ask for anything I'll be getting via the station network through the back door. People might become nervous and check up on things when they deny a request. Once our special paths are in place, the chances of being discovered are slim. However, while I'm hacking away, I can be caught red-handed in a snap. And that would be embarrassing as hell."

"Is that how it happened on Starbase 25?"

"No comment, sir."

# — Seven —

"Under no circumstances, Major."

"May I ask why, Chief Administrator?"

Movane's face, never the most cheerful sight at any time, was even more pinched than the day before. His question only deepened the frown and tightened the lips. She remained silent for a few moments, expressionless eyes studying the Marine.

"I think my reasons should be obvious. Your people have absolutely no training underground, let alone in an airless environment. Ore extraction, under such circumstances, presents enough dangers without a bunch of untrained idlers getting underfoot. And it would cut into productivity."

Captain Engstrom, in whose office they were, had remained silent from the start, preferring to let Movane do all the talking. Now, he spoke up in a regretful voice that sounded just a tad insincere to Delgado's ears.

"I'm sorry, Major, but I must agree with Chief Administrator Movane. She's right about the safety considerations, and I can't imagine how the mine galleries would even figure in your defensive planning. Please consider the matter closed. Was there anything else?"

Delgado, who'd expected a refusal, shook his head. "No, sir."

"In that case, you may return to your duties."

The Marine stood, saluted, and turned on his heels. Fortunately, he had another course of action open to him before the sole remaining option meant ruffling a lot of feathers. He hoped that his first impression of the man had been right.

On his way back to the Marine barracks, Delgado left a message in the small Miner's Union cubicle near the *Reach*. Limix was a team boss on the alpha shift and wouldn't be off until sixteen hundred hours. Meanwhile, Delgado had work waiting for him in the command post.

**

Delgado and Hak entered a busy cafeteria for the midday meal and stood in line with the civilian workers as they picked up trays and served themselves at the food dispensers. Afterward, they found an empty corner table from which they could watch the room and sat.

Anything like normal conversation seemed impossible against the background noise of a hundred separate discussions, and they didn't even try. At least the food was good, if plain. It wasn't up to Fort Arnhem's standards, of course, but the hydroponics farm provided fresh greens for everyone.

As before, the station's civilian complement ignored the Marines, deeming them part of the background scenery, automatons who crisscrossed every module, walked up and down every staircase, and took every lift while others toiled. Only once in a while did they do more, and those incidents were over almost instantaneously. The hardship bonuses paid by Assenari were too generous for drunken shenanigans which might land someone on the blacklist and removed from Tyrell forever.

A kilometer beneath them, on Level Fourteen, the members of Team Four, alpha shift, were also enjoying their midday meal. Each Gallery had a portable, pressurized control module from where the operators oversaw the excavation droids and conveyor belts and fixed any mechanical issues that didn't need intervention from the mine's engineering team.

But they spent their shifts in pressure suits anyhow — with the helmet visor up for a modicum of comfort and so they could eat and drink. That way, if the control node lost integrity, they could button up in seconds and return to the station with their integral air reserves and rebreathers. But eight hours in a pressurized suit was a long time, and it was a relatively small, uncomfortable space for three adult humans wearing bulky gear.

The team leader finished his sandwich, downed half a thermos of coffee, and burped, then he leaned back against the bulkhead and looked at Harry after making sure the node's automated voice recorder was off. Technically, he shouldn't be capable of disabling it. Still, it was understood that sometimes people wanted a few minutes of privacy, and the operations center turned a blind eye to brief and infrequent unauthorized breaks.

"Tell me about those Marines again."

"Something's happening, Lyle. These guys differ from the previous batch or any rotation I've seen. Sure, they wear the insignia of the 42$^{nd}$ Marines, a regular line unit, but they remind me too much of the special operations guys I saw when I was in the Corps. They're fitter, leaner, meaner, and their eyes miss nothing. Plus, they're under a major instead of a captain. If that doesn't tell us strange doings are afoot, I don't know what else I can say."

"But you're working on nothing more than a gut feel." Lyle Fournier sounded skeptical.

"When has my gut ever been wrong?"

Joey, the third member of Team Four, snorted derisively.

"Whenever you eat too much spicy food, my friend. Everyone in our block can smell the wrongness."

Harry gave his colleague the rigid digit salute.

Joey blew a kiss at him. "Love you too, buddy."

"Look," Lyle said after downing the rest of his coffee, "it doesn't matter what they are. There's only so much any Marines can do around here besides busting heads when idiots drink too much and go stupid. No patrol ever left the habitat and entered the shafts. That old sourpuss Movane doesn't want any Fleet idiots in the mine, and whatever she wants, Engstrom gives her. I wouldn't be surprised if she was running her own little racket, the way she acts. If it makes you happier, we'll be more cautious for a while, but we won't become rich by jumping at shadows. If the Fleet suspected anything, it would send military police, not special operations people. And we're not even sure they're anything more than regular jarheads who happen to look sharper than the usual Marines sent here. I, for one, am planning on a comfortable retirement running my own restaurant after a few more tours here, and I won't let anything interfere. Capisce?"

They nodded at him one after the other. "Understood."

"Alright then, back to work, guys."

Although he appeared unconcerned in front of his cronies, Lyle Fournier was a worried man. He knew Harry from way back and trusted his gut instincts more than those of anyone else. Sure, these new Marines who took over the rotation earlier than usual might simply be here because of the rumors that one of the recon droids found something unusual. However, they could still ruin his plans if they were sharper than regular troopers.

Surely, they wouldn't stumble on his operation and shutter it now. Only a few more shipments, and they would be home free while the penalty for losses was more than he cared to contemplate.

The rest of the shift went by quickly enough, but even Joey saw Lyle's mind wasn't on his work. While the former didn't connect the lunchtime conversation with the team leader's unaccustomed absent-mindedness, Harry caught on, and a worried Lyle was cause for concern. Harry knew things Joey didn't. He'd met Jannika Hallikonnoen and knew what kind of hold she exerted on Lyle and their little money-making operation.

# — Eight —

Delgado's communicator chimed, interrupting Sergeant Testo's progress report on infiltrating Tyrell's computer core.

"Delgado here."

The miner's honest face appeared.

"Ed Limix, Major. You left a note for me at the Miner's Union."

"Yes, thanks for calling back so fast, Mister Limix." The call-back had been prompt — alpha shift came up from the ore face a scant half hour ago. "I'd like to buy you a drink and chat. When are you free?"

Limix gave Delgado an amused look. "Fishing expedition, Major, or is there something you want from me."

"To be perfectly honest, Mr. Limix, there is something I'd like to ask you, but over a drink."

"Okay, Major. You buy, you bend my ear. Meet you in the *Reach* in twenty minutes." Limix faded out as he cut the link.

Once again, the noise and heavy aromas threatened to overwhelm Delgado as he stepped into the dimly lit bar. He saw a group of off-duty Erinyes in one corner, and they nodded politely at him before returning to their animated discussion. Ed Limix, who'd spotted the Marine, stepped out of a booth and waved his arm high over the crowd. Delgado walked over, followed by a waiter who'd obviously been warned by Limix.

Limix and Delgado shook hands before sitting. Then, as promised, the Marine ordered drinks for both of them. They made some small talk while waiting, Delgado deliberately steering away from his reasons for the meeting. Marine officers rarely interacted with trade unionists, and it felt strange to be here socializing with the local boss.

After all, officers were considered management, but Limix seemed perfectly at ease, though his eyes were wary, searching, wondering what Delgado wanted.

The drinks appeared, and the Marine thumb-printed a chit. With the waiter gone, he sat back, leaned his head against the divider, and took a sip.

"Tell me, Mr. Limix, how's the atmosphere on Tyrell? I mean, between labor and management?"

"Call me Ed, Major. Everybody does." The big man grinned, friendly and open. Likable. "We get along pretty well at Assenari. To tell you the truth, though, it wasn't always that way. A couple of years ago, we were represented by the Amalgamated Mineral Workers Union, and they were cutting shady deals with the big corporations, especially the ComCorp outfits. When they started bullying us at the Norden Mines, out on Hesperia, we threw the bums out and went on strike to make Assenari recognize our new union. Those were pretty rough days. We had a few scraps with company security and Amalgamated toughs who were doing dirty tricks for the local chief administrator. That's when I enjoyed my first taste of union work."

Limix paused for a sip of whiskey.

"Couldn't stand the slimy asshole who was the local boss at Norden. He never worked underground a day in his life and lived off both our union dues and kickbacks from the mine administration. Probably was connected with the mob, too. What finally broke the whole thing wide open was when we found proof that Amalgamated reps were selling illegal drugs to the miners in connivance with the chief administrator. We pushed the evidence through to head office. They immediately sacked the administrator, recognized our embryonic Assenari Miner's Union, and compensated the guys busted up in the fights. Couldn't convince federal prosecutors it was worth an indictment, of course. It didn't take long before the other mines threw Amalgamated out and formed locals of the new union. Since those days, I've been active in one way or another. This is my third tour at Tyrell and my second stint as the local shop steward. Things have been smooth. Yeah, we see eye-to-eye with Assenari."

"How about Chief Administrator Movane?"

"What's this leading up to, Major?" Limix frowned as he studied Delgado. "I'm not an Amalgamated crook if you're looking for drugs, contraband, or someone to stir up trouble."

Delgado held Limix's gaze as he raised his glass before replying.

"I'm a combat soldier, not a cop. My only interest is protecting Tyrell and everyone here. I needed to know about your relationship with Movane before I ask you for a favor. I don't want to get you in trouble, and your answer will decide whether I go it alone and piss everybody off or see if we can't come to an understanding."

Limix didn't answer for a moment, though his eyes never wavered.

"You strike me as somewhat different from the usual Marines who come through here. They're only concerned with a trouble-free tour and don't ask funny questions. In fact, this is the longest conversation I've ever had with one." He paused and looked at the crowded room before turning back to Delgado. "I pride myself on having a good instinct for people. You come across as someone trustworthy."

Delgado acknowledged the compliment with a slight nod.

"Movane, as chief administrators go, is average. She's not what you would call a people person. She works hard, knows her stuff, and keeps her eye on the profit margin. That's fine with us. This place works on a per-share bonus system, and the more productive we are, the richer we become. Low productivity means less bonus pay. In other words, what's good for Assenari and the Fleet is good for us. You need to understand that most of us are here so we can make a bundle, enough for early retirement, before hard work underground ruins our bodies.

"Hell, another tour after this one, and I'm chucking everything by the board to buy me a nice little tavern back home because I'll be flush for life. Old sourpuss Movane's the same. I heard she came up through the ranks, started as a heavy equipment operator, and clawed her way to the top. You could say we understand each other. We want to make money and enjoy a long retirement. For that reason alone, Movane keeps the relationship between the company and the union on an even keel. Does that answer your question?"

"Thanks, Ed. Let me order us a refill, and I'll tell you what I'm contemplating."

Delgado signaled for a waiter. Both men remained silent, watching the crowd while they waited for the drinks. When they arrived, the Marine raised his in a silent toast and took a sip. Limix responded in kind.

"As I said, my chief concern is keeping this place safe and operational. For that, my people and I must be familiar with every square centimeter of this place, and I mean familiar by having been there. The difference between seeing a place in person instead of only in a virtual projection can easily become the margin between life and death during an emergency. Bottom line is my people should see the shafts and walk the galleries at least once. Movane won't allow us to go underground, and Engstrom is playing along with her. They don't understand that the minor inconvenience of letting us into the mine proper could be repaid by saving dozens of lives."

Limix's frown returned.

"What are you concerned about, Major? While not a secret, this place isn't known much outside of Assenari circles, and what we refine won't attract raiders, pirates, or other assorted scum. Too bulky for the value," Suddenly, Limix's eyes lit up. "Aw, crap. The rumors that a recon droid found something unholy are true, aren't they? Is that why the Fleet replaced Captain Jerrold with a Major and much tougher looking Marines?"

Delgado figured either Limix was a superlative actor or Engstrom and Movane didn't keep him in the loop on everything, which meant no real triumvirate. And the union boss didn't seem like a practiced dissembler, but Delgado had been wrong about people many times before.

"I couldn't possibly comment. If an emergency occurs on my watch, I'll be ready, no matter what Movane or Engstrom, or you, for that matter, may think. I'd rather someone around here cooperated willingly, but if I must, I'll do things my way because I'd rather not risk lives because of turf wars."

Limix nodded, his expression carefully neutral.

"Understood. I'll help you — just say the word. Engstrom and Movane make a big deal about me sitting at the table with them, but I'm not part of their little command group. I don't get a say in matters beyond worker safety or when one of my members submits a grievance. Oh, they'll listen politely, but most of the time, it's forgotten two seconds after I leave Engstrom's office. However, you and I share a common concern — staying alive and keeping the mine productive. I'll talk with the team leaders over the next few shifts and convince them to take a patrol into the galleries. Strictly off the books, of course. There are ways of making sure operations don't notice.

"Mind you, I can't force them, especially if Movane said no, but I can convince most. Big Ed Limix's word carries a lot of weight in Tyrell. I'll let you know what the guys say. Not everyone will risk running afoul of Movane, and not all of them like the military either. They have their reasons, which are as good as anyone else's. One thing, though, nobody's stepping into the shaft cars without an orientation briefing. I'll organize a couple of quiet sessions for you." He finished his drink. "Just be warned. No Marine garrison ever entered the mine proper, and the rumor of a recon droid finding something has reached every last ear on Tyrell, so most will make a connection."

"Thanks, Ed. Knowing I can count on your support makes my job a lot easier." Delgado drained his glass and rose. "You can contact me anytime you want. Just call my command post, and they'll put you through. If you drop by the barracks, I'll give you a quick tour of my outfit, which usually ends with a dram of Glen Arcturus."

"I'll take you up on that, Major. Since I'll be working hand-in-hand with a management representative, I might as well enjoy the perks." The shop steward chuckled as he and Delgado shook hands. "Talk to you later."

Across the dimly lit room, in another darkened booth, a man and a woman had watched Delgado and Limix talk. Though they couldn't hear what was being said, plainly, the union boss and the Marine had come to an agreement. But about what? Thinking of Harry's claims about the new troopers, Lyle Fournier felt his stomach churn with worry.

Big Ed Limix was known as a straight arrow, the guy who'd kicked the Amalgamated Mineral Worker's Union out of the Assenari operations because of drug-dealing and corruption. He was well-liked by most of the honest miners and respected by the rest. He was the kind of shop steward who drew the line at how much protection a brother or sister would receive, especially when it offended his sense of morality.

However, Fournier, a short, sharp-faced man in his forties, never got along with Limix and still held a grudge against the union boss. He'd done well during the Amalgamated days — plenty of money, power, and status. Now, with the squeaky-clean AMU, he only accumulated what he scraped together himself through his little side business.

He looked at his companion, a solidly built woman of indeterminate age with short blond hair and washed-out blue eyes.

"I don't like it. Limix has no business socializing with Marines, let alone an officer. Do you think Big Ed suspects something? And if so, will he tell this Delgado character?"

"Relax, Lyle. If Limix knew anything, he'd have acted before this. He's the kind who figures he doesn't need outside help to keep his own turf clean. Even if he found out, he wouldn't call in the military unless he couldn't handle it anymore. Before that happens, we'll know and can silence him. Just let it go for now. If we act scared and jump at every shadow, we'll just attract attention to ourselves, and that *will* put us right in it."

The woman looked hard at Lyle, enough so to make the miner swallow nervously. Then she spoke in a very soft tone, filled with menace.

"You and your buddies will not, under any circumstance, do anything beyond watching your backs more carefully when you're about our business. We will not change our plans or procedures. If I find out you've been panicking, I will make sure *I'm* covered." She made a slicing motion across her throat. "I hope you catch my drift. Those Marines, whoever they are, don't scare me."

# — Nine —

"Whatever you do, don't put your fingers on the conveyor belts, don't touch the mining equipment, and don't go wandering off into old galleries. They're partially blocked by boulders painted in red, but anyone can get past. If you do visit them and run into trouble, we won't come looking for you. Those old galleries haven't been inspected since they were shut down and are *dangerous*. If you don't believe me, go ahead and try. Just don't expect us to come and dig you out. We don't have time to waste on lost tourists."

The mining team leader, a large, muscular man with angular features and deep-set, intelligent eyes, paused to see his audience's reaction, Command Sergeant Faruq Saxer's Delta Troop.

"Sounds like a great idea for a survival exercise," Lance Corporal Carlo Torres muttered to his winger, Sergeant Osmin Sberna. "No light, no map, a failing rebreather, and two hours of air. Now make it back. I know a few people who could conveniently vanish that way."

The miner frowned at Torres. "Any objections, Lance Corporal - is it?"

"No, sir. I was merely telling the sarge that you seemed like a knowledgeable and competent gent to whom we'd better listen." It was said in a voice oozing with so much feigned innocence that the rest of Delta Troop couldn't keep a straight face, and many chuckled openly.

To everyone's surprise, the team leader put on a genuine smile.

"I see there's a comedian in the ranks. Good. It can get boring as hell down below. Just remember, once you step into the lifts, your survival depends on your smarts. I'm dead serious about safety. You've seen what happens to a body when a suit gets punctured."

The Marines nodded soberly. It was a common sight aboard ships raided by pirates.

"Every so often, a miner screws up, someone who fools the safety checks and makes it into a gallery drunk or stoned. None of us like to carry the body back up. We don't even bother removing the remains from the suit before we ship it home in a sealed casket." The miner glanced at Command Sergeant Saxer. "That's it. How did you want to split up your people?"

Saxer pushed himself away from the wall.

"How many troopers are you willing to take with each team?"

"Two or three. Preferably two. The pressurized control modules are pretty small, and we don't keep extra oxygen supplies for more than six in each gallery."

"No sweat, Mr. Isenar. We work in fire team pairs anyhow. Our rebreathers are fresh off the production line, and we'll bring our own spare oxygen canisters, but I don't think we'll stay for more than a few hours at a time. Certainly not for an entire eight-hour shift. As for the old galleries, we'll just take our chances if the major orders us to scout them. We've done crazier things over the years."

Isenar shrugged dismissively. "It's your funeral, Sergeant. Ed Limix asked us to take you guys down because the chief admin was against the idea. What you do there is your business, just as long as you don't interfere with operations or endanger us, which means no going in front of the control modules. Behind them? Be our guests."

"Fine with me, Mr. Isenar. How many pairs can we send per shift?"

"Six on the alpha shift, five on the beta shift, and seven on the gamma shift, because that's the number of teams who agreed to take tourists with them. The first time, you'll enjoy a grand tour. After that, you're on your own."

"Understood. I'll give you a list of my people and the shifts with which they'll go."

\*\*

Sergeant Sberna finished checking Lance Corporate Torres' pressure suit integrity and clapped him on the shoulder.

"You're good to go, Carlo." His words came through Torres' helmet speakers since both were buttoned up.

Torres, in turn, checked Sberna and gave him a similar tap when he was done.

The latter flicked his helmet radio to the miners' frequency and glanced at their guide.

"We're ready, Mister Johansen."

The Marines and Johansen's team — himself and two others — were in one of the airlocks leading to lift cars. Other fire team pairs were preparing in adjoining airlocks.

"Okay." Johansen grinned at his two mates through the helmet's transparent visor. "Let's make room for our tourists, and don't forget to point out the sights along the way."

He then made a little bow at the Marines and swept his right arm in front of his body.

"Welcome, welcome, gentle guests. Please step aboard and hang on to the rookie bar. We don't want you flying all over the lift cage when we plunge into the planet's murky depths. Complimentary barf-bags are available on demand."

The lift door slid shut. A flashing alarm light started to strobe to the piercing scream of a siren, while a toneless voice warned the occupants of the imminent depressurization of the lift car. The heads-up display on the inside of Sberna's helmet faceplate gave him a running readout of the surrounding pressure. When the red digits reached zero, and they could no longer hear the siren, the lift dropped out from under their feet.

Both Sberna and Torres felt their stomachs leap up into their mouths, and they struggled to keep their breakfasts down. It was as if someone had cut the lift free of its cables, and it was falling uncontrollably toward the bottom of the shaft, several kilometers below.

"It isn't the fall that kills you. It's the sudden stop at the end," Sberna muttered.

Banishing thoughts of impending death, Sberna stared at Johansen. The miner smiled back, clearly enjoying the Marines' discomfiture. Sberna wouldn't be surprised if he found out that the miner deliberately rigged the lift's speed controls to play a little trick on them. He was wrong.

"How do you like it, Sergeant? Our very own rollercoaster ride. Surprises us the first time too. Fastest mine lifts in the sector, here at Tyrell."

"It's just dandy," the Marine replied in as casual a tone as he could muster. "Reminds me of jumping from perfectly good shuttles in low orbit — that's our version of your rollercoaster ride."

The lift slowed, imperceptibly at first, and then with enough force to make the occupants flex their knees. Finally, it came to a stop and the massive doors slid open on a dream world of harsh light and dark shadow.

Johansen and his two men stepped out, followed by the Marines.

"Beauty, isn't she, Sarge? Welcome to Hades. Level Sixteen is the lowest level of Shaft Number One and the deepest in the mine, period. We're thirty-five hundred meters below the station. This chamber here was once filled with high-grade ore."

Lance Corporal Torres let out a soft whistle tinged with awe. The lift had stopped at the bottom edge of an enormous cavern whose roof vanished into the darkness. It was huge. A dozen light globes illuminated the cave but couldn't pierce the gloom sufficiently to show the far walls.

The lift they'd taken was one of three serving this particular shaft. From the outside, the lift tubes looked like shiny rods clustered around a large trunk. As Sberna knew from studying the mine's setup, the trunk was an anti-grav vacuum that sucked extracted ore up to the smelter. Four conveyor belts coming from four widely spaced active galleries fed it ceaselessly.

Since this was shift change, the cavern slowly filled with suited figures. Those coming off work appeared from the galleries aboard small vehicles with oversized wheels, while others, like Johansen and his team, stepped out of the lifts. The miner led them to the large module in the center of the cavern.

"Shaft boss," he explained, using his team's private frequency. "We check-in, so he knows who's here in case there are problems."

The module had a large window with several terminals below it facing the miners. Inside the pressurized habitat, three suited figures, minus helmets, worked on a status board. At one end of the shaft boss' office, a door with a prominent red cross pierced the smooth metal surface. An airlock on the outside, also marked with the red cross, showed the way to the emergency medical facilities, including stasis pods.

Sberna unconsciously nodded with approval and pointed the door out to Torres. He made a note to check out the functions of the other modules before leaving this place. A good reconnaissance always included knowing where the emergency facilities were.

"Sarge, you and your mate just need to punch in your names and serial numbers using that terminal. Don't forget to come back here and punch out before heading to the surface when you're done."

"Sure thing, Mr. Johansen."

"Sarge, it's time you stopped calling me mister. Around here, life's dangerous enough without wasting time on social niceties. My name's Olaf."

"Okay, Olaf. Mine's Osmin."

"Come on, Osmin, ours is Gallery B, and that's our vehicle over there." He pointed at each in turn. "I figured you'd ride with us and then walk your way back, so you can examine the gallery at your leisure."

"Sounds like a plan."

The miners and Marines piled atop the automated car while nearby, more buddy pairs teams from Sberna's section did the same with other teams, and the various groups of Marines waved at each other, gesturing obscenities in their private hand signal language. The car pulled away from the waiting area with a barely perceptible jerk and sped toward the gaping hole that marked Gallery B's entrance.

The tunnel was a smooth granite tube, laser-drilled, with a flat floor. It was lit at intervals by glow strips embedded in the ceiling. As the car sped by, Sberna caught sight of several red splashes on either side of the tunnel — painted boulders marking abandoned galleries that led off into the black heart of the rock. The tunnel was broad enough for the car and the conveyor belt, with room to spare, but its low ceiling momentarily made Sberna feel the weight of the planet's crust bearing down on him.

Several minutes later, the tunnel widened into another, smaller cavern, brilliantly lit by work lights. The pressurized control node sat to one side, with tools neatly arrayed along its outer shell. A hulking beast slumbered at the very end of the conveyor belt — the remotely controlled miner-borer, silent between shift changes.

"What happens now," Johansen said, breaking the silence that enveloped them since leaving the lift cavern, "is that we check the machinery and the control node's integrity. That gets done every shift change. Then we make sure the miner-borer is still aligned with the main ore seam. After that, we three climb into the module and put everything in motion again."

"Why isn't everything controlled from the lift cavern or, better yet, the surface? Can't an AI run the machine itself?" Torres asked.

"Because problems happen, and when they do, you need people to fix stuff without delay. The miner-borers work hard and need regular maintenance. If something breaks and the thing isn't stopped fast, it'll self-destruct and take a section of conveyor belt with it. An experienced operator, on the other hand, can tell when something's about to go wrong and stop it immediately. Considering the cost of a new machine versus pay for three operators per shift, the company would rather pay us to be here with it than several kilometers away, reliant on tunnel transmitters."

"I see. Interesting."

"We should start. Otherwise, we'll hear about it. Please stay behind the control node while we're working and give me a shout when you're leaving so I can tell the shaft boss."

Sberna nodded. "Wilco."

The Marines watched the miners go through the preparatory cycle and then enter the control node. Sberna nudged his winger and indicated the tunnel behind them.

"We're off, Olaf."

"Enjoy the walk. Why don't you guys meet us for a beer at the *Reach* after the shift? We can celebrate your first time in the pit."

"Sure thing."

"Enjoy spelunking."

**

"Pretty spooky, Sarge. I can't imagine spending my life doing this."

The two Marines had been walking back alongside the conveyor belt for nearly an hour, scanning and recording every inch of the tunnel. It was tedious work.

"I hear you, Carlo. Me neither. Give me open spaces and breathable air under a warm sun."

As he did every few minutes, Sberna looked behind them at the empty tunnel that led to the ore face and Olaf Johansen's team. Ten minutes earlier, the Marines passed an abandoned gallery, and its opening was still barely visible at the edge of a bend in the main tunnel. A trio of waist-high boulders painted blood red blocked the entrance, and neither their lights nor their night vision visors could pierce the deep, brooding darkness beyond a sharp curve two dozen meters in.

Major Delgado had ordered them to stay in the active galleries for now. A look from the entrance and a quick scan was it. Later on, perhaps... But Sberna felt uneasy at the idea.

As he turned to face their direction of travel again, his instincts took over. He froze in mid-movement, a spine-tingling sensation of fear raising the hairs on the back of his neck. He could have sworn he saw movement at the mouth of the abandoned gallery out of the corners of his eyes.

Sberna reached for his handheld sensor and aimed it at the gaping maw of the lightless tunnel. Nothing.

"What's up, Sarge?"

"My eyes playing tricks on me. When I was looking at the abandoned gallery's entrance, I saw a shadow move, but my sensor isn't picking up a thing."

"Let me." Torres imitated Sberna. "Nope. Nothing, but I'll tell you what, we're deep in this planet's crust, and our little battlefield units are blind beyond a few meters of solid rock. We can't even pick up Johansen's miner-borer from here, and its reactor is pretty powerful. Want to turn back and recheck the side tunnel entrance?"

Sberna glanced at this helmet's heads-up display to see how his rebreather was doing.

"No. Let's make a note in the log. The more I think about it, the more I figure my imagination is playing tricks on me. Harsh lighting and jagged shadows will do that."

Sergeant Sberna took one last look behind, just before the abandoned tunnel disappeared in the distance, and felt the tiny hairs on the back of his neck stand up again as he spotted the outline of an unknown watcher behind the blood-red boulders. Or was it his overactive imagination?

# —Ten—

"Show me exactly where you saw that possible contact, Sergeant." Delgado glanced at Sberna. "This may be a thoroughly unfamiliar environment for us, but you're a trained observer. If you think you saw something, then you did. Maybe not a human being, perhaps not anything living, but you saw something that wasn't supposed to be there."

A holographic projection of Level Sixteen hovered over the command post's map table, and Sberna pointed out where he and Torres were when he saw the shadowy movement at the mouth of the abandoned gallery.

Along with Sergeant First Class Testo, Delgado had led him through a full accounting of his movements, from the moment they left the barracks until they returned, tracing every step of the way on the schematic maps projected by the computer. Each fire team provided such a report upon returning, and usually, Testo debriefed them on his own. Still, because Sberna reported a possible contact, the operations sergeant figured Delgado should hear about it in person.

"Movement attracts the eye, sir," Testo said, "even at that distance. Since there's no atmosphere and therefore no air currents to generate random activity, it was either a dislodged rock that caught Osmin's attention or an unauthorized human."

First Sergeant Hak patted Sberna on the shoulder. "And he's not known for seeing things that aren't there, Skipper."

"Right." Delgado climbed to his feet. "Spread the word that I want to hear about any other ghosts in the galleries, even if our people figure they're figments of the imagination. Sometimes, those figments are hiding distinctly human activities, the sort we ought to know about."

"Aye, aye, sir."

Delgado gave Sberna a nod. "Thanks, Sergeant. You can head for the barracks now."

"Sir." He briefly came to attention, then pivoted on his heels and walked out.

Delgado, Testo, and Hak turned their eyes back on the holographic projection.

"Any chance Osmin might be seeing things because of nerves?" Delgado asked. "Thirty-five-hundred meters below ground, no atmosphere, and an unfamiliar environment can make even the least imaginative of us nervous."

Hak nodded. "True, but I stand by what I said. Osmin has solid nerves. Could it be an optical illusion? Sure. But since we're here for a reason and know the opposition could have its own people in Tyrell already, I figure we should take it as real until proved otherwise."

Testo made a grimace. "But why would someone be screwing around that deep? And how did they bypass the safeguards that ensure only those with business there enter the galleries?"

The first sergeant snorted with amusement. "Friends in the right places, just like us. Do you think the chief administrator's office will see the names of our people in the daily log?"

Testo shook his head. "No. Whoever Limix enlisted in the cause will make sure they're wiped once they pass the surface checkpoint on their way back to the barracks."

Delgado, who'd been leaning against a workstation, pushed himself upright.

"So, there could be a lot more happening in the mine than what's recorded."

"Without a doubt, Skipper. We went in despite the chief administrator, who'd have heard of it by now if the security logs weren't being doctored. Why not others."

"But why?" Delgado tapped his fingertips on his chin as he frowned. "What could be happening in the deepest pits of Hades?"

"Seems like a strange place for the sort of illegal stuff common on outposts like Tyrell." Hak shrugged. "Smuggling?"

"Let's allow a few shifts to pass so we can see if our folks encounter more ghosts in any of the galleries on any level.

If they don't, we can send a properly equipped patrol into that abandoned tunnel Osmin mentioned."

"Which might become interesting, sir," Sergeant Testo said. "The maps of Level Sixteen reveal a few minor gaps, Osmin's tunnel included."

Delgado cocked an eyebrow at the operations noncom. "Such as?"

"Details on the abandoned galleries. It could be a fluke or sloppy record-keeping or computer core degradation, but the Level Sixteen maps are the only ones with missing information on the abandoned areas."

"Are we talking just one or two galleries here?"

"No, all of them have something missing. It's like someone is covering their tracks by spreading the blanks around."

"When can we plausibly schedule another patrol of Level Sixteen?"

Testo called up the patrol plan on his console.

"Not for six or seven days, sir. We still have the galleries in Shafts Two and Three before we can give Shaft One a return visit without attracting attention."

Delgado stroked his chin while Hak and Testo watched him think. The Erinyes had been tossed in here with very little information beyond the fact that their job was ensuring no one absconded with the Second Migration War-era munitions before the Fleet could organize an orderly and highly secret retrieval.

Sberna's sighting and Testo's discovery of faulty maps were the first unusual occurrences, even though they probably bore no relation to the potential outside threats identified by Naval Intelligence. Still, he didn't like the idea of something unknown occurring on his watch. After all, Erinye Company was responsible for the station's security, notwithstanding the core mission. If someone was using the lower galleries for illegal activities, he should stop them.

Delgado turned to Hak.

"Or you and I could visit the galleries, starting with Shaft One, Level Sixteen, Top. We'll take our wingers and go an hour or two after the shift change, under the excuse that we should also be familiar with the environment. I'll let Ed Limix know."

"No, sir. Bad idea. That's a job for sharp-eyed youngsters, the sort who already went underground and know what's what."

Delgado was about to reply when the command post's communicator chimed. Testo reached over and touched the screen.

"Station security office, Sergeant Testo speaking."

"This is Captain Engstrom, Sergeant. I need to speak with Major Delgado."

Testo stepped aside, and Delgado took his place.

"I'm here, sir. How can I help you?"

"I understand that contrary to my orders, your people are wandering through the mine galleries." Engstrom was trying for a severe expression and tone, but it didn't quite work, at least in Delgado's opinion. "What do you say about that?"

His quick sideways glance betrayed the presence of another person in his office, probably Chief Administrator Movane.

"Sir, as far as I recall, you said that I *shouldn't* go underground, not that I *couldn't.*"

"As I recall, Chief Administrator Movane forbade you from entering the mine."

"Sir, with due respect, Administrator Movane has no authority over the station's security complement. I'm answerable solely to you."

"Major, you're skirting rather close to the line between argument and insolence. *Chief* Administrator Movane runs the mining operation. Tell me, are you one of those bloody guardhouse lawyers? Should I record everything I tell you?"

"I'm sorry you feel that way, sir. We are doing this in the best interests of Tyrell Station. My duty is ensuring its safety and the only way we can do that is by reconnoitering every nook and cranny, the mine included."

Engstrom turned his head to one side again, but this time it was more than just a glance. His mouth moved, but no sound came through, proof he was conferring with Movane. He turned back toward the video pickup and restored the sound.

"Major Delgado, you will desist from your reconnaissance of the underground shafts and galleries. Stay out of them. They're no place for inexperienced tourists."

"Sir, we've already almost completed our reconnaissance of Shaft One. The miners kindly briefed us on the safety rules and procedures, which we followed to the letter. They also guided my people during their first descent, and we've not interfered with production. Furthermore, we are highly experienced operating in an airless environment, more so than the average miners on their first tour. Since we've already done close to one-third of the mine proper, I suggest it would be more profitable if we finish. I can live with a one-time visit of the active galleries."

"Oh, you can live with it, can you, Major? You assume a lot, especially for someone who's only been here a few days."

The sarcasm was forced, unconvincing. Delgado suddenly formed the idea Engstrom was uncomfortable about something.

"Sir, I'm here for a specific job, and that's keeping Tyrell safe from all threats, internal *and* external." He held Engstrom's eyes and let his words hang between them for a few heartbeats. "If you prevent me from carrying out my duties, I have no choice but to inform Fleet HQ."

Delgado hoped Engstrom would understand his unit wasn't just another Marine company on a routine tour of duty but realize their arrival was connected with the recon droid's classified discovery. A distinct air of hesitation crossed Engstrom's face, perhaps at the mention of Fleet HQ rather than Delgado's putative superiors in the 42nd, and the Marine pressed his advantage.

"Captain, just let me finish Shafts Two and Three, and I won't need to go underground again except in case of an issue involving Tyrell's security." Delgado put on a wholly feigned, albeit vague, air of embarrassment, determined to lay it on thick. "To tell you the truth, sir, my Marines prefer wider spaces and don't necessarily enjoy going into the mine. Therefore, I'm as anxious as anyone to finish our reconnaissance. I'd rather spend the rest of my tour above ground."

Engstrom's eyes took on a wary expression, and he studied Delgado, who fought to keep his face guileless as he stared back.

"You say you've already finished Shaft One?"

"Almost, sir."

Again, the burly naval officer cut the sound and turned to his unseen partner. This time, the conversation was longer. Finally, Engstrom came back on.

"Major Delgado, as long as your troops obey the safety regulations and do not interfere with mining operations, you may complete your recce. Once you've done Shafts Two and Three, your unit *will* stay above ground. I hope that's understood. I don't want any further dubious interpretations of my orders. Advise me when you're done. Engstrom out."

The screen went black.

Testo let out a low whistle. "Skipper, I think that naval gent appears concerned about Shaft One."

Delgado nodded, smiling.

"That was my impression as well. I hope Captain Engstrom doesn't play poker because he'll lose with a face like that. You will note he did not specifically forbid us from revisiting Shaft One while we're walking the other two. What's not specifically forbidden is permitted, right Top?"

"That's how I understand it, sir, and I'm sure Colonel Decker would wholeheartedly agree."

"If I were a betting man, I'd say that once Engstrom found out we already did Shaft One without reporting strange occurrences, he saw no reason to keep us away. Or he's the best actor I've ever seen, and he's just deliberately pointed us at Shaft One so he could hide something else."

"Engstrom doesn't seem like a subtle enough guy for that," Hak said. "So, what's he hiding?"

"The Almighty knows, Top, but I'd re-phrase your question: what are Engstrom and Movane hiding? I wouldn't be surprised if they both harbored secrets they'd rather we didn't uncover, but I just can't see them engaged in something sordid, like smuggling or drug running. Movane may be an uncomfortable customer, but she's got an honest reputation."

"A bonus mystery?"

Delgado shrugged.

"Perhaps. Considering the Migration War bunker isn't anywhere near Shaft One, Level Sixteen, it's the only thing I can figure."

# — Eleven —

An insistent chime interrupted Delgado's dream of a dark future where he helped conquer entire worlds and instantly woke him. Like most of his breed, he was a light sleeper during missions. He reached for his communicator, sitting on a shelf beside his cot while noting that the barracks were still plunged into gamma shift's nighttime darkness.

"Delgado."

"It's Rolf, Skipper. I have the duty," Command Sergeant Painter replied.

If Delgado hadn't already been wide awake from the communicator chime, Painter, whose troop worked gamma shift, calling in the middle of the night would do the trick.

"What's up?"

"One of my patrols — Sergeant Greaves and Lance Corporal Ng — found a dead body in Storeroom Twenty-Seven-Charlie at oh-three-fifteen. The storeroom contains supplies for the administrative offices and should normally be locked, but Greaves and Ng found the door wide open.

**87**

Greaves entered and discovered the body of a female lying on the floor. Although there is no immediate evidence of foul play, he secured the site as a potential crime scene. I've called the station infirmary, and the duty surgeon should arrive momentarily. I also informed the operations center who'll take care of warning the CO and the chief administrator."

Delgado absently scratched at his side, thinking. Technically, he was Tyrell's provost marshal, the local sheriff, so to speak, and any suspicious death became his responsibility. A dead woman in a normally locked storeroom definitely qualified.

"I'll visit the scene right away, Rolf."

"Roger that, Skipper."

"Delgado, out."

By the time he'd slipped on his uniform, First Sergeant Hak materialized, no doubt warned by Painter.

"We found ourselves a stiff, I hear." Hak was dressed as well and armed with his needler in an open holster at the hip.

"You don't need to come, you know. Grab some more sleep."

"And miss our first murder investigation? Not a chance, sir."

"We only have a suspicious death, Top." Delgado strapped his gun belt around his waist and put on his beret. "So don't become overly enthusiastic about playing detective."

The station seemed just as busy in the middle of the gamma shift as any other time since mining and smelting operations went on twenty-four hours a day. However, they still reached Level Two within minutes and quickly found Storeroom Twenty-Seven-Charlie.

As they approached, Sergeant Greaves and Lance Corporal Ng, standing guard by the open door, snapped to attention, and the former saluted.

"Good morning, sir. The body's still inside the room. We've been careful not to disturb anything. Sergeant Rankin is busy looking for a crime scene kit — apparently, our predecessors didn't store it in the right spot — and the duty surgeon hasn't arrived yet. Would you like to take a glance?"

"Lead on, Greaves." He glanced at Hak. "Probably best if you stay here, Top. The fewer tourists shedding DNA in a potential crime scene, the better."

The storeroom was small, by usual standards, and filled with row upon row of ceiling-high steel shelves holding boxes of various sizes and colors. Behind one of the rows, hidden from the door, lay the sprawled body of the unidentified woman.

She had auburn, shoulder-length curly hair, thin lips, a pointy nose, and a slender build that made her seem very different from muscular miners, let alone tough Marines. Her clothes, a simple two-piece dark blue suit, and soft shoes marked her as an administrative worker.

Delgado saw no signs of a struggle, although her body was contorted in a fashion that hinted at an uneasy death, something the Marine had seen often enough to know. He examined the body, careful not to touch it but saw no signs of violence, meaning her death could stem from natural causes or a drug overdose. Nothing that would warrant a murder investigation. Delgado stood and adjusted his gun belt. The body at his feet looked infinitely sad, like a broken doll.

The station's doctor, a tired-looking civilian under contract to the Navy, arrived moments later. He nodded once. "Major. I don't believe we've met. I'm Franklin Blake."

"Curtis Delgado, sir."

Blake didn't offer his hand, and Delgado stepped aside to let him work while two medics with an anti-grav stretcher — civilian contract workers as well — waited in the hallway.

After running extensive scans, Blake climbed wearily to his feet.

"My preliminary conclusion is cardiac arrest since I can't detect any underlying cause for death. But I wouldn't be surprised if blood analysis shows she died as a result of consuming illicit substances. It happens from time to time, no matter how much we try to educate the miners and the support staff."

"How often?"

He shrugged.

"Two or three a year. Assenari writes them up as having died from work-related injuries to avoid intensive law enforcement scrutiny and questions from families. This is a bleak place, as you'll find out. People crave momentary escapes, and where there's a demand, you'll inevitably find a willing supplier. Just one more thing Assenari would rather keep from the public. What this place really needs is a Constabulary detachment, not Marines without law enforcement experience — no offense intended."

"None taken."

"You seem remarkably sanguine about this, Major." Blake gave Delgado a curious stare.

"I've seen my share of death." A shrug. "In this line of business, you either become inured to it, or you find something else."

"Lots of time on the frontier hunting reivers, then?"

Delgado nodded. "You could say that. Did a hitch in the Service yourself?"

"No, but one of my cousins was a Pathfinder command sergeant. You remind me a bit of him."

"What's his name?"

"Hal Tarra. He retired, joined a private military corporation, and vanished into the Protectorate Zone, never to be seen again. This happened a few years back. Did you know him?"

"I've heard the name, but we never crossed paths."

A Marine sergeant first class carrying a metal case appeared in the doorway. "Sir, I finally found the scene-of-crime kit and can start if you'll give me room. The sooner I'm done, the sooner the medics can remove the body."

Delgado glanced at Blake, who nodded and followed him a few meters to one side. They watched Sergeant Rankin scan the body and its surroundings, record images, and take samples from the floor and the nearest shelves.

"Are you equipped to collect samples from the body and the clothing, Doctor?" Delgado asked.

"Yes. There is a protocol when dealing with fatalities, and recording evidence for a possible inquest is part of it."

After a bit, Sergeant Rankin packed up his case and glanced at Delgado.

"I have everything we need, sir."

"Thanks. Let the medics know they can pick up the body on your way out."

"Yes, sir."

Once the dead woman was gone, Delgado ordered the room sealed with one of the portable locks Sergeant Rankin brought up from the command post and dismissed the patrol to its duties.

As they returned to the barracks, Delgado asked Hak, "Ever run across a Pathfinder command sergeant by the name Hal Tarra? The doc is a cousin of his. Says he became a merc and vanished in the Zone."

Hak grimaced. "Yeah. Hal was one of Colonel Decker's closest buddies in the 902nd Pathfinder Squadron and his troop sergeant. Tarra died saving the Colonel's life during an undercover mission many years ago, from what I was told. A good man and a solid Marine."

"Small galaxy, isn't it?"

"And the Pathfinder family is even smaller."

After breakfast a few hours later, Delgado headed for the station infirmary, hoping for more information about the dead woman. He found Blake in his office, looking even wearier than before.

"Good morning."

Startled, the man looked up. "Oh. Good morning, Major. Although it feels like I've already done a full shift. Please come in and sit."

"Who was she?"

"Terry Evans, thirty-six, a logistics specialist from Assenari Mining on her first tour in Tyrell. She worked the alpha shift."

"Did you determine a time of death?"

"Midnight, give or take a few minutes on either side."

"A bit late for an alpha shift worker."

Blake merely shrugged, indicating that he considered the habits of others beyond his concern.

"What's the cause of death?"

"Cardiac arrest." When Delgado frowned, he allowed himself a faint smile. "Yes, when the heart stops beating, we die, but there is generally an underlying cause. Yet, in the case of Terry Evans, I could find none. She was young and healthy in every respect — no signs of injury, trauma, or chronic issues. Her organs are in perfect condition, heart included, and I didn't find traces of any noxious substance in her blood, so it wasn't a drug overdose. At this point, I'm stumped."

Blake fell silent, and he frowned in turn, head tilted slightly to one side as he studied Delgado.

"Why do I get the impression you just figured something out?"

The Marine hesitated for a moment. "I may know of one way a heart would stop beating, even though there's nothing whatsoever to show why that happened. Did you ever hear of a procedure called conditioning against interrogation?"

Blake shook his head. "No."

"Can't say I'm surprised. Those who use it don't discuss the matter. In essence, it makes a person incapable of answering certain questions. If an interrogator persists or uses drugs, a conditioned individual can die from simple cardiac arrest. Don't ask me how the procedure works. I do not know."

"Good heavens. Why would someone agree to it?"

Delgado shrugged. "Condition of employment, so that if an intelligence operative, for example, falls into the wrong hands, he or she can't reveal secrets."

"So, you're saying Evans was a spy? A Commonwealth government agent?"

"An operative of some sort, sure, but the government isn't the only one with its own intelligence network. The big zaibatsus, like ComCorp or even Assenari Enterprises, run theirs, meaning she could have been working for one of many organizations. If I'm right, of course. Did you examine the body for injection marks?"

"No. But now I will. However, as I said before, I found nothing out of the ordinary in her bloodstream."

"There are sedatives to force compliance and interrogation drugs which dissipate rapidly. She died at midnight and was found at oh-three-hundred. By then, all traces would be gone."

"You sound as if you're rather familiar with such matters." Blake gave Delgado a searching look.

"I read a lot, Doctor." Delgado climbed to his feet. "Let me know what you find."

# — Twelve —

"Someone's already been here." Hak grimaced with distaste as he squatted by the door of the second-level cubicle. "And didn't bother hiding the fact. Or Evans was a real mess."

Delgado turned to Command Sergeant Painter, a craggy-faced, dark-haired man in his late thirties who wore what often seemed like a faint yet permanent smile, as if life in general amused him.

"Rolf, question the people in this module and see if anyone noticed somebody climb into Evans' cubicle in the last nine hours." He paused. "In fact, consider yourself the head of our criminal investigation detachment until further notice. I'll reassign your troop's routine duties to the other three and let you concentrate entirely on police work."

"Can do, Skipper. Call me Detective Command Sergeant Painter, CID." He saluted and turned on his heels.

As Painter walked away, Delgado called the command post.

"Testo here, sir."

"We need to find out when Evans was last seen moving under her own power or, better yet, if anyone saw her enter the storeroom."

"I'll put out a query on the station's public information net, but I don't think we can expect much. The miners may be a friendly bunch, but we've just become the closest thing to cops around here, and you know how it is, especially on isolated outposts like this one."

"Probably, but it's part of the procedure. Maybe we'll get lucky."

"Aye, aye, sir."

"Delgado, out."

He watched Sergeant Rankin and one of Alpha Troop's corporals pack up the dead woman's belongings, then returned to the command post.

Moments after sitting to write a report for Captain Engstrom and add to his daily report for Naval Intelligence, Blake called.

"So?" Delgado asked the moment the doctor's face appeared on the primary display.

"You were right. I found two recent puncture marks, made before death and less than twelve hours old. One on the neck and one in the left forearm, above a vein."

Delgado nodded. "The first would have been a quick jab to immobilize her. Something she wouldn't see coming. The second was likely a more deliberate injection with something to loosen her tongue. But we'll never know for sure."

"As I said, you seem surprisingly familiar with such procedures."

"Can I ask that you not include my theory in your report?"

"I wasn't intending on it since I only found tiny puncture marks which could stem from other causes."

"Will you mention them?"

"In the official autopsy report, yes. There's no choice, but my report for Captain Engstrom will only contain the facts we know about her death — she died from sudden cardiac arrest, cause unknown. It's extremely rare in healthy people but does happen. In any case, that's it. Blake, out."

Once his image faded, Testo chuckled with amusement.

"If only the man knew what we do for a living." Then his serious expression returned. "You think the victim was conditioned, sir? If so, what the hell does that make her? Naval Intelligence would tell us about an agent in place, right? Or the Constabulary, for that matter."

"Considering we're intelligence's direct action arm, I'm pretty sure Admiral Talyn wouldn't hold back. As to who Evans worked for, your guess is as good as mine. Constabulary is a possibility, but so are many corporate intelligence organizations, including Assenari Enterprises' own in-house service. One thing's for sure, though. There's a pro in our midst."

\*\*

Nothing remained secret for long in a closed environment like Tyrell, and news of Evans' suspicious death was already making the rounds when Blake told Delgado about the puncture marks. Conversations in the cafeteria and the *Reach* were of nothing else.

In an isolated corner, Jannika Hallikonnoen quietly fumed at the untimely incident. Evans had been a helpful tool, with direct access to the primary data nodes. This would force a change in plans. Fortunately, she'd cultivated another well-placed associate, one she'd kept quiet until now. A sort of ace in the hole who enjoyed access at the highest levels.

Chewing on her lower lip worriedly, Hallikonnoen knew she must find out how Evans died. Word around the station was cardiac arrest, but Evans was young, healthy, fit. And in a storeroom when she should be sleeping? If this damned Major Delgado and his Marines probed too deeply into the dead woman's background, they might uncover things that should stay hidden. And that meant a few folks would start earning the money they'd been promised, though they wouldn't like it.

Jannika smiled cruelly at the thought. Lyle and his merry fools might come in handy after all, and if things went right, they wouldn't be around to tell tales afterward.

But the smile quickly vanished as she realized there could be more of her kind in Tyrell, operatives on their own missions who could compromise hers.

\*\*

"So far, we're drawing a blank. Nobody saw anything around the storeroom last night. Nobody saw Evans wandering around. It's like she turned into a ghost well before someone sent her into the Infinite Void. Even the surveillance pickups in module two didn't spot her."

Delgado looked up at Testo. "What?"

"Someone tampered with the surveillance, Skipper. According to the station's logs, no one entered the corridor leading to the storeroom between twenty-three-hundred and oh-one-hundred. I'm running through the entire station's logs right now, and there's no trace of Evans in the two hours leading up to her death. It's almost as if someone magically transported her from her cubicle to the storeroom. And, of course, no trace of whoever made those puncture marks. That's serious record tampering."

Testo gestured at Sergeant Kuzek, who functioned as assistant operations noncom when he wasn't watching Delgado's back.

"It'll probably take Carl a few hours to even find the precise points at which they were altered, but that's the only way of reconstructing the closest thing to a timeline."

At that moment, Command Sergeant Painter entered the command post and took one of the visitor's chairs.

"Any luck in the accommodations module, Rolf?"

Painter shook his head. "Negative, Skipper. Nobody saw anyone trash Evans' cubicle, but I'm sure a few of the buggers are hiding something. Same deal with Evans leaving last night when she should be in bed.

Unfortunately, short of slapping the module's inhabitants around, there's no way to obtain a straight story."

"Damn."

"What do you want first, sir?" Testo asked. "Run through the tampered records or dig into Evans' workstation?"

"The workstation."

"On it."

Delgado turned back to Painter. "Anything else?"

"No. The Top is searching Evans' personal effects with Bernie Rankin, though I doubt we'll find anything useful. Oh, and Bernie uploaded the scene-of-crime kit data. Not that it'll do us much good."

"In that case, stand down your troop and get some rest while we process everything. You'll be back sleuthing soon enough."

"Roger that, Skipper." Painter stood, sketched a salute, and left the command post.

Delgado glanced at the time and stood as well. "I'm off to Captain Engstrom's office."

Kuzek glanced over his shoulder. "Need close protection, sir?"

"Negative. He's as harmless as they come for a squid."

The sergeant gave him thumbs up. "Roger that, sir. Enjoy."

\*\*

"You're sure it was simple cardiac arrest and not drug-related?" Delgado sensed Engstrom seemed eager for a confirmation that would let him dismiss the whole matter as another of those things that happened in a harsh outpost like Tyrell.

"Doctor Blake found nothing in her bloodstream, and she was uninjured. He can't explain why her heart stopped but said it happens in rare cases. What Evans was doing in that storeroom at midnight when she's on the alpha shift is something we'll likely never figure."

Movane shrugged, her expression as pinched as ever.

"She worked in the logistics section, and we don't stand on principle with working hours. Yes, she was part of the alpha shift, like most support staff, but could do more work at any other time of the day if she so chose. What I still can't grasp is someone young and healthy simply dropping dead."

The fourth person in Engstrom's office, Ed Limix, looked equally sour.

"That's three deaths so far this year. But it's the first time in my entire career with Assenari that someone keels over, and we don't know the cause. Usually, it's a drug overdose, a fight that got out of hand, or a careless miner who didn't button up his suit correctly and no one caught it."

Delgado stared at Limix. "How is that even possible?"

The big miner grimaced. "When all three in a given team are still running on alcohol or drug fumes, fatal mistakes can happen. And they do. Especially if they bought a bad batch of wacky pills."

"Lovely." Delgado turned his gaze back on Engstrom. "We'll continue investigating it as a suspicious death, seeing as how there are no discernible reasons for Evans' cardiac arrest, but at this point, Doctor Blake is calling it natural causes."

"Thank you, Major. Please keep us informed of developments. You may return to your duties."

Delgado stood, saluted, and left the office.

\*\*

When the door closed behind him, Limix looked at Movane and Engstrom, grimacing.

"I think our boy here knows or suspects more than he told us. Delgado's a smart Marine. That makes him dangerous, a loose cannon, and his closed-mouth attitude worries me. He and his people aren't the regular sort we see as garrison, so I wonder what's really going on. Think you can order him to open up, Nero?"

Limix found his answer in the uncertain expression on Engstrom's face and sat back. "Question withdrawn."

"Isn't it strange Ed," Romana Movane asked, in a vaguely acrimonious tone, "how your chumminess toward Delgado has changed into suspicion? Do you think it was worth giving him access to the mine without my permission?"

Limix didn't immediately reply, glaring at Movane with an expression that hinted he wished he could wipe the mocking grin off her face.

"That was then. This is now. Delgado is hiding things from us. It's a fine way of repaying my generosity. Tell me, are you scared of something? Or simply concerned a support staffer's death might reflect badly on you, considering most fatalities come from the mine and smelter?"

Engstrom raised both hands before the discussion could descend into acrimony.

"Thank you both for coming. Romana, I'll leave you to handle the arrangements for repatriating Evans and informing Assenari. This too shall pass."

# — Thirteen —

Jannika Hallikonnoen found sleep hard to come by that night. Lying on her cot in a darkened cubicle, eyes wide open, she couldn't stop wondering about the Evans investigation. She'd hoped to hear from her associate and learn what the Marines thought, knew, or suspected but found no way of doing so before slipping into bed.

With those hard-eyed, unsmiling Marine noncoms asking everybody questions, she knew Delgado was lying when he called Evans' death a simple case of sudden cardiac arrest. She knew if the Marines dug deep enough, they would find traces of Evans' extracurricular activities, and that might jeopardize the entire business.

Hallikonnoen never failed her employers, and she wasn't about to start, especially not because of some busybody Marines playing sheriff. Fortunately, she wouldn't need to keep them distracted for long. Besides, experience had taught her a trick or two that would keep uniformed automatons running around in circles while she struck.

**

A few modules over from where Hallikonnoen tossed and turned, Ed Limix and Curtis Delgado were sitting in the latter's office cubicle, enjoying a wee dram of Glen Arcturus from the Marine's private stash. Limix had ostensibly come to apologize for Movane's asperity, but in reality, he wanted something.

"Friends of mine were telling me your Sergeant Painter and his people are going around asking questions about Terry Evans. Now granted, we're not keen on dealing with cops, even if they're Marines doubling as the local police, but my friends speak with me, knowing I enjoy a direct line to the company commander."

Delgado nodded, waiting patiently for Limix to come to the point. Rolf Painter and Alpha Troop weren't getting much from the station's workers so far.

"So anyway, I understand from a solid source that Movane and Evans were close friends, closer than a chief admin normally gets to her staff."

"Lovers?"

Limix shrugged.

"Doubtful, but I'm sure it gets lonely at the top. I thought you might like to know." The miner raised his big hands. "But don't misunderstand me. I'm not accusing Romana of anything. For what it's worth, I think she's a straight arrow. But if she and Terry Evans were friends, perhaps she knows more than she's saying, or someone else does. It's a matter of asking the right questions."

Limix took a sip of whiskey while watching Delgado for a reaction.

The Marine cocked an amused eyebrow. "Are you on a fishing expedition, Ed?"

"Just trying to help."

"And I appreciate it. At this point, we're simply tying up loose ends. There's no evidence of foul play, and, as the doc said, sometimes, albeit rarely, the heart simply stops beating with no warning signs. As a wise man once said, we're given a finite number of heartbeats in this life. The only thing we can do is make sure we use them in the service of good rather than evil."

"A philosopher in uniform." Limix raised his glass. "What a concept. Here's to us having many heartbeats left."

Delgado picked his glass up and touched Limix's. "Here's to us."

They downed their drinks, and the miner stood.

"Thanks for the wee dram."

"My pleasure. Enjoy the rest of your evening."

Delgado, a thoughtful expression on his face, watched Ed Limix leave the barracks module. Why would Limix point his finger at someone he claims to respect for her integrity and honesty? So what if Evans and Movane were friends even though the latter was the former's superior? Unless Assenari Mining forbade fraternization among its staff, it was a non-issue. But Limix certainly had an agenda.

He stood, stripped off his uniform, and grabbed his toiletries bag. A quick shower, and then an early bedtime.

**\*\***

Deep in the bowels of the planet — Gallery B, Level Sixteen, Shaft One — Sergeant Moses Singh of number two section, Bravo Troop, and his winger, Corporal Raldy Rezal, carefully made their way around yet another set of red boulders and into one more abandoned gallery.

So far, on this shift, they'd explored three of the old tunnels, slowly filling-in the spotty map to a distance of one kilometer from the main gallery. It was a tiring job, climbing around or over small rockfalls, retracing their steps constantly after either hitting a dead end or reaching the maximum distance while pausing every few minutes to watch and scan for anything unusual.

He looked at the time in his helmet's heads-up display, then consulted the map on his tablet. There were two more abandoned tunnels leading off from Gallery B marked by Sergeant Testo as areas of interest, meaning the base's main computer had forgotten bits and pieces. Then he checked the state of both his and Rezal's rebreathers.

"I'm calling it a day," he said over the private frequency.

"Thank the Almighty. I'm ready for a shower and a cold one."

The Marines made their way back to the gigantic cavern and patiently waited for the lift, ignored by the people in the control module once they'd signed out.

Moses Singh, able to detect an IED at fifty meters and a detonator ticking away from twice that distance, was disoriented in this environment, let alone after spending hours in a closed pressure suit. He never noticed the shadowy figure watching from the mouth of Gallery B.

\*\*

Delgado sat at his desk, trying to concentrate on the words marching across its primary display. An amateur military historian, like so many Marine Officers, he often plunged into humanity's past so he could, as the philosopher Santayana aptly said, avoid repeating the same mistakes as his predecessors. But this time, even Douglas's enthralling dissection of the Second Migration War's most hard-fought ground battles didn't hold his attention.

Unfortunately, with the investigation essentially frozen, no word from Fleet HQ about when an expedition to retrieve the biological and chemical warheads would arrive, and his company carrying out its duties like a well-oiled machine, he felt a tad useless.

The only bright spot was Sergeants Testo and Kuzek worming their way into Terry Evans' account and discovering she enjoyed way more access than a simple logistics specialist should — at least in Delgado's opinion. On the other hand, she might not be an isolated case, but he didn't want Testo to trigger any hidden safeguards by checking the accounts of other administrative staffers.

As if he could sense his commanding officer's restlessness, First Sergeant Hak poked his head into the office cubicle and held up a thermos bottle.

"Ready for a midmorning cup of what passes for coffee around here, Skipper?"

"Sure. There's nothing better on offer right now." Delgado gestured at the spare chair as he pulled out a mug liberated from the station cafeteria.

Hak settled in and poured, then sat back, a thoughtful expression on his face.

"You know, Skipper, I've been thinking. If I wanted to neutralize Tyrell on my way to recovering those warheads, I might do it in one of two ways. First, there's the outside attack, say, a couple of mercenary ships hired by the opposition. Flatten the station, then help yourself to the payloads. The problem is, those three-hundred-millimeter plasma cannon could really ruin my day. Okay, then, sabotage the guns ahead of time. For that, you need an insider. If I infiltrate one or more operatives to take out the guns, why not also go after the comms, power generation, the garrison, anything else that would give me the best edge possible."

Delgado nodded. "That's pretty much what I've been figuring. Which makes Terry Evans' death somewhat more significant, considering the sort of access she enjoyed all over the station. But if the opposition plans to neutralize Tyrell from the inside before they retrieve the warheads, they'd be looking at something more complicated than simply messing with the various systems. Physical rather than virtual targeting, which would take a little more preparation time, especially if the insider's goal is surviving intact."

Hak tapped the side of his nose with an extended index finger. "And who can do things around here without raising an eyebrow?"

"Movane, Engstrom, a couple of the department heads, like Chief Engineer Sakamoto, and perhaps Ed Limix. He got us into the mines easily enough." Delgado took a sip of his coffee. "And they seemed nervous when we met yesterday."

"Could be there's a way of making them feel confident we're running after a wild hare, Skipper. And people who are confident when they shouldn't be often screw up somewhere and betray themselves."

"How?"

"Simple..."

When the First Sergeant finished his explanation, Delgado admitted it might even work. And if it didn't, there was no harm done.

# — Fourteen —

"I'm telling you, Lyle, those damned Marines are snooping around like they know something. What'll keep them from finding our stuff? And why did that dumbass die right after they replaced the regular garrison?"

Harry Zbotnicky's whining grated on Lyle Fournier's nerves. At least his buddy Joey wasn't around to echo each complaint. Lyle ignored the man and stared at the busy dance floor, absently swirling the greenish hooch in his glass.

He'd met Jannika Hallikonnoen an hour earlier, and the woman was worrying him. As much as she thought it didn't show, irritation at Evans' death and the Marines' sticking their noses in every corner of the station was breaking through her icy demeanor. But Lyle couldn't figure out why.

She was a dangerous woman, he knew that, but so far, she hadn't made too many demands on Fournier and his little gang of smugglers and petty crooks. A bit of information gathering here, some rumor spreading there, a few deliveries — package contents unknown — and a warning to stay ready for more important stuff.

Hallikonnoen had promised Fournier ample rewards if he did her bidding and a few choice words in the ears of the Marine garrison commander if he didn't. Fournier, like everyone in Tyrell, was here for the money. Still, he could tell she was working on something else.

He took a sip of his Shaft Slammer, letting the booze burn a hot path down his throat. Whatever that something was, it would happen soon. Otherwise, she'd let the current uproar die away.

"There's a shipment coming in five days on the resupply ship, Lyle. We should do something. These Marines will watch everything pretty closely, that's for sure. More so than the usual sort."

"Shut up, Harry. They won't find a damn thing and lower your voice. There's always a few of them over in the other corner watching and listening."

Unseen in the next booth, Jannika Hallikonnoen allowed herself a cruel smile as she decided. A distraction was what those Marines needed, and her tame smugglers would give them one. She could manage without them when the time came. Delgado and his people were welcome to Harry and his moronic sidekick for all the good that'd do them. But Lyle?

She watched Fournier and his acolyte leave the *Reach* as a plan crystallized in her mind. It would take a few days to set up, but the timing should be perfect. Absolutely perfect.

**

Deep in the bowels of Shaft One, Sergeant Sberna and Lance Corporal Torres emerged from the first of the two abandoned galleries, giving off Gallery B, Level Sixteen, with nothing extraordinary to report. Only one more tunnel to do, and with any luck, they'd get another assignment. Something fun, like preparing the base for demolition or giving this forsaken planet a new orifice using high explosives.

At the blood-red boulders blocking the way into the second gallery, Sberna pulled out his handheld battlefield sensor once more to check the surrounding rock for cracks or instability. The machine wasn't exactly designed for such work, meaning precision and effectiveness were less than optimum, but it gave him and Torres a certain sense of security.

Sberna studied the results, then slipped between the boulders and into the abandoned gallery. As they left the harsh yet comforting light of the main tunnel, their helmet visors' night vision function took over, showing them a gallery bathed in an eerie, faintly green glow.

Underfoot, regular dimples in the floor showed where the conveyor belt which once moved ore to the vacuum tube in the great cavern had been bolted down. Otherwise, there were no indications of the tunnel's former role.

The smooth walls receded in the distance, blending with the black of the dead planet's innards beyond the night vision visor's range. This was the tunnel at whose entrance he may or may not have seen something. But Sberna didn't believe in ghosts or other supernatural manifestations. And after trudging through dozens of abandoned galleries, he didn't think there was such a thing as secret hideouts three and a half kilometers underground either. He'd probably seen a natural shadow cast by the glare of the industrial lighting and let his imagination fill in the blanks.

Still, Sergeant Testo's patrol schedule ensured Sberna did that particular one last so as not to alarm anyone if it was being used for nefarious purposes.

As they walked in complete darkness, they spotted secondary galleries branching off from the main and investigated each, determining they were dead ends. And onwards they went, deeper and deeper into the old tunnel.

After another couple of dead end branches, the gallery came to an abrupt halt at a rockslide. Sberna and Torres searched the sides and top of the slide for anything hidden in the shadows, perhaps a way through. Then they turned off their visors and switched on powerful flashlights. Aiming them at every nook and cranny of the slide, they concluded it was impossible to pass without excavating.

As Sberna studied it, something tugged at the edge of his consciousness, something which drew from his intimate knowledge of explosives and their application in every context. After a few moments, he looked up at the ceiling, bathing it in light. The entire scene felt wrong, though he couldn't quite put his finger on the why quite yet.

"What do you make if it? Natural or unnatural?"

Torres picked up a melon-sized boulder and examined it. He tossed it aside after a lengthy examination and he climbed up the unstable pile of rocks until he reached the fractured ceiling to inspect it with his eyes and his sensor.

"A small charge might have created this, Sarge. I'm neither seeing nor picking up any fractures."

Torres climbed down again. "The slide isn't that wide — around five meters. No telling when it happened. Could be two years ago or this morning."

Sberna thought for a few moments but decided against further exploration, not without the Skipper's permission and not without tools and more people.

"Let's do an in-depth scan and head for home. If the major wants to go further, we can always come back."

"Roger that, Sarge."

# — Fifteen —

The following day, shortly before eleven-hundred hours, Delgado entered the command post after his daily briefing in Engstrom's office.

"So, how did they react to your tale?" Hak, ensconced in one of the hard chairs, took a sip from his unending coffee thermos.

"I am looking for an honest man," Delgado declared in a sonorous tone. "Diogenes."

"He the guy who used to live in a barrel?"

"So they say, Top. As the story goes, Diogenes wandered through ancient Athens carrying a lamp in broad daylight. When people asked why that's what he answered."

"By quoting the old Greek cynic," Testo said, grinning wryly, "I gather that our three friends did not come out of it smelling like roses, Skipper."

"Yeah. When I finished, Engstrom looked like he'd seen a ghost, Movane didn't react in any way, which is even more noteworthy, and our good pal Limix became vehement in his indignation."

"I think thou dost protest too much. I can't remember who said that. So even Limix shone like pyrite."

"Oh, did he ever. Can we stop the quotation festival for a while and talk seriously?" Delgado looked at the sergeants, Kuzek included, eyebrows raised.

"You started, sir," Testo replied with an air of wholly feigned innocence.

"My privilege," he replied, pointing to his rank insignia. "Where do we stand with our investigation and the other business?"

"We nearly completed the job of tapping into Tyrell's systems," Testo replied. "A few more days, and we'll enjoy complete access to the station's primary nodes. It doesn't mean we'll be able to do everything we want undetected but close enough. We hit a wall on the Evans side of things, though. Whoever set up her unauthorized access to various areas didn't leave any traces. I'm getting the sneaking suspicion that there's a little virus at work, erasing every clue the moment we're within detection range. We just about completed the survey of Shafts Two and Three. Nothing to report and no discrepancies between reality and the blueprints.

"Moses Singh and One-Two-Charlie will head down today and check out what's behind the rockslide Osmin Sberna and Carlo Torres found on Level Sixteen. Rolf Painter and his people are still checking out Evans' associates. Apart from Movane, she was friendly with a team boss called," Testo glanced at his workstation's display, "Jannika Hallikonnoen. Rolf will follow up on her."

"Okay," Delgado nodded. "You can stop chasing Evans' computer ghosts. When you're not busy hiding Moses Singh's moves, start working on the changes I want to the primary command-and-control files."

He placed a microchip on the table.

"Your defense plan, Skipper?"

"A few notions I came up with last night, nothing more. Whoever will try to seize the warhead stockpile might well do it by paralyzing Tyrell from the inside, and you can't plan properly against an enemy in your midst. We can only make sure we find out as soon as they act or, better yet, get a short warning period if we're lucky. And of course, make sure nobody can catch us with our pants around our ankles by using the base's main computer core."

Testo nodded thoughtfully. "If I come up with any more ideas..."

"Please feel free, Sergeant. Top," Delgado continued, turning toward Hak, "prepare a few discreet planning and preparation sessions for the troops."

"Ship defense?"

"Yeah. Being on the other end of the stick will be a bit of a change for everyone."

"Understood, sir." Hak nodded.

"If there's nothing else...?"

They shook their heads.

"Then let's do it. I'll be in my quarters, dreaming up a few more notions. Oh, that's right." Delgado snapped his fingers, remembering something. "When's the next ship from Assenari due?"

"In four days," Testo replied, glancing at his workstation again. "Why?"

Delgado grinned. "Think about it. We figure the opposition might already have a spy in place, perhaps even two. But I doubt a full saboteur team is sitting around, just waiting to be caught by smart Marines like us."

Metellus Testo's face lit up with a broad smile.

"But of course. The replacement workers. If you're right, Skipper, then our window of greatest danger is in the day or two after the Assenari ship leaves. That doesn't leave us much time to prepare. Not if we don't want the resident tangos to figure out that we've figured out."

"Right. We need something that'll divert attention from our actual activities."

"*Maskirovka*," Hak grumbled, chin against his chest. "What are you thinking, sir?"

"A little witch hunt? I've already sown the seeds this morning. All that's left is watering the soil."

\*\*

"The Marines figure Evans was involved in some drug thing, and her death might be suspicious?"

"Yeah, that's right. But I think Delgado just wants us to believe that. I'm sure the bastard was lying through his teeth. He's pulling a con. You wouldn't know anything about Evans' death, though, would you? I mean, you wrapped Lyle Fournier and his morons around your little finger, right?"

Hallikonnoen's eyes glittered dangerously as she looked at her informant. She thought she'd compartmentalized her help, but if he found out about Fournier, then so be it. There was nothing she could do now. Evans' unexpected death was a sore point. Hallikonnoen had not planned on killing her until she was no longer useful. Now she needed alternatives.

"I may not know how Evans died, but I will know everything about your death if you don't watch your step."

He raised his hands, palms facing outward. "Hey, we're on the same side."

Her face tightened briefly with contempt. He was nothing more than a tool, but a useful one and should be treated with care until he was no longer required.

"We are," she replied. "See if you can find out more. I don't believe Delgado and his people are incompetent. On the contrary. I'm worried they picked up something. The sergeants playing detective seem much too clever to be blundering around like amateurs. And before I forget, with Evans gone, you'll be ensuring I can still access the main computer core."

"Sure, but just don't expect to mess with the classified data banks or the programming. There's only so much I can do. The security protocols are not only code but terminal sensitive."

"Then you'll obtain what I want from the secure areas."

"I'll try, but I'm not a technical genius. In any case, I hope I can count on the generosity of your employers to pay a little extra for more hazardous duties."

Hallikonnoen answered with a noncommittal grunt. In her chosen field, she was as much a professional as the Marines were in theirs, and not only despised people who sold out for money, helpful as they were, but had a healthy respect for Delgado and his troopers. Too bad she had no time to cultivate another tool as backup for the greedy fool in front of her. Still, how much could the Marines do, even if they found out? Tyrell was a big place, and they were few. No, the plan could not fail.

She shrugged off her worries, and without another word, left her informant sitting in the booth. It was high time she set a few distractions loose among the unsuspecting and did something about Fournier, who'd become a liability now that the informant knew about him.

**

Engstrom, Limix, and Movane ate in silence, the ripples of Delgado's revelations that morning still roiling their thoughts. Movane was the first to finish and sit back. She stared at Engstrom with her usual sour expression.

"Delgado's hiding something, Nero. Use those stripes on your collar and make him answer."

Limix grunted in agreement as he chewed on a mouthful of hydroponics-grown lettuce.

Engstrom finished his last piece and carefully placed his fork on the empty plate.

"He won't talk to me, Romana. You saw for yourself that he doesn't trust either of us,"

"Why don't you tap into his security network," Limix said around another mouthful. "That way, you can keep track of what he's doing."

Movane nodded. "Ed's right. For the safety of Tyrell, we should use every means available to keep tabs on that loose cannon. Set it up properly and you can override any protection he's using. If you're really careful, you can even prevent him from knowing about it. And as you once mentioned, information systems are not only your specialty but your hobby."

"And if he finds out?"

"Tell him he should jump in a black hole."

"Oh, alright," Engstrom replied with a frown of irritation. "I suppose you'll want copies of what I find?"

"Don't we always run this place as a team?" Movane asked, smirking, convinced Nero Engstrom would be happy to share responsibility for the act. The man's weaknesses came in handy at times.

"Sure, a team." He didn't sound convinced, but Movane knew he'd do it.

\*\*

That evening, while Sergeant Singh and his section were in the abandoned tunnel off Gallery B, Level Sixteen, this time carrying excavation gear, Curtis Delgado was contemplating ideas to bolster his control over Tyrell. A knock on the office cubicle's door frame broke through his meditative state, and he looked up as Sergeant First Class Metellus Testo poked his head through the opening.

"Got a moment, Skipper?"

"I have nothing but moments, Sergeant. What's up?" Delgado gestured at the much-abused chair fronting his desk.

"Two interesting bits of news," Testo said once he was seated. "First, despite your orders to the contrary, one of our three luminaries upstairs spoke out of turn. The whole base is abuzz with rumors of drug smuggling and murder. To use an old cliché, the cat is among the pigeons."

"Even if it doesn't tell us much about the troika's loyalties, it confirms that one of them at least cannot be trusted. Good, it'll make our witch hunt deception that much more plausible. Next?"

"We picked up a peeping tom."

Delgado sat up and frowned. "Pardon?"

"Someone's trying to tap into our computer node." As Delgado made to speak, Testo raised his right hand, palm facing outward. "Carl Kuzek's already on it, Skipper. The sensitive stuff has been moved to a node not connected with the station's net and is now being replaced with plausible garbage. Whoever it is hasn't breached the first level of safeguards yet. And no, we can't tell where it's coming from yet, except that our hacker is skilled. We won't be able to run a trace until we put the deception data in place. Offhand I'd say you did a good job spooking the station's top brass."

Delgado sat back and smiled.

"You know, this is a golden opportunity to feed the opposition choice bits of crap so we can trap them. In the immortal words of Sun Tzu, all warfare is based on deception. Hence, when able to attack, we must be seen unable; when using our forces, we must seem inactive..."

"When we are near," Testo continued, "We must make the enemy believe we are far away, and such good stuff. Definitely an opportunity, Skipper."

"Did I just hear Metellus quote the Master?" Hak asked, stepping into Delgado's office.

Testo gestured at his commanding officer. "Don't look at me, Top. He started it."

"The highest form of generalship is to balk the enemy's plans," Delgado intoned sententiously. "We've cast bread upon the waters, and a fish has risen to feed. The good sergeant and I were discussing what kind of net we should use."

Hak rubbed his hands gleefully and sat on the remaining chair, an expectant air on his seamed face. "So where do we start, sir?"

# — Sixteen —

"You damn fool. Now Delgado will know one of us blabbed."

The rumors about Evans' death and the ugly thought of drug smugglers on the station made the rounds like wildfire, thanks to Hallikonnoen's network of stooges. It was the chief topic of conversation, even in the darkest corner of the *Reach*, where people could meet without being seen.

Hallikonnoen shrugged, struggling to contain her irritation.

"It's better this way," she replied, keeping her voice carefully neutral so she didn't spook her informant. She still needed a way into the Marines' command-and-control node. "Even if Delgado threw you a red herring, he's stuck acting on the rumors or at least pretending to do so. Especially if I send some tidbits his way. That'll keep him distracted. Besides, I'll bet my tour bonus he doesn't trust any of you, so what does it matter?"

"Just make sure your little tidbits don't get me fingered. Remember, I'm your only conduit to the information you need."

"Do your job, and you'll be amply rewarded." Hallikonnoen drained her glass and placed it on the stained tabletop. "Keep me informed of anything you find in their files, and I'll see that my employers reward your extra efforts lavishly."

She rose and cast a last glance at the informant. Greed struggled with nervousness in a face that increasingly repelled her. Then, she left the *Reach* and returned to her quarters.

\*\*

"Our friendly hacker just circumvented the first level of protection, Skipper," Sergeant Testo announced when Delgado entered the command post the following morning.

"It's about time." Delgado scoffed. "Amateurs. Any longer, and I'd think our magnificent works of fiction would stay unread."

"The moment he or she starts the investigation files, I'll launch a trace." A pause. "And here we go. They're reading the fake summary."

Delgado grinned at his operations noncom. "I hope the reviews will be favorable. It's so hard to find an appreciative audience for pseudo-fiction these days."

**

Deep below Erinye Company's command post, Staff Sergeant Singh and his Marines stood in front of a now dismantled rockslide, their excavation tools propped against a sidewall behind them. After a quick scan, which revealed nothing, Singh sent a fire team through the narrow opening they'd created.

A few minutes later, the section's radio frequency came to life with a single word.

"Clear."

Singh left one fire team behind and crawled through the opening with the rest of his Marines.

The gallery on the other side held no surprises. It disappeared into the darkness beyond the reach of their night vision visors, straight as an arrow and as smooth-walled as every other tunnel.

Slowly, the Marines moved deeper and deeper into the bowels of the planet, stopping every few minutes to scan ahead with their battlefield sensors until the tunnel abruptly stopped at a blank, smooth rock wall. Singh and his troopers stood there, puzzled. They saw no secondary galleries, and their sensors detected nothing more than solid rock.

"If this is a dead end, then why the suspiciously artificial-looking rockslide, Sarge?" Corporal Rezal asked.

"Beats me. Let's give it a good scan, then head home and see what the major says."

**

"You told us you discovered something, and I hate being kept needlessly waiting." Movane toyed with the food on her plate while staring at Engstrom.

The latter had organized an impromptu working supper, gleefully hinting at new developments.

"After coffee." Though Movane scowled at him, Engstrom could not keep a smile of triumph from tugging at his lips.

Limix and Movane seemed to have reversed roles tonight. Where the chief administrator usually kept a reserved countenance, she now displayed unusually and uncharacteristic impatience. Limix, on the contrary, seemed far from his ebullient self.

Dragging out the suspense as much as he dared, Engstrom relished each sip of coffee, returning a superior smile for each of Movane's dirty looks. Finally, he put down his empty cup, wiped his lips with a napkin, and stood.

"It's time, my friends, to gaze into the looking glass."

"Looking glass? What kind of garbage is that?" Limix demanded.

Movane threw him a withering look. "Lewis Carroll. Alice in Wonderland. Not an exact quote. Try reading some classics, Ed. It'll do you good."

Limix grunted dismissively as he joined his two companions at Engstrom's desk. Like a piano player, the latter theatrically raised his arms and stretched his fingers before dropping his hands to touch his workstation's control screen. His fingers danced for a few seconds, then a line of writing appeared on the screen. Movane whistled appreciatively.

"Nicely done, Nero. So, they found perimortem needle punctures on Evans' body and figure her death could stem from an intentional overdose of a drug that broke down in the bloodstream before she was autopsied."

Engstrom raised a hand. "It gets better. They found a small stash of an illicit substance in Evans' quarters and figure she fell out with persons unknown but active in the trade. Evans could have been a dealer. Her work as a logistics specialist gave her full access to shipments brought in by the regular Assenari transports and made her an ideal conduit for illegal substances. Delgado plans on searching everything that comes off the next one. And there's more."

The text on the office's primary display dissolved and was replaced by a different paragraph.

"They figure on setting up automatic scanners by the change room airlocks to pinpoint miners with traces of banned substances clinging to their clothes. But without telling me or anyone else."

"Can Delgado do that on his own authority?" Movane asked.

"Technically, no. But if I let on that I found out, he'll know someone hacked into their node. Best I let him chase his own tail looking for smugglers who don't exist."

Movane let out a skeptical grunt. "I don't know if that's a good idea, Nero."

"Trust me. The Marine mentality is rather straightforward. Delgado isn't the sort capable of playing four-dimensional chess. Getting into their files wasn't much of a challenge."

"That's what worries me."

Limix patted Engstrom on the shoulder. "Nicely done in any case. At least now we can keep up with what they're doing behind our backs. What else do you plan on digging up?"

"If the rest of their protective layers are like the first one, we can probably read every single record. So what do we want? Personal files to discover hidden vices? Delgado's secret plans? You name it, I'll find it."

Limix grinned at him. "Why not everything. It'll make for amusing after-dinner reading."

**

Several modules below the executive deck, Sergeant First Class Metellus Testo looked up from his command post workstation display and allowed himself a smug smile. He tapped the communicator.

"Niner, this is Zero."

A few seconds later, Delgado's face appeared on the main screen.

"Niner here. The Top is with me. What's up."

Hak appeared beside him seconds later.

"Someone hacked into our node from the station commandant's office this time, Skipper."

"Figures that a professional engineer with an all-access pass to the entire outfit would be the one. But I somehow doubt he's in the opposition's pocket. He's not a good enough actor to be useful." Delgado ran his fingers through his close-cropped red hair. "Which leaves us with Movane and Limix as possible culprits."

"Seen much of our friendly shop steward lately, sir?"

"Now that you mention it, no. I don't think he's actively avoiding me. I just don't run across him, although it could be for many reasons. Still, Limix got us into the mine against the wishes of Engstrom and Movane."

"To pull the wool over our eyes?" Hak asked.

Delgado chuckled, though it was devoid of humor. "A man can twist his brains into tight little knots just thinking about the possible blinds and double blinds. Anyway, we have a conduit to disseminate disinformation. I guess the next step is leaving an erroneous defense plan for our hackers to find. That'll give us an edge if the opposition tries something other than a bombardment from high orbit, beyond the range of Tyrell's guns."

"Which we now control, by the way, sir."

Hak gave Testo thumbs up.

"Good." He glanced at Delgado. "What about the witch hunt?"

"We give them exactly what they expect, now that they've read our fictional case file."

"The miners won't like it."

"Tough." Delgado paused as his brow crinkled in thought. "No, wait. Tell our barflies to spread the word that Engstrom and Movane pushed us into it, Top."

Hak let out a grim chuckle. "The Admiral would approve, sir."

# — Seventeen —

Moses Singh was nothing if not a methodical man, a trait he shared with most in Ghost Squadron who routinely faced extreme danger. As per Major Delgado's orders, he took his section back to the rockslide, and they re-examined every square centimeter of the tunnel beyond it.

By the time they reached the blank wall, Singh felt almost ready to admit there was no mystery. Not even a little one. But he put his people to work scanning the abrupt dead end with the larger crew-served sensor package, nonetheless. After a few minutes, Corporal Raldy Rezal pointed out the apparent discrepancy.

"Sarge, this wall here doesn't look like a mining mole touched it. Otherwise, there'd be a deep dimple in the middle. Moles have pointed snouts, as I remember from our orientation visit."

"Right." Singh drew out the word. "Could be they used lasers or plasma borers."

"Nope. Check the floor, walls, and ceiling around the dead end. They're smooth. Mole smooth, just like we saw

**134**

in the active galleries. That, as they say, is impossible. The mole's snout is a meter long. Therefore, the smooth sides should stop at least a meter from this wall." He tapped the dead end for emphasis.

"When you've eliminated the impossible, whatever remains, however improbable, has to be the truth," Lance Corporal Hobart Lee intoned. "Sherlock Holmes. Perhaps this wall is a blind, Sarge."

Singh gave the short, squat Marine a look of surprise.

"How is it you can quote ancient English philosophers, H. L?"

"Because I read the classics and not just modern trash, Sarge?" Lee retorted, amusement dancing in his dark eyes. "But seriously, why don't we try picking at this wall. A bit of laser, a bit of plasma..."

"And then we'll find an old English philosopher on the other side. Okay, Rezal, Maiikonnen and Drake, let's go."

A few minutes later, Raldy Rezal swore as he shut off the laser borer. "By the Almighty, this is impossible. I may not be a geologist, but it isn't granite, even if it looks and scans like granite."

"But there's no denying it absorbs the laser beam as if it were a giant heat sink."

"Let's try a shaped charge," Lee proposed.

Singh shook his head. "We don't know the condition of the rock around here. Using explosives could bring the roof on our heads."

"I guess that rules out the portable rocket launcher. Sad."

Singh gave Lee an exasperated glare. "Your fascination with blowing things up always worries me."

"Hey, Colonel Decker enjoys solving problems with high explosives, which means I'm in good company."

"Can anyone come up with better ideas?"

Rezal said, "Nope. But if the wall absorbs a steady stream of energy, maybe it'll choke on a concentrated burst."

"Ah, yes," Singh nodded and pulled his blaster out of its holster. "Here it goes."

He snapped off a shot at the center of the wall. To the amazement of the watching Marines, the round vanished into the rock. It didn't splash or create a hole but simply sailed right through.

"By the Infinite Void," Singh said, "if I were a betting man, I'd wager we're looking at the best hologram I've ever seen."

"How about a holographic projection covering a force field, Sarge?" Raldy Rezal suggested. "Force fields stop matter but absorb energy, like the ones they use to keep the air in when opening space doors."

"Except they let spacecraft through."

"Yep. Countervailing energy emissions on spacecraft hulls along with slow velocity crossing the field."

Singh contemplated his winger for a moment. "So how do we create a countervailing field on our tin suits? They're built to be stealthy, not to emit."

"How about we collapse the field?" Lance Corporal Drake said. "It surely has a limit on how much energy it can absorb in a short time before the emitter shuts off. I'm going to guess this thing here isn't equipped with a failsafe like space door emitters either."

"You're suggesting we simply open fire on this?" Singh gestured at the blank wall.

"It's gotta be worth a try. But from a distance, I'd say, Sarge."

When Singh seemed to hesitate, Rezal said, "If we bring this idea to the Skipper, he'll tell us to try. Might as well save ourselves a trip and just do it."

"Okay. Let's back up thirty meters and give it a few volleys dead center."

Singh and his Marines withdrew and, at his command, adopted firing positions.

"Aim." Six red dots appeared on the wall and quickly merged into one. "Fire."

Plasma rounds lit up the tunnel as bright as day.

"I swear I saw a shimmer, Sarge."

"Me too."

"Let's try this again. Five rounds, rapid fire. Aim. Fire." A pause. "Another five rounds, fast as you can. Aim. Fire."

As soon as the flare of light from the plasma volleys died away, Rezal let out a whoop.

"It's flickering and sparking."

Singh aimed again and squeezed off two quick shots on his own, and the seemingly impossible wall vanished. He stood and slung his carbine.

"Shall we go see what was behind illusion number one?"

When they reached the spot where the fake obstruction used to be, they found nothing more than a pair of emitters bolted to the walls on either side, both connected to a black power cord that vanished into the darkness beyond.

"Whatever kept the illusion up is at the end of that power cord, Sarge." Drake took a few steps deeper into the tunnel.

"Still master of the obvious, eh." Singh pointed at Maiikonnen and Lee. "You two stay here and take intensive scans of the emitters. The rest, with me."

"Roger that, Sarge."

They didn't go far. A few meters beyond the bend, they encountered an armored door, one with a coded lock. The cord ended at a blank rock wall beside the door. Singh shook his head, exasperated at the feeling of wandering through a holographic role-playing game.

He scanned the door, scrutinized its lock, then turned his section around to head for home. The major would decide on the next steps. Weird was no longer the operative word around here. They'd gone well beyond that.

\*\*

"I don't like this, Lyle. The Marines are about to grab us by the short and curlies." Harry Zbotnicky and his pal Joey looked like a pair of anxious rabbits, cowering in the dark corners of the booth.

Around them, the *Reach* lived and breathed as usual, except for anxious, angry, or self-righteous mutterings about the Marines' upcoming crackdown on smugglers, something that seemed to attack the very freedoms miners considered as their sacred right. Especially the freedom from random searches, even if they weren't hands-on.

"Shut up and let me think, Harry."

For all his bluster, Lyle Fournier was a worried man. If the Marines caught him red-handed, guys like Ed Limix would make sure he never worked again. The Marines supposedly used battlefield sensors that could spot camouflaged enemy troops from hundreds of meters away, which meant they could sniff a stash from up close without a problem.

But in an airless environment, perhaps not so much. As far as Fournier could tell, police sensors relied on airborne particles to detect banned substances. Did their sensors also rely on airborne particles? Jannika should be able to tell him. She knew things no honest miner should. If he was lucky, she might even help. They'd done enough jobs for her lately.

"Wait here and don't move," Lyle growled at his two companions. He left the booth to search for Hallikonnoen, and it didn't take him long to spot her.

"Hey Jannika, how's it been?" Lyle grinned as he approached her table.

"What do you want, Fournier? I told you I make contact, not the other way around."

Her harsh tone and angry glare stopped Fournier dead in his tracks. After a moment, he closed the remaining distance and leaned over so he could speak without being overheard.

"It's this Marine drug search thing. Me and the boys are still holding, and we'll be getting more on the next ship. I was figuring you'd know a thing or two."

Hallikonnoen fought her antipathy for the smuggler and tried to give him an attentive ear. She'd planned on using him as bait for Delgado's troopers but remained undecided on how at the moment. However, Fournier might unwittingly give her ideas. She motioned for him to sit and speak.

"Okay, we agree the Marines' battlefield sensors are top-notch. Are they good enough to sniff out well-packed merchandise from a distance?" Fournier asked, peering around the room.

"Yeah. They can detect minute concentrations that would escape the best genetically enhanced police dog — if they program them to search for something in particular. There are limitations, but essentially, that's it."

"Meaning if I hid my stash underground, where there's no air, they can't find it, right?"

Hallikonnoen nodded, a sudden idea nearly making her smile. She gave Lyle a calculating glance.

"Right. And I think I figured a way of helping you with that."

"Really? I appreciate it, Jannika. If there's anything I can do for you, just say the word. When shall I bring you our remaining inventory?"

# — Eighteen —

"And finally, we came across a worker by the name Jannika Hallikonnoen who struck us as a rather interesting individual, Skipper." Rolf Painter called up an image of her on the primary display.

"She's a team boss, which means this is not her first tour in Tyrell, yet no one can remember her previous tours. Or if they do, they're holding back. Either way, that's mighty strange. Hallikonnoen knew Terry Evans, but people who saw them together didn't think they were exactly friends, not in the way Evans was friendly with Movane if we can believe Ed Limix. One witness thought Evans behaved in a subservient attitude toward Hallikonnoen as if she worked for her in some capacity. As a personal observation, most people here seem hesitant to talk about Hallikonnoen, and we got the impression a few consider her dangerous. Other than that, apparently, she doesn't speak much about anything beyond work."

"Perhaps she's someone we should watch," Testo suggested.

Painter shrugged. "Might be a little difficult. She frequents the *Reach* when off-duty and not in her cubicle, where she usually occupies one of the rear booths from which you can see without being seen. However, we noted that sometimes, she's neither in the bar nor her quarters when she's off-duty. None of the others in her module are aware of her movements or aren't saying."

"Try to find out, will you, Rolf?"

"Already on it, Skipper."

As Painter left, Hak glanced at the time.

"Ready, sir?"

Delgado nodded and stood.

"As ready as I'll ever be. You have the watch, Top."

"Aye, aye, Skipper. Sergeant Singh and One-Two-Charlie are waiting for you in the locker room."

Something on his workstation screen attracted Testo's attention. "It seems the hacker in Engstrom's office has nearly broken through the second level of protection."

"Persistent bugger, ain't he or she?" Delgado sketched a salute and left.

\*\*

Curtis Delgado, wearing an armored pressure suit and combat harness like the Marines of Singh's section and carrying a plasma carbine loosely slung over his shoulder, stood where the fake wall once was and studied the emitters.

"Hologram on top of a force field. Interesting."

"It was pretty realistic, sir."

"I can't imagine moving the power pack that'll feed it, though," Delgado replied, eyes tracing the black cord nestled at the foot of the tunnel wall. "Let's take a look at that door you found."

When they reached it, Singh checked the tiny tell-tales he'd left on his last visit.

"Seems like no one opened it since we were here last." He gestured at Raldy. "Time you used your skills for good rather than evil."

Sergeant Testo had spent most of the night shift looking for evidence the door lock in front of them was plugged into the station's network, but without success, meaning it was most likely a standalone, which suited Delgado.

He stepped aside, leaving Raldy to squat in front of the lock and scan it. After a few moments, he stood again.

"No need for my subtlety, Sarge. Although it may not seem so to the untrained eye, that there is a Hopkins-Payne model one-three-five-zee beneath the skin." The designation meant nothing to the other Marines, and Delgado made a come-on signal, encouraging Raldy to elaborate. "Sorry, sir. This model is a standalone lock. It won't be connected to any network. If we blow it off, no one will find out unless they come down here and see for themselves."

"I'd rather we didn't use high explosives, Corporal. It's best if we leave no traces of our passage."

"No sweat, sir. I'll pop this for you in a moment with no one being the wiser."

Raldy crouched again, stuck his sensor against the lock, and ran through what looked like an esoteric search sequence, but the Erinyes were confident he would find the proper release code. After all, Raldy was Bravo Troop's designated lock pick, a skill he'd developed in his younger days before joining the Corps.

Less than two minutes later, a green light blinked, and Raldy stepped back.

"Done."

Singh reached for the small wheel in the middle of the door and turned it counter clockwise. When the wheel stopped, he pushed the slab of steel inward, and it swung back easily, revealing a well-lit scene beyond the threshold.

"What the hell is going on here?" Singh asked no one in particular as he moved aside and allowed the troopers designated as point into the chamber, one of them scanning with his battlefield sensor, the other one covering him with his carbine.

\*\*

Harry Zbotnicky felt his heart catch as he passed through the airlock leading to the miner's change room. Joey, hard on Zbotnicky's heels, cursed under his breath. Without bothering to hide their presence, several Marines were installing automatic sensors in the room itself. Both men were carrying their remaining inventory in satchels so they could give it to Lyle Fournier, who'd found a good hiding place underground.

Talk among the miners and smelter operators had acquired an indignant edge, fed by warnings of a Marine crackdown and stirred up by militants within the unionized ranks. Rumors that Engstrom and Movane ordered the action made no impression on the workers, and they almost immediately shunned off-duty Marines in the *Reach*, cafeteria, and other public spaces.

The emerging consensus viewed the automated sensors as a violation of civil rights in the form of unwarranted searches. Who knew what else those infernal machines could detect without the miners knowing? While the hardy and mainly honest men and women did not want smugglers within their ranks, they refused to live in police state conditions.

Ed Limix promised to discuss the matter with Engstrom, but the other team bosses sensed his reluctance. Most put it off to Limix's experiences with drug dealers on Hesperia III. Still, within a few shifts, the opposition coalesced around Limix's primary opponent, and there were mutterings of recalling him as shop steward because his cozy relationship with management suddenly seemed like a sellout.

However, a few workers appeared untouched by the growing controversy, but no one noticed, something for which Jannika Hallikonnoen was thankful.

It was shift change time, and the air in the locker room buzzed with animated discussions. In a corner, Hallikonnoen was waiting for Lyle Fournier. The seeds of distraction she'd sown were sprouting healthy little offshoots, and she was pleased — the Marines now faced growing hostility from the workers.

As she had hoped, underestimating the military mind for once, they embraced their policing powers with gusto. A few more touches, something that would really set the pot roiling, and she would be free to act. Soon. Very soon. And that fool Engstrom was playing right into her hands. Because of her informant, she knew everything he uncovered in the Marines' files. Once she had their defense plan...

Sudden movement nearby jerked her back to reality. Lyle Fournier nervously smiled at her above his pressure suit collar. He carried a full satchel under his arm.

"I've got it, Jannika. Just as you said. I owe you big for this."

Hallikonnoen grunted as she stared at him. Wordlessly, she held out a bag, and Fournier dropped his satchel into it. She squeezed the bag until it was emptied of air, sealed it, and shoved it into her own satchel.

With a swift motion that caught Fournier off-guard, she grabbed the smaller man by his suit's carrying handle, just below the collar, and lifted him single-handed against the bulkhead until his feet dangled a few centimeters above the metal-mesh floor.

"You tell anyone about this, and you're taking an elevator ride into the mine without a suit." Her tone, soft as it was, conveyed a menace like none Fournier ever faced before.

"Sure thing, Jannika," he croaked. "Even Harry and Joey don't know what I'm doing with the stuff."

"Make sure it stays that way." She let him drop, and his boots hit the deck with a metallic clang. The few miners who saw the incident couldn't hear what was said but were aware enough about Hallikonnoen's habits to ignore her doings.

# — Nineteen —

Nero Engstrom worked away at his console alone in his office, feeling powerful, perhaps even omniscient. The undetected tendrils he'd sent into the Marine garrison's node gave him an advantage over that insufferable major who ignored Engstrom's more senior rank and his authority as the station commander.

If Delgado persisted in refusing to share his plans and findings — oh, he did it ever so politely, but still — Engstrom would obtain what he wanted via other means. Especially anything about the Evans matter. Delgado's investigation was quickly turning a placid mining operation upside down.

He finally broke through the second level of protection and accessed the company's personnel files, never wondering why they would bother loading them into their command post node.

"Interesting," he muttered as Delgado's file came up.

Contrary to the Marine's claims he was recently promoted but left in place as company commander until his next posting was available, he'd been a major for some time and sent back to command a rifle company after prematurely leaving a more senior position. From what little the naval officer knew about the Corps, it could only mean Delgado either stomped on the wrong toes or screwed up sufficiently for a punishment tour but not enough for more formal measures. And he'd taken his sweet time reaching the rank of major in the first place after officer candidate school, which told Engstrom that Delgado wasn't one of the Corps' shining lights.

First Sergeant Hak's career summary was equally unimpressive. Busted to private from buck sergeant once; not selected for a commission after four years as a command sergeant leading an infantry platoon; no special qualifications, just like his company commander, and many years as first sergeant, bouncing around from one assignment to the other.

After perusing the senior sergeants' files, Delgado's company seemed like a collection of sad sacks good only as garrison troopers. And as Sergeant First Class Metellus Testo, whose own faked record was dull, hoped, Engstrom swallowed every bit of it, chuckling to himself as he thought up ways of humiliating Delgado.

He scheduled another quiet evening meal with Movane and Limix and would again amaze them with his findings, especially the news Tyrell's workers had nothing to fear from the Marines.

\*\*

Delgado, astonished beyond words, stepped through the open doorway and into a smooth-sided chamber lit up bright as day. One by one, the other Marines joined him and became rooted to the spot as they gazed around open-mouthed.

"We're not in Kansas anymore, Toto," H.L. said in a soft tone.

Predictably, the quote earned him a questioning "Huh?" from Singh.

"The Wonderful Wizard of Oz. Early twentieth century children's story," H.L. replied, not making things any more straightforward for his section leader.

Singh knew when he was beaten and grunted. "You spend way too much time following in Colonel Decker's footsteps and memorizing useless old sayings."

"And you'll note that it's *Colonel* Decker these days, Sarge, when once upon a time, he wore the same lance corporal hook as the rest of us. Maybe memorizing trivia is what got him there."

"All right." Delgado raised a gauntleted hand. "Our time is limited, so fan out and scan."

The tunnel section beyond the armored door was approximately twenty meters long by ten meters wide, twice the width of standard galleries. But instead of the faintly rough walls left behind by mining moles, these were slick, shiny, as if carved by a high-powered laser or subjected to the intense heat of a nuclear blast.

The tunnel ended with another closed door. However, this one bore as little resemblance to the one they'd just cracked open as the first biplanes to modern dropships.

Besides the far door, the most notable feature was a small elevator base unit adding a bump to an otherwise straight wall. It was recognizable as a human construct, like the armored door, and Delgado gestured at Singh.

"Make sure you check out the lift with exceeding delicacy, Sergeant. Let's not activate it since we don't know where it ends."

While the Marines, battlefield sensors in hand, carefully scanned each square centimeter of the tunnel, Delgado headed for the slick gray door, which screamed alien to his experienced eyes. He'd been on enough non-human worlds to develop a clear sense of what was manufactured by his species and what wasn't, and this one gave off an awfully familiar if strange vibe.

The small elevator base unit proved that someone human from the station worked down here. But nowhere was this section mentioned in Tyrell's database. Testo hadn't even found traces of an extra elevator shaft, distinct from those serving the mine galleries, which meant its upper terminus was well hidden.

"Mystery is another name for our ignorance," Delgado muttered, studying the strange door's surface.

"Pardon, sir?" Sergeant Singh asked.

"Never mind. Just something I remembered from one of the old books Colonel Decker donated to the regimental library."

Lance Corporal Lee let out an amused chuckle.

"I guess the major is bucking to become a colonel as well. Another wise man said, if you go directly to the heart of a mystery, it ceases to be a mystery and becomes only a question of drainage. If you'll step aside, sir, I'll work my sensor magic and see if the mystery of this door will drain away."

Delgado stepped to one side and reminded himself he was a tourist while watching his Marines work under Singh's direction. But it proved in vain.

The inner door resisted attempts at analysis. They found no apparent locks, no release mechanism, and no hinges. The sensors picked up a large space on the far side but couldn't say what, if anything, might wait for whoever found a way through.

Only the elevator shaft revealed a few of its secrets. It was a simple anti-grav cage in what seemed like a perfectly straight borehole leading upward, presumably to the station's inhabited modules. It drew power from a pair of contact strips lining the borehole. Those strips, in turn, were connected to a small portable fusion unit embedded in the elevator's base, which, judging by the cable, also fed the force field emitters. The lift cage was currently resting at the bottom of the shaft, though they found nothing to indicate when it was last used.

Delgado fought back the temptation to send Singh up with a few troopers and find out where it ended, figuring the upper terminal would be monitored and locked. They could easily calculate the probable location by plotting their current position and assuming the shaft was absolutely straight.

"I guess we're done here, sir," Singh finally said.

"Yep. Let's head for home and run your scans through the tactical AI."

"Spooky, though, isn't it?"

"You got that right, Sergeant."

# — Twenty —

"Our friendly hacker in Engstrom's office spent a leisurely afternoon browsing through the doctored personal files, sir," Sergeant Testo reported the moment Delgado joined him and Hak in the command post after returning to the surface. "I asked Rolf to check on the triumvirate, and only Engstrom was in the office. He may not be working for the opposition, but he surely has an agenda."

Hak shrugged.

"Someone told them about the Second Migration War ammo bunker, and Engstrom is one of the few here who knows what the recon droid found, if not the specifics. He might well be the leak. Perhaps he was even a Black Sword member who escaped detection and the subsequent purge. So, what strange and wonderful things did you discover, Skipper? Moses Singh seemed pretty subdued when he checked in."

Delgado, dressed once more in his black battledress, shook his head.

"I don't know, Top. Let's run the data Moses and his people collected through the tactical AI and see. But only after it's disconnected from the rest of the station's systems. Since Captain Engstrom is weaseling his way into our node and we tapped into every other node, there could be unknown hostile elements lurking among the data streams, waiting for a misstep on our part."

"It's disconnected, sir. And running the analysis of the scans." Testo keyed through the visual record while the AI digested the sensor scans.

The first results appeared on a side screen, and it seemed that the vaunted special operations tactical AI was drawing blanks.

Delgado tapped his chin with extended fingers.

"Hmm. Substance of the door, unknown. Age, unknown. No EM traces, no signs of hidden mechanisms." He fell silent for a few seconds. "You know, this reminds me of things we saw a few times during raids in the Zone, the sort that have only one explanation."

A faint smile twisted Hak's lips. "You too, Skipper?"

"Yeah. Tell me we didn't just score a twofer by stumbling across a L'Taung era cache, which just happens to be in the general vicinity of a Second Migration War ammo bunker."

"The old proto-Shrehari civilization from a hundred thousand years ago which collapsed after establishing a huge interstellar empire?" Testo asked. "I always figured they were a myth. And from what I read, the present-day Shrehari think so."

"They're real. We found sufficient evidence of an ancient star-faring civilization in this part of the galaxy, which vanished when our ancestors were still roaming across Earth, hunting for food with stone-tipped spears. Whether they were proto-Shrehari is still up for debate."

"Bit of a coincidence, though, finding a L'Taung trove here," Hak said in a dubious tone. "And you know how I feel about coincidences, Major."

Delgado glanced at his first sergeant.

"This planet had an atmosphere at one point, not that long ago in the grand scheme of things based on geological evidence. Perhaps it was still inhabitable during the L'Taung era. It might even have lost its atmosphere because of some ghastly attack as the civilization collapsed rather than from violent natural causes."

"Okay." Hak nodded. "I'll buy the idea that the L'Taung owned this rock at one time and stuck a cache well below the surface to protect it from orbital bombardment when their society cracked apart. Perhaps as a way of preserving things that could help them rebuild their empire. But how the hell did one of the Migration War factions end up placing an ammo bunker in the same area, except at the bottom of a canyon and not three and a half klicks beneath the surface? It's a big planet."

Delgado grimaced. "I can't answer that, Top. Sheer coincidence? Or perhaps when the bunker's builders were looking for a stable spot on a planet that's still geologically active, they came to the same conclusion as the L'Taung. Perhaps on top of being a stable spot, something about this vicinity makes it more impervious to orbital scans because of how the bedrock is structured along with the abundance of mineral deposits that are Tyrell Station's reason for being."

"Sounds plausible, but it's still a stretch."

Another shrug. "There are more things in heaven and earth, Horatio, than are dreamt of in your philosophy."

"Say what now, sir?"

"William Shakespeare, from his play *Hamlet*. The whole business of unknown unknowns. But here we are. Why isn't anyone at Fleet HQ aware of this? Clearly, someone built the lift we saw in recent times, probably before the Fleet bought Tyrell from Assenari."

"Could be HQ knows, and Admiral Talyn didn't think we needed to for this mission, sir."

"Anything is possible. But I wonder whether the opposition is in on it."

Sergeant Testo made a face. "They heard about the Second Migration War ammo bunker quickly enough, Skipper, and we don't know how long ago this supposed L'Taung artifact was found, but it wasn't yesterday. Considering it's at the end of a gallery abandoned while Assenari still owned Tyrell, I think we can assume knowledge of its existence has been circulating for at least a year, perhaps even longer."

"I doubt many people are aware. When a secret is worth keeping, those in charge of enforcement become pretty heavy-handed." Delgado ran a hand, fingers splayed through his hair. "But yeah, the opposition could be aware, which means they might gun for both targets. In any case, we won't speak of what we found to anyone."

"Moses already briefed his people on the importance of staying *stumm*, even within the company, sir," Hak said.

"Good. Now, as much as I'd like to find out what's behind that door, I'm equally interested in finding the lift's upper terminus. If the opposition tries a two for one, that's where they'll be looking."

"The AI is running a search while it analyzes the data from the mystery of the deep, sir."

"How long before it spits out results?"

"An hour or so."

Delgado turned to Hak. "Buy you a coffee while we wait?"

"Sure thing."

When they returned, Testo was waiting for them by the command post's primary display, which showed a picture of the mysterious door.

As they sat, Delgado asked, "What do you have, Sergeant?"

Testo pointed at the image.

"See here, right in the middle, sir. A normal visual scan shows nothing visible to the naked or even enhanced eye. But if we examine it under heavy magnification, you can detect a small line running straight from top to bottom dead center."

Delgado nodded. "Meaning it opens in the middle. Now we need a door handle."

"Since that's the only thing the AI found on the door itself, we can reasonably determine the opening mechanism isn't part of it. Next, the AI analyzed the scans of the wall on either side."

The image of the door vanished, replaced by what Delgado recognized as a composite representation of the slick stone surface, with each of its constituent minerals in a different shade.

"See that black rectangle, sir? It's the only part the AI can't identify. I suspect it's made out of the same material as the door and might be a smaller one."

"But we saw nothing, even with the enhanced eye, so it was well camouflaged. Interesting."

"Indeed. And that's pretty much it, sir. The AI can't figure out how the door and that rectangle are related, let alone if the latter opens the former."

"Okay. Find me the upper terminal of the lift. Tomorrow, I'm headed back there with Sergeant Singh's section and see if we can't figure things out. And let's keep the witch hunt going full bore. Now we really need a distraction to cover our steps. In the meantime, I'd better prepare a report for the Admiral and Colonel Decker. Things are getting a little strange around here."

\*\*

At supper that night in Nero Engstrom's quarters, the conversation centered on Delgado's drastic measures to stomp out the suspected illicit substance trade. His companions so far showed little interest in what he'd found in the Marine's computer node.

Ed Limix wore a worried expression on his ordinarily bluff features, and when he spoke, it was with a mixture of anger and nervousness. Romana Movane, looking as pinched as ever, took affront at everything and anything the others said.

"Oh, come now." Engstrom's tone, meant to be soothing, came across as more jittery than he intended. "There is no drug smuggling in Tyrell, and the Marines will seem like the zealots they are. So, the workers are offended. Ed can remind them this is a military installation and that they live under Fleet regulations, which are fair and even-handed. They have nothing to fear if they've done nothing wrong."

Movane snorted contemptuously.

"Military law is to law what military music is to music. Or something like that. The workers don't like it, and they're right. Even if the Marines are bumbling fools, which I doubt, you'll find a mess of labor troubles on your hands soon enough."

"She's right," Limix interjected. "There's talk of replacing me as shop steward if I can't convince you to make them stop. They will vote Hendrik Isenar in, and he won't be as accommodating as I am. In fact, you don't want to know what he thinks of you, Nero."

"Oh, very well," Engstrom sighed after a few moments during which he studied his companions. "I'll speak with our overzealous major tomorrow morning. Of course, you're right. There is no trade in illicit substances around here."

He clapped his hands once, a clear punctuation to their discussion.

"Who wants to see the most recent on our brave Marines?"

When Nero Engstrom finished proudly displaying his latest bits of knowledge, both Ed Limix and Romana Movane knew there was something wrong with the files. Yet neither voiced that fact. Some things were better kept unsaid. But it begged the question of whether the witch hunt was real or a distraction. And if the latter, what were the Marines really doing.

**✳✳**

"So, nothing new?" Jannika Hallikonnoen asked abruptly when the informant slid into the booth across from her.

"Nothing you can hang your hat on. Our glorious leader enjoyed himself by reading the sordid details in the Marines' personal files."

"I'd rather you find me something more tangible, like what they want to do if this place is ever subjected to an external threat."

"Wait for it, Jannika. Our friend Engstrom is still digging, and they buried the defense plans behind the highest levels of security."

"Sure," she replied dryly. "What about the supply ship?"

"Still on time. I've arranged for the people you named to work at reception. The computer virus that'll distract the Marines' security scanners is in place, ready for activation."

"Not too early, or they'll track it down."

"Don't worry. I've as much at stake in this as you."

With that, the informant stood and left Hallikonnoen to her thoughts. Something felt wrong, out of her control, and she didn't enjoy the sensation. Delgado's measures, for instance. They'd caused a significant uproar, something he surely knew in advance. Plus, there were better ways of finding actual smugglers, ways that didn't cause a great big stink.

So why? Was this a case of waving the right hand in your opponent's face while the left hand went for the kill? Marines weren't supposed to be that subtle. What did Engstrom find in the personal files?

After downing her drink, Hallikonnoen left the *Reach* and slipped into the maintenance tube, where ladders allowed covert access to the executive housing level.

When she reached the top, she opened the customarily locked door and stepped into the corridor, deserted at this time of the gamma shift. But she didn't count on the surveillance sensor placed in one of the air circulation ducts at Delgado's orders. It alerted Sergeant Rolf Painter, who once again stood watch in the command post, and he allowed himself a faint smile.

Gotcha.

# — Twenty-One —

The following day in the main cafeteria, Tyrell's workers gave Delgado and Hak a wide berth, leaving them to enjoy an entire table alone, even though most of the rest were crowded.

"Don't like us much anymore, do they?" The first sergeant commented as another trio walked by, scowling openly. But he took pleasure at returning every rude or angry stare with a friendly smile and did so again this time.

"I'd be annoyed as well if someone decided he'd scan every hard-working employee because of a few suspicions," Delgado replied.

"Doesn't seem fair, though. They're nice people, on the whole."

"I know, Top. But it's the best way of stirring things up to cover our moves. And maybe help us find out if *Sécurité Spéciale* operatives are plotting mischief."

"Who might also know about the other thing we haven't yet fully figured out."

Delgado nodded, then drained his coffee mug. "Rolf should show up with his daily report soon. Are you coming?"

"Wouldn't miss it."

Painter was chatting with Testo when they entered the command post. Both looked up at Delgado, and the former said, "Good morning, Skipper. I hope you enjoyed a good night's sleep."

"I did, thank you. A little birdie tells me something interesting happened during the night watch." Delgado and Hak took their accustomed chairs at the conference table.

"That birdie would be right, sir. The sensor we installed on the executive accommodations level picked up Jannika Hallikonnoen appearing in the corridor via the maintenance tube and entering Chief Engineer Iago Sakamoto's private quarters."

"Really?" Delgado's eyebrows rose in surprise. An unprepossessing, balding fifty-something with a slight paunch, Sakamoto oversaw Tyrell's entire infrastructure and was Romana Movane's second-in-command.

"Please tell me Carl Kuzek's trick of turning the executive level bedroom communicators into listening devices worked."

A predatory smile briefly lit up the normally dour command sergeant's square features.

"It did, and you're about to hear things you can never unhear, Skipper."

"How many obscenity laws does the recording break?" Delgado asked, grinning.

"Hardly any. Our esteemed chief engineer doesn't sound like much of a lover, which should not surprise those of us who've met him." He glanced at Testo. "Might as well share the pain."

Testo reached for his console, and clear voices filled the room. "Be grateful it's audio only, Skipper."

Painter was right. Sakamoto didn't sound like someone highly active in bed, nor did Hallikonnoen seem to enjoy herself much. When the recording ended, Delgado leaned back in his chair and steepled his fingers beneath his chin as he mentally separated the chaff from the kernels of truth.

"If I may, Skipper?" Painter waited until Delgado gave him the nod to go ahead. "I figure it's clear Hallikonnoen is in this relationship with Sakamoto to collect information about Tyrell. You may have noted that she skilfully interrogated him during and afterward, something he didn't seem to realize. If you'll recall, I did a tour at Camp X as an instructor back when Colonel Decker was a major, and we trained agents in interrogation techniques. In my professional opinion, she's more in our line of business than that of extracting rare ores from the crust of a dead planet."

"*Sécurité Spéciale*, then." Delgado gave Painter a knowing look.

"That would be my guess. But something else struck me. The questions she asked and the way she asked them makes me believe Hallikonnoen used him to confirm or expand on information she already has."

Hak let out a soft grunt. "Meaning Hallikonnoen is using other informants, people she may not entirely trust."

Painter nodded. "That's what I figure."

"Then what's her game? She arrived here well before the recon droids found the Migration War bunker, so not that." Hak looked at Delgado. "Do you figure she's here to monitor the Fleet's newest gambit — extracting the resources it needs to build starships and weapons instead of buying them from the Assenaris of the galaxy at market rates? Or is it because of the thing in the basement?"

"Or both. I'm sure the *Sécurité Spéciale* is interested in how the Fleet handles this. They probably placed agents or informants in every mining and production operation we bought, just to see why we did so. Heck, it wouldn't surprise me if they already know we found Migration War records presumed lost and are buying properties around suspected weapons caches. Whatever's on Level Sixteen is merely a bonus."

"So, we use the assumption that Hallikonnoen is *Sécurité Spéciale*, Skipper?" Testo asked.

Delgado nodded. "Until we find out otherwise. Which begs the question whether she's involved in the death of Terry Evans."

"No tangible evidence," Painter replied. "We've not yet asked anyone direct questions concerning their whereabouts that night, and if we assume she's *Sécurité Spéciale*, then we definitely won't speak with her."

"Agreed. I think she feels reasonably secure at the moment, seeing as how she has no qualms about visiting Sakamoto during the night shift and asking him questions about Tyrell's infrastructure oversight protocols. Let's keep it that way but focus our surveillance on her and the people she interacts with when off-duty. Discreetly, of course."

"Roger that, Skipper. If there's nothing else for me?"

"You're free to go."

Once Painter left, Delgado turned to Testo.

"Next order of business. I'm headed for Level Sixteen with Singh's section again during the beta shift to see if we can't open that mysterious door. How's the search for the unmarked lift's upper terminal going?"

Testo touched his workstation console again, and a three-dimensional holographic projection of Tyrell Station materialized above the table.

"If it reaches the station proper, it could be in many of the stacked modules ending with Hydroponics Three at the very top, but so far, I've found nothing in the system about any additional lift coming from below. Not even a hint that something was added in recent times."

"Okay. Keep searching. How about the sensors at the airlocks?"

"In place and scanning," Testo replied. "And annoying the workers to no end. But I doubt they'll detect anything smaller than a couple of micrograms liberally sprinkled on some idiot's clothing."

"It's mostly for show, anyway. And if it makes the guilty nervous, then so much the better. Is everything in place for the arrival of the ship tomorrow?"

The operations noncom nodded. "Yes, sir. We should be ready for any eventuality."

"Good. I'll do a final review of my contingency plans when we're done here. Once the amended version is up, I want both of you to poke holes in it. I want us ready for anything by the time the replacement workers arrive because that'll be the *Sécurité Spéciale*'s only chance of slipping extra operatives into Tyrell. They must know the Fleet can show up at any time with the resources to remove the Migration War payloads." When both nodded, Delgado said, "Captain Engstrom summoned me to his office at ten hundred hours. It might get interesting. Did you turn his office communicator into a listening device yet?"

Testo made a so-so gesture and grimaced. "It's a tad harder to penetrate than those in the private quarters."

"Try your best. I'd love a recording of whatever we discuss."

Delgado stood and, with one last glance at the holographic projection of Tyrell, left for his cubicle.

**

Delgado stepped off the lift and into the executive office corridor a few minutes before the appointed time. Though most doors were open, he heard few voices and nothing more than the mechanical hum of an outpost on an airless world, whose tightly contained atmosphere was constantly cycled through environmental scrubbers.

He stopped at a broad, transparent aluminum window and looked out over the planet's tortured landscape, stark against the cold, black majesty of space. The rays of the midmorning sun were painting a tableau of harsh light and deep shadows wherever jagged peaks rose above the surface and craters dropped beneath it.

Delgado couldn't help but wonder what Keros looked like a thousand centuries ago when the proto-Shrehari L'Taung civilization — if his assumptions were correct — dug out a room deep beneath the surface even as it collapsed. Was the planet alive, lush, and teeming with strange life forms? Or was it a marginal, hardscrabble world like some he'd visited, such as Andoth?

Unbidden, the troubling words of the early twenty-third-century poet Hiroshi Yamagata, who died during one of the First Migration War's many massacres, came to mind.

*Born in darkness*
*It will die in darkness*
*The universe ever changing*
*Never changing*
*Violent and peaceful*
*With harmony ever out of reach*

It took an effort to tear his eyes away from the savage panorama and prepare himself for what he figured would be a confrontation.

He crossed the corridor and entered Engstrom's office antechamber, where his administrative assistant greeted him with a bland expression.

"Major Delgado for Captain Engstrom as ordered."

"One moment please." She tapped her workstation console. "Major Delgado is here, sir." She listened for a moment to words only she could hear and then smiled apologetically at the Marine. "I'm sorry, sir, Captain Engstrom is unavoidably detained for a few more minutes. Please take a seat. He won't be long."

Delgado nodded, unsurprised at the delay. Engstrom was playing the oldest game in the book, making him wait to show his superiority. He sat, composed himself, closed his eyes, and slipped quickly into a light meditative trance, restful and calming.

If Engstrom wanted to make him wait, then he would wait for as long as necessary. The man's games were meaningless and allowed him to clear his mind and focus. Gradually, Delgado felt an inner calm, a feeling of balance and harmony slow his heart rate. His body relaxed and he knew he had already won the conflict that lay ahead.

# — Twenty-Two —

Engstrom played the game to the limit, making Delgado wait for nearly half an hour. When the staffer finally ushered him into the station commander's office, the Marine wore a smile on his face. Per protocol, he halted a pace in front of Engstrom's desk, came to attention, and snapped off a salute that would have done Regimental Sergeant Major Augustus Vanlith proud.

"Major Delgado reporting to the Station Commanding Officer as ordered, sir."

Engstrom returned the salute negligently, in another calculated gesture.

"Sit, Delgado. We have much to discuss." The Marine detected an undercurrent of uncertainty in the man's voice.

For a brief moment, Delgado wondered what Engstrom's reaction would be if he played the recording of Sakamoto and Hallikonnoen. And if Delgado mentioned she might be a *Sécurité Spéciale* operative on top of that? Tyrell's chief engineer compromised.

His amusement at the idea must have shown in his eyes because Engstrom frowned.

"Is something funny, Delgado? If so, please share your thoughts. I enjoy little enough humor around here, especially with your Marines playing cops and robbers."

"Just remembering something I heard this morning. A man who should know better making idle boasts."

For a moment, Delgado figured Engstrom was about to suffer from a stroke. His face turned beet red, and the veins in his temples throbbed. Robbed of speech, he could merely stare at the Marine in both wonder and horror for a few heartbeats before looking away. Clearly, a display of guilty conscience that proved he thought Delgado meant him. Interesting.

After a moment, Engstrom said in a somewhat strangled tone, "Major, I command this station and outrank you. That means you work for me and will show me the proper respect.

"Yes, sir. You outrank me, and I deserve any rebukes for failing to treat you accordingly." Delgado wondered about mentioning that his status vis-à-vis Engstrom in policing the station wasn't quite as clear. He wasn't in the latter's chain of command because he reported to Fleet HQ but thought better of it.

After taking a few breaths while his face returned to its normal color, Engstrom met Delgado's eyes again.

"I want the truth about the Evans investigation. I also demand to know what the hell you believe you're doing chasing fictional illicit substances across my station, throwing labor-management relations back to the dark ages. As well, I want to see any plans you've made about the station's defense and security."

"With due respect, sir, you know as much about the Evans case as I do. As for the suspected illicit substances, we collected enough evidence to investigate under the relevant Armed Forces Orders and Regulations, specifically Volume Two, Chapter One-Hundred-Six, Section One."

Hak, the Erinyes' disciplinarian and expert on regulations, dug up the reference, although it didn't really apply here and wouldn't hold up in front of a court-martial. Before Engstrom could protest, Delgado continued in a conciliatory tone.

"I'm sorry labor-management relations are affected, but that's not my responsibility, sir. You enjoy the confidence of a shop steward who has no reason to love those dealing in illicit substances and a chief administrator who apparently has the respect of the workers. Between them, they should be able to smooth ruffled feathers, no? Besides, you're the commanding officer and sole master of Tyrell after the Almighty. I'm merely here at the Fleet's orders to make sure you can run Tyrell free of internal and external threats. And I will do my utmost."

Engstrom seemed mildly flustered at Delgado's patient, respectful reply and eyed him with suspicion for a few moments. Then he appeared to gather his courage.

"Major, I have been checking up on you and your outfit, and I don't think you're in any position to take this kind of lackadaisical attitude with me."

"I'm not sure what you mean, sir?" Delgado kept a straight face even though he was smiling inside.

"You misrepresented yourself and your unit."

"Sir?"

"Do you recall stating you were promoted to major while in command of H Company and are waiting for a suitable staff position to open in the 42$^{nd}$ Marines? Well, I have it on good authority you already held said staff position and were returned to command a rifle company, somewhat of a punitive step backward in my eyes. Moreover, your company was formed expressly for this assignment from those in the regiment who've made missteps and need a hardship tour. In other words, you and your people aren't the best the 42$^{nd}$ can offer."

A faint air of triumph crossed Engstrom's florid face as he sat back and dared Delgado to rebut him.

"You may have been able to get away with your shenanigans before, but I remind you that Tyrell is a Class One activity of the Fleet's Chief of Procurement. I doubt he'll look upon your attempts to circumvent the proper chain of authority with much favor. I warn you, if you do not cease, I will ask you be relieved of command and returned home."

"Sorry you feel that way, sir. But you misunderstand the situation. Marine regiments tasked to provide subunits as security for outposts like Tyrell generally put together ad hoc companies from carefully selected volunteers under an experienced commanding officer. My Marines and I are far from being here on a punishment tour. Quite the contrary.

We were all temporarily detached from our parent units for this mission because we are the most suitable." Delgado gave Engstrom a sad glance. "I believe you've either been misinformed or misinterpreted what you were told, sir."

As Delgado watched Engstrom parse his words, he saw the naval officer's gaze begin to waver with uncertainty. Since most of Delgado's statement was the truth or almost the truth, he clearly sounded convincing.

"I'll tell you what, sir. You'll see my updated contingency plans on your desk by the end of the day. For your eyes only, of course." Delgado paused for effect. "And if I may, there's one thing I would like you to take into consideration. Should I be wrong about the traffic in illicit substances, you've lost nothing more than the workers' goodwill for a time. But if I'm right, then by letting me take action, you'll be well-positioned to prevent incidents that can impact production or even cause fatalities."

By now, Engstrom seemed more confused than uncertain, let alone choleric, as if he no longer knew what he should believe or accept. And that was precisely how Delgado wanted him — off balance.

"One last thing, sir. May I suggest you remind the senior staff they should take better care about what they tell individuals who do not have the need to know? I'm certain the civilian heads of department, like Chief Engineer Sakamoto, might benefit from a quick word."

While Engstrom stared at the Marine, unable to formulate an answer that didn't make him seem foolish, Delgado stood, saluted, and left the office.

**

"How did he react?" First Sergeant Hak looked at his commanding officer expectantly as the latter entered the command post and tossed his beret on the table before pulling out a chair.

"I don't think he'll be obstructing us. At least not openly. But he acted rather guilty when I hinted at senior people talking out of turn, which makes me wonder what he's been up to that we don't know about. Hopefully, he'll follow my suggestion and remind his and Movane's direct reports — I used Sakamoto's name as an example — that discretion is a part of the job." Delgado shook his head and exhaled. "Sergeant Testo, see that Rolf's people keep an eye on Sakamoto as well."

Testo nodded. "Will do."

Delgado's eyes narrowed as he noticed Testo's expression. "What?"

"While you were upstairs, we received an anonymous tip fingering an illicit stash."

"How did that happen?" Delgado asked, frowning.

"Lanny Greaves was having a beer in the *Reach* and went to the heads so he could vent his ballast tank," Hak replied, beating Testo to the punch. "While he was washing his hands afterward, a miner tucked a piece of paper in his shirt pocket."

"Did he see him?"

"No. The heads were pretty full."

"What do you figure?"

"Not enough data, sir," Testo made a slight grimace. "Lanny is probably known as one of our investigators by now. Rolf is already on it."

"So, where is this supposed stash?"

"Shaft Two, Level Five, in an abandoned branch off Gallery F. Behind a small pile of tailings."

"What do you guys think?" Delgado asked both Testo and Hak.

The former flatly said, "It's a trap."

"Probably, but even so," the first sergeant replied, "We should go see. It might tell us something about the people who set it. Mind you, it could be genuine. An anonymous tip is a good way of giving us what we're after and distracting us. I gather our increased scrutiny finally had some effect. Most miners don't like users, anyway. Too dangerous in unpressurized environments."

When Delgado's eyes narrowed in thought, Testo said, "I alerted Delta Troop. Faruq has Salford Lambrix and one-four-alpha on standby."

"Okay, send them in, fully armed. At the slightest sign of funny business, he stops and reports. We'll take it from there. The more I mull this over, the more I figure it could be a move to keep us preoccupied just as the regular ship is due."

"I'll send the orders out right away."

"And make sure they bring Delta Troop's droid."

About as large as a medium-sized dog, the semi-autonomous anti-grav propelled machine with four articulated arms was routinely used to replace humans in perilous situations, such as bomb disposal, and Erinye Company brought its normal one per troop allotment.

"They already liberated it from QM stores, sir."

# — Twenty-Three —

Staff Sergeant Salford Lambrix checked his Marines, making sure the suits were operational and that each trooper carried the proper armament, munitions, tools, and emergency air tanks, in case their suits' scrubbers failed. Satisfied, he reported to the command post and led his section into the waiting lift. The time was thirteen hundred and the alpha shift wouldn't end for another three hours, which meant the locker room and lift area were deserted.

After a week of patrolling, Lambrix and his people knew their way around the station, the mine, and the smelter. None of them so much as flinched when the lift floor dropped away, and they were whisked one and a half kilometers into the bowels of the dead planet.

Within moments, it slowed to a gentle stop, and the broad, curved doors slid open. Level Five of Shaft Two did not possess the majestic grandeur of Level Sixteen Shaft One. There was no gigantic cavern, no ceiling reaching into darkness, just a wide, circular hub from which half a dozen galleries headed to the various ore seams. The ceiling was low enough that the shaft boss module and the anti-grav ore transport tube seemed wedged between it and the floor.

Lambrix stepped off the lift first and headed for the shaft boss while Sergeant Sberna mustered one-four-alpha near the entrance to Gallery F using hand signals. He waved at the shaft boss, who gave him a curious look through the transparent aluminum window, then entered the names of his Marines and their destination using the outer terminal.

Major Delgado had impressed upon him that everything must be done precisely by the rules, especially since the target might be a trap which, this deep underground in an airless environment, could spell death. Better everyone knew where they were. That way, if anything happened...

His duty done, Lambrix joined the others.

"Everyone ready?" He asked over the patrol frequency.

Lance Corporal Carlo Torres raised his armored fist. "Yeah, Sarge. What do we do if we come across an interested buyer on the way back? The unit fund needs a little top up, and so does the Torres beer and retirement account."

Sergeant Sberna smacked Torres on the arm. "What did I teach you about anticipating things too early?"

"Someone else might take my idea and run with it?"

"Yep. And that means the Torres beer and retirement account is definitely out of luck on this one."

The rest of the section chuckled.

"All right." Lambrix pointed at Gallery F. "Let's move out."

**

"If at first you don't succeed, destroy any evidence that you tried," Testo said, spinning his chair around to face Delgado. "I've concluded we won't find the upper terminal of a non-existent lift sitting behind a computer console. Nothing in the data hints at its existence. Nor is there anything in the blueprints that even remotely resembles a camouflaged lift station. And yes, I'm ninety-nine percent sure at this point."

"What would your best guess be?"

"The hydroponics module. It's mostly automated, which means only a daily visit by the environmental systems maintenance crew. Since it's at the same level as the administrative and executive modules, it has way less routine traffic than the ones below. But we'll need to go see for ourselves, sir."

Delgado glanced at Hak. "How about the Top and I pay Hydroponics Three a visit? You can open the way for us without station operations noticing, right? And I assume the maintenance team has a schedule?"

"Yes to both." Testo nodded. "Maintenance visits it at ten hundred hours every day, which means they've been and gone until tomorrow."

"Good. If we find something, like an unregistered airlock or an extra power distribution panel, we'll note the position and not let on we're searching. I'll decide whether we make further inquiries once we know what's what."

"Have fun among the ferns, Skipper."

\*\*

Jannika Hallikonnoen lay in her bed, chewing on her lower lip, thinking. The cubicle's curtains were drawn, giving her as much privacy as Tyrell's workers got. Sakamoto had called her shortly after Engstrom sent a reminder to senior staff concerning the unauthorized release of restricted information, clearly feeling himself the target of the memo.

She did not know what angered her more. Him risking her anonymity by contacting her directly to say their relationship was over and giving the Marines a chance to find out about it — if they haven't already. Or the fact that she no longer had the means to confirm the data she collected from her various sources.

The only thing that kept Hallikonnoen from getting too worried about the memo so soon after her last tryst with Sakamoto was the ship's arrival in less than twenty-four hours. After that, everything would happen, and there was nothing the Marines could do.

They were still flailing in the dark, playing little power games and running after small fry. Even if what Engstrom found in the personnel files wasn't wholly accurate, garrisoning Tyrell wasn't a choice assignment, so she doubted they were handpicked volunteers rather than troopers who ended up on their commanding officer's blacklist. And even if they were good fighters, how bright were they compared to operatives like her? She didn't for a moment believe Zbotnicky's assertions that they seemed like more than just regular line infantry.

She looked at her watch. Hell should break loose any time now, covering her final preparations before the arrival of her strike team.

**

Delgado and Hak casually strolled into the tube connecting Administration Module One to Hydroponics Module Three. Beyond the transparent aluminum windows piercing the tube at regular intervals, Keros' sun painted the desolate landscape with its harsh rays.

To their right, the tube overlooked the landing area, and they saw the massive space doors of the hangar. On the other side, they admired the dark abyss that split Keros' crust less than a kilometer from Tyrell, its shadows just as hard-edged as the sunlit peaks.

"Pretty little place, ain't it, sir. I might just see myself retiring here. Probably live longer than on most colonies with no other human beings to screw you around." Hak remarked in a conversational tone.

"Pass. I prefer living without the need for canned air and regular resupply ships."

The two Marines tore themselves away from the remarkable and somewhat humbling view and headed for the airlock leading to the 'glasshouse' as hydroponic installations were nicknamed because of their transparent roof and sides.

There, Delgado reached for the lock pad, hoping Sergeant Testo's eyes were on them. The pad changed from red to green as they heard the mechanical sounds of the heavy door latches retracting. Technically, no one except the maintenance crew responsible for the hydroponic farms was allowed inside unescorted, not even the Marine security detail. All previous patrols had been performed under supervision.

They stepped through and into a radically different atmosphere, where the warmth and humidity reminded them of a living, breathing world, not Keros' stark environment or the utilitarianism of Tyrell's other modules.

A veritable jungle filled the space as far as the eye could see, yet its core was orderly, with wide, shallow trays containing lush, healthy food plants stacked one above the other and side-by-side, like oversized steps leading from the floor of the module upwards. As they stood there, taking in their surroundings, overhead sprayers gently misted the plants and deposited a light sheen of moisture on the Marines.

Hak let out a soft grunt. "Nice place. A little too humid for my taste, but it soothes the nerves?"

"Yep." Delgado pulled a handheld sensor from his harness. "Shall we?"

"Aye, sir." Hak imitated his commanding officer.

They strolled between the stacks of trays, dodging hanging plants while enjoying the rich scent that accompanied the profusion of life around them. After ten minutes, they were back at the airlock, no wiser than before.

"If that lift ends in this module, it'll be under our feet, in the mechanical room." Delgado gestured at a closed door in the corner nearest to the airlock. "If I recall correctly, there's a circular stairway behind it that leads to the environmental machinery, water recirculation, fertilizer recuperation and the other things that make plants grow."

He touched his communicator.

"Zero, this is Niner."

"Zero, here," Testo replied within seconds.

"Can you unlock the door to the stairs leading down?"

"No problems. Wait one." Then, "It's yours."

"Thanks. Niner, out."

The module's lower level was crammed with pipes, tubes, vats, and other unidentifiable machinery. A pungent mixture of organic aromas filled the Marines' nostrils, and they glanced at each other, grimacing.

"It smells much better upstairs if you want my opinion, sir."

"Agreed. Let's scan the place and leave."

They spent a good twenty minutes walking through every corridor and passageway, entering every compartment and recording every last detail so the tactical AI could compare their readings with the station's official blueprints.

"I think that's it," Delgado finally said when they were back at the foot of the stairs. He pocketed his sensor. "Time to head home."

Hak pointed at the lower level's own airlock. "How about we leave that way and see how the maintenance tube looks like around here?"

"Right." Delgado tapped his communicator again. "Zero, this is Niner. We'd like to exit via the module's maintenance airlock."

"This is Zero. On it," Testo replied.

Moments later, the heavy door swung open to reveal a windowless corridor whose walls were covered in grimy conduits, condensation, and signs of mold.

"Ugh." Hak grimaced. "Makes you wonder about the quality of the salads in the cafeteria."

"You think I should tell Engstrom his cleaning crew needs added motivation?"

"Nah. We'll be out of here soon enough, Skipper." A pause. "I hope."

**

Romana Movane's private communicator chimed insistently, never a good sign, and she frowned when she retrieved it from her tunic pocket while touching her desk's control surface to close the office door. Only two people in Tyrell used the private, encrypted Assenari communications network, one neither Engstrom nor the Marines knew about.

"Yes?"

"We may have a slight problem, Chief Administrator."

Movane recognized the voice of the undercover operative from the Assenari Enterprises Corporate Security Division, Valenti Nabakov. He ostensibly belonged to the environmental engineering team but, in reality, monitored things for the *zaibatsu* and reported to Movane, who thought of him as a necessary, but uncomfortable presence in Tyrell. Of course, the Fleet didn't know Assenari left an intelligence and security specialist behind when it withdrew the corporate police detachment.

"What is it?"

"Delgado and his first sergeant just toured Hydroponics Three and spent an inordinate amount of time scanning both levels."

"How in Hades did they enter? Operations would tell me if they try."

She could picture Nabakov shrugging. "I suspect the Marines tapped into Tyrell's network and can temporarily take over certain segments with no one knowing."

"Did they find it?"

"Not that I can tell, but if they compare their scans to the specs, they'll uncover inconsistencies."

"Which means they found the lower end."

"That's my assessment."

"Damn." Movane struck her desktop with a clenched fist.

"What's done is done, Chief Administrator. Best we don't let on that we know they know or that we suspect they tapped our systems. I've concluded that these aren't ordinary Marines, but specialists sent here for a specific purpose, highly trained professionals."

"The recon droid discovery."

"Likely. But I figure Delgado sensed a mystery, which is why he's been snooping. And yes, before you say so, Evans' death was unfortunate in that it triggered his suspicions, but I thought I might circumvent ComCorp Security's conditioning. They've improved their formula. Besides, we couldn't let her go on for much longer without compromising security."

Movane stared at the communicator, eyes narrowed. "All right. We do nothing. If Delgado is here because of the recon droid find, he'll soon be gone once the Fleet acts on it, and we can go back to normal. But tell the researchers they're not allowed down until further notice."

"As you wish, Chief Administrator."

# — Twenty-Four —

"Nothing, Sarge." Osmin Sberna shook his head inside his suit, a reflexive gesture unseen by his section leader as he looked up from his sensor.

"Go in," Lambrix replied.

Corporal Martin Davros and Lance Corporal Guillermo Coronadas, who were walking point, stepped around the red boulders, and slipped into the abandoned gallery, every movement cautious and considered.

They made intensive scans on the far side before leaving the bright lights of the active gallery behind and slipping into darkness while Sberna set the rest of his squad in motion. Lambrix would keep the other half of the section in the gallery standing guard.

The tip they'd received said the cache was less than thirty meters from the junction, under a small slide in a side pocket. And sure enough, the Marines on point found it. They signaled Sberna, then moved past to secure the squad's flank.

He and Carlo Torres, battlefield sensors in hand, approached the haphazard pile of small and medium-sized rocks and subjected it to intense scrutiny while the remaining two Marines, Corporal Horace Yu and Lance Corporal Piotr Olenga, stood a few paces away, watching their surroundings.

"Looks like a plastic package about fifty centimeters below the slide's surface, Sarge," Torres eventually said over the dedicated squad frequency.

"Concur. Now to check if the bait comes with a hook." Sberna chuckled. "Did I ever tell you about the time I was on a military assistance gig with the Hispaniola National Guard? Now, this was long after the uprising—"

"Didn't Colonel Decker fight in that one when he was a buck sergeant, back before the dawn of time?"

"Yep. Anyway, the hardcore terrs were still around in my day, and they'd amuse themselves by leaving attractive prizes lying around, readers — booze, food, and gear, hooked to primitive booby traps our sensors didn't always detect. More than one Guard dumbass lost a bit of himself because he either wasn't paying attention or trusted his gear too much. Sometimes, his buddies also paid the price."

"I can pick up nothing other than rock around the package, Sarge." Torres, eyes on his sensor's display, sounded somewhat dubious.

"What is it, Carlo? I know that tone."

"For a nanosecond, I could have sworn I spotted a blip, but it's probably either a sensor ghost or my imagination. It wouldn't be the first ghost we picked up. Something about the planet's crust around here does funny things to sensors."

"Likely a result of it being so rich in certain ores, but what do I know. Okay. You and I keep scanning, Carlo, while Horace and Piotr remove the rubble stone by stone to make sure there are no surprises." Sberna turned toward Yu and Olenga and pointed at the rockslide.

"Roger that, Sarge." Yu led his winger over, and both dropped to one knee.

They carefully cleared out the area, each gesture deliberate as Sberna and Torres kept a close watch for anything unusual. Eventually, a rectangular red plastic toolbox emerged, one no different from those stored in every mining mole and module throughout Tyrell's rabbit warren. Fifty centimeters long by thirty-five wide and forty high, it bore signs of hard use along with the station's logo.

"It's definitely full of something, Sarge," Torres said. "But I can't figure out what."

"As long as it's not connected to something else." Sberna gestured at Yu and Olenga. "Step aside, gentlemen. I'll make the last few moves. Sergeant's privilege."

They obeyed without a word, knowing Sberna not only had more experience and expertise but wouldn't hide behind one of his Marines when things turned risky.

He knelt by the tool case and scanned it once more with his sensor at extremely close range. It sat flat on the gallery floor with the top and four sides exposed, leaving the underside as a possible hiding place for a trigger that could spring a lethal trap.

But something nagged at his subconscious, and he remained motionless for so long that Torres asked, "What's up, Sarge?"

Sberna raised a hand. "Something's not right. Call it a gut feeling."

"Roger that." Torres took an involuntary step back because he knew from experience that Osmin Sberna's intuition had saved lives many times before.

The latter switched his radio to the section frequency. "One-Four-Alpha, this is Alpha-Two. I'm evacuating the gallery so we can send in the droid."

"You think it's a trap," Staff Sergeant Lambrix replied.

"I can't detect anything, and the box's contents seem inert, but my gut is telling me otherwise. No idea why, but it's best if none of us are nearby when we try moving the package."

"Acknowledged. Prepping the droid."

It wouldn't take long. Corporal Leroy Taggart, Lambrix's winger, was carrying the lightweight machine in a special backpack and simply had to power it up and make sure it spoke politely with the remote control station.

Sberna picked up his sensor and stood while switching his radio back to the squad frequency.

He pointed toward the main gallery. "We're leaving."

Five hands shot up, acknowledging the order, and, as per standard operating procedures, they extracted in reverse order, with Davros and Coronadas taking the rear guard position. As soon as they rejoined the rest of one-four-alpha, the droid, floating a hand-span above the gallery floor, maneuvered around the red-painted rocks and vanished into the darkness.

Corporal Taggart, leaning against the main gallery's far wall, eyes on the control station, watched the view from the droid's own night vision device as it slowly approached its target while a pair of Marines from Lambrix's half of the section stood guard on either side of him.

"Anything specific make you extract?" The latter asked Sberna.

"Nope. But if there's funny business, better the droid than yours truly."

"Roger that, old buddy."

Both sergeants walked over to where Taggart stood and patched their helmet visors into the control station's video feed, so they could see the same thing as the droid and its pilot.

"Seems pretty ordinary," Lambrix commented when the old toolbox appeared.

"You can pack a lot of stuff that goes boom into it, though."

"But you didn't pick up anything that looked like a detonator."

"Negative, although they're not that hard to hide if you know what you're doing. From what the sensor picked up, there are several packages of various sizes jammed together, some with metallic elements."

Taggart reached out and tapped Sberna's arm. "What should I make Ozzie do?"

"Ozzie?" Sberna guffawed. "You gave the droid a name?"

"Sure. Seemed like the right thing to do if we're sending him in as your replacement, Sarge."

"Smart ass." Sberna grinned at Taggart.

"Better that than being a dumb ass, right? So, what about Ozzie's next move?"

"Tell him — it — to pick up the box using the handles at each end, making sure the thing stays horizontal."

"Wilco."

"Then bring it out." Sberna turned to Lambrix. "Assuming Taggart's little buddy fetches the box without causing nasty surprises, what next? Having Ozzie crack it open down here doesn't strike me as a great idea. I'd much rather we do that out on the surface, preferably a few hundred meters from Tyrell, but that means taking it up in the lift, through a few modules, and out via the hangar."

"Which in turn means we need a boom box."

"This place should have a few, in case a demolition charge hangs fire, and they need to get rid of it safely."

"Let me call—"

Before Lambrix could finish his sentence, a brilliant, albeit noiseless flash lit up the abandoned gallery. Almost at once, they felt a wave of vibrations course through the soles of their armored boots as the energy released by the explosion propagated through the rock. Simultaneously, a geyser of small and medium-sized stones erupted from the tunnel entrance, pelting them with enough force to knock over the Marines in the strike zone, Taggart, Sberna, and Lambrix included.

\*\*

It didn't take the tactical AI long to discover a discrepancy between the scans and the official specs, indicating where the mystery lift's upper terminal might hide.

Sergeant Testo swiveled his chair around to face Delgado and Hak, sitting at the command post table.

"Found it." A pair of three-dimensional holograms appeared above the table. "The blue projection is as per the official plot; the green is based on your scans."

A small section of the green projection turned red.

"And that is likely a hidden door. If the mystery lift runs straight, that's pretty much where it would end up."

Delgado gave his operations sergeant a pleased grin. "Nicely done. Can you set up discreet surveillance on that hidden door so we find out who uses it?"

"No problems. I'll do it right away."

Before Delgado could reply, a deafening alarm siren rang through every module.

"What the..." Delgado half rose from his seat, taken by surprise.

Testo swung back toward his workstation.

"Accident in the mine — looks like a cave-in — Shaft Two, Level Five. They're scrambling a rescue team now."

Delgado and Hak looked at each other with bleak expressions.

"Crap."

# — Twenty-Five —

"Sarge."

Osmin Sberna's eyes fluttered open, and for a moment, he wished they hadn't. He was on his back, facing the bright main gallery lights whose glare pierced his ringing skull like the hottest daggers of hell.

Then Lance Corporal Torres' concerned expression swam into focus.

"Wh-what?"

"Are you okay, Sarge?"

"C-concussed?" His voice came out as a croak.

"Probably. Seeing the dents in your armor, those rocks came flying out real hard." Torres shook his head. "Can you imagine if we were still in there, standing around like idiots? The regiment would be holding a half dozen military funerals in two weeks — if they dug our bodies out."

"The others?"

"Salford and Leroy are still out of it. Same deal — dented suits, but no breach of integrity. The rest of us got a bit of by-blow, but not like you three." When Sberna made to sit up, Torres held him back. "No go, Sarge. Your suit's medical scanner says you're okay, but we don't want to take chances. It can't detect everything. Stay still while we wait for the rescue team. Zero says you, Salford, and Leroy are headed straight to sickbay in your suits. Martin's taken over the section for now, so everything is in hand."

**

"Station operations confirm the rescue team with three stretchers are suited up and preparing to enter the lift," Sergeant Testo reported in a flat tone. "Tyrell's chief geologist has also been called out to investigate."

"Chief Administrator Movane for you, sir," Sergeant Kuzek, working the command post communications station, said.

"Yes, Chief Administrator?" Delgado put on a neutral expression as he faced the woman on the primary display.

"You're aware the rescue team is about to head down and fetch your injured?" Her tone and expression matched Delgado's, something for which he was thankful.

"I am. Thank you for the quick response. Do you need any extra assistance?"

She shook her head.

"No. The last thing we need is more Marines milling around uselessly where they shouldn't be in the first place. My people are experienced in these matters. Yours, not so much. Now, would you please tell me what happened?"

"Someone tried to murder a half dozen of my troopers with an improvised explosive device hidden under what I assume was a fake rockslide in an abandoned tunnel."

"You'll need to lay this out for me, Major."

"We received an anonymous tip about a stash of illicit substances hidden in that tunnel, and in my role as the station's provost marshal, I sent a patrol to look at it. When—"

"Without telling Captain Engstrom or me." She frowned. "Why? Do you not trust us?"

"The sergeant in charge of finding the stash dug it up — a Tyrell Station toolbox seemingly filled with inert material," Delgado continued, ignoring her questions. "But he's an experienced noncom who's dealt with IEDs before, and something told him it might be a trap, even though his sensor detected nothing. He evacuated his squad from the tunnel in question and sent in a remotely controlled droid. When the droid lifted the box, it exploded with enough force to send a cloud of stones into the main gallery at high speed. If my people weren't wearing armor, the three who took the brunt of it would be dead. As would any miner wearing one of your pressure suits. This was clearly meant to kill. The culprit or culprits simply didn't count on the finely honed instincts of the noncom in charge. And now you know as much as I do."

She nodded silently, absorbing his words. "Thank you for your openness. If someone is after you for some reason or other, my people could easily become collateral damage, and they don't need additional risks when this job already has more than its fair share of them. That being said, please do us a favor and keep your Marines out of the mine shafts. I'm sure Captain Engstrom will speak with you in due course about this incident. Movane out."

When her image faded away, Delgado, Testo, and Hak looked at each other.

"If she's behind the IED, she's a damn talented actress," Hak finally said in a low voice.

Delgado shrugged.

"At this point, everyone in Tyrell, other than the Erinyes, are suspects. If we didn't have our hands full before, another investigation would do it." He paused for a few moments, forehead creased in thought, then said, "And that was probably the point of this incident. In any case, Movane's request we stay away from the mine shafts notwithstanding, once things settle, I want a team back there to take samples from the blast zone for analysis. If nothing else, determining the nature of the explosive used could be helpful."

"I don't think we'll find the time for that sort of crime scene analysis, Skipper." Testo looked at his workstation display when it chimed softly for attention. "The regular Assenari ship *Thunder Bay* just dropped out of FTL at Keros' hyperlimit twelve hours early. She'll be in orbit shortly."

"It never rains, but it pours," Curtis Delgado gave his first sergeant a bleak smile.

"Not on Keros, cause of the lack of atmosphere, except maybe in the hydroponics modules, but we didn't sign up to sit around and watch the mold grow on the environmental ductwork anyway, sir. So, the more, the merrier."

"Yep. Join the Corps, they said. You'll see the galaxy, they said. What they didn't say is that you find yourself way up the hind-end of human space chasing druggies while waiting for the good guys to show up and make that bunker full of nasty crap vanish. We might as well have stayed home and kept pounding the 1st MLI with object lessons." When Hak, Testo, and Kuzek gave him surprised looks, Delgado raised both hands and grinned. "Wouldn't miss this show for all the gold and platinum in the universe."

∗∗

As word of an improvised explosive device, one which almost killed a half dozen Marines and left three injured, made the rounds of Tyrell Station, the workers' anger at Delgado and his troopers quickly evaporated. Sure, they didn't like being treated as potential suspects, but this incident proved there were clearly rotten apples in their midst.

And if those rotten apples would try murdering those who upheld law and order, what chance did miners in unarmored pressure suits stand if ever they crossed the wrong person? Delgado immediately noticed the change in atmosphere as he, Hak, and Sergeant Kuzek walked through the station to the infirmary to check on the three injured. Workers gave them grave nods in passing rather than icy stares or turned backs, knowing it could have been miners targeted by the IED rather than Marines trained in dealing with such things.

Doctor Blake greeted them with a faint smile of relief when one of his medics fetched him from the examination room.

"Your people are bruised and shaken, but the armor saved them from greater injury. I'd like to keep them under observation for the next twelve hours if you don't mind. Just in case something is developing that the scans can't pick up yet."

"Certainly."

"If you want to take their armor and equipment, feel free, but I don't know that it can be recycled. We forced some of the joints damaged in the explosion. It must have been one hell of a bomb."

Delgado shrugged. "We'll probably never know. Confined spaces such as mine galleries tend to funnel an explosion, so it need not be that big."

"You're the expert."

"Can we see them?"

"Sure." Blake turned on his heels. "Follow me."

Delgado glanced at Kuzek, who correctly guessed what his commanding officer wanted.

"I'll organize a work party to bring their gear back, sir."

Blake looked over his shoulder, "It's stowed securely in my office, Sergeant. I'll show you where."

He directed them to the recovery room where the three Marines, alert and quietly talking among themselves, occupied diagnostic beds beneath silvery medical blankets. The moment Delgado and Hak entered, they fell silent.

"How are they hanging?"

"Still one lower than the other, sir," Staff Sergeant Lambrix answered. "A bit shook up, though. Mind you, if Osmin hadn't listened to his instinct, it would have been much worse."

"Yeah," Corporal Taggart added. "But it's still a shame about Ozzie."

"Ozzie?" Delgado cocked an eyebrow at the grinning Marine.

Sberna let out a grunt. "That's what he baptized the droid before sending it in. Called it my replacement."

"And it was a damn fine thing you pulled out and let Ozzie at it. Any idea what triggered your gut feel?"

"Not a clue, sir. I was kneeling in front of the thing with my sensor when a little voice said, stop. Can't explain it any better than that."

"Your little voice earned its danger pay. In any case, well done. Doc wants to keep you overnight, just in case. We'll take care of your gear, but apparently, the suits are done for."

"They did their job," Lambrix replied. "I'd hate to think about the damage if we were wearing those used by the miners. Good thing we brought spares."

"Anything you need right now — other than a stiff drink, which the doc will surely forbid?"

A chorus of 'no, sir,' greeted Delgado's question, which he expected. If they wanted something, including a quick shot of whiskey, they'd call on their section mates, who were even now being debriefed by Sergeant Testo for the incident report. It would go out to HQ as soon as possible. Someone had upped the ante, and the Admiral needed to know as quickly as possible.

# — Twenty-Six —

"Was that IED your idea, Jan?"

Jannika Hallikonnoen kept her eyes on the foamy depths of the beer mug in her hands. The *Reach*'s main bar was crowded as usual, even though it was shortly after midnight, Tyrell time, and talk was of nothing but the bomb that almost killed a bunch of Marines underground.

A flash of anger lit up her eyes, and she forcefully repressed a desire to strangle the informant, sitting in the next booth and whispering over the divider

"I told you not to speak to me until I gave the signal."

"The Commanding Idiot is beside himself, scared stupid, and has backed away from digging into Delgado's node. He won't even let me at it. What should I do now?"

"Nothing. But we'll take care of him when we need access through his terminal."

"Then they'll know—"

"It'll be too late," Hallikonnoen interrupted. "Find a way to dig up what I asked or suffer the consequences. Now leave and don't approach me again until I say so."

She watched the informant leave, fighting back her growing annoyance that the plan had failed. The Marines were supposed to be buried by a cave-in, with no one knowing a bomb caused it. But once again, Delgado's people proved they were brighter than she expected, and knowing there was a bomb maker in Tyrell would merely motivate them to search harder. Fortunately, the ship was early, and that would at least partially make up for it.

\*\*

"Shuttles on final approach. Everything's green." The voice of the Tyrell controller echoed through the command post, courtesy of Sergeant Testo's tap into the ops node.

They'd watched the gigantic Assenari Mining Corporation bulk hauler *Thunder Bay* enter orbit and gobble up the refined product cubes flung up by the station's powerful electromagnetic rail gun before releasing a trio of large commercial shuttles.

The command post's primary display screen now showed the beetle-like craft slowly dropping toward the slagged rock tarmac, riding on columns of pure energy. One was configured as a passenger shuttle, the other two for cargo. The first would bring in fresh workers and take those whose tour was back home while the rest carried food, spare parts, all-important alcohol for the bar, and other consumables.

Both cargo craft would enter the hangar, but the passenger carrier would dock externally, where a pressurized gangway tube extruded from the personnel arrivals and departures module immediately beside the hangar.

Command Sergeant Bassam and half of Bravo Troop, wearing pressurized armor and carrying scatterguns, were in the hangar, standing guard, as per Tyrell's standard operating procedures. His troop sergeant and the remaining Marines were in the personnel module to scan the new arrivals and check off the departures from the list provided by Movane.

As the shuttles' downward movement ceased, leaving them to hover a meter above the surface, the hangar doors slid open, revealing the shimmering curtain of the force field keeping the atmosphere inside. One by one, the cargo units crossed the energy barrier and settled on the marked spots while the third gently landed on the external spot.

"Landing maneuvers completed. Standby for disembarkation. Stevedore crews to the hangar," the same disembodied voice said.

Delgado leaned forward, elbows on the table. "Okay, Sergeant, let's see what we've got."

The primary display switched to a split view, hangar on the right, and personnel module on the left. In both, they could see Bravo Troop Marines ready to run the station's multipurpose scanners to check for signs of contraband, weapons, explosives, and other forbidden items. In addition, the one in the arrivals and departures lounge would register the newcomers' biometrics.

While the scanner's data feed was for the operations center only, Testo ensured the command post saw the same thing.

After a few moments, the Marines in the lounge stiffened, signaling that the first arrivals were coming down the gangway. Before any fresh faces could appear, the primary display blanked out.

"What?" Testo turned to his workstation and tapped the controls, swearing beneath his breath as he took on an increasingly intense look of frustration. "The system crashed. The entire damn arrivals security system and I can't get it back online again."

Delgado frowned. "A glitch or sabotage?"

"Must be sabotage, sir." Testo gave him a disgusted look. "I checked the programming myself only half an hour ago. I even put in a few redundancies, just in case. But it went pear-shaped."

"So now we have no way of knowing what and who just came on board?"

"Nothing beyond what Bravo Troop can pick up on their handheld battlefield sensors. I'm alerting them now."

Delgado sat back and sighed. "I suppose we'd better assume that more hostiles are joining whoever planted the IED. Give Rolf a list of the new arrivals and tell him to run in-person checks. They won't like it, but too bad."

"He's already investigating who could have planted the IED. In fact, he should show up with the results of his combing through the blast site at any moment."

"Right." Delgado nodded. Command Sergeant Painter and his troop were somewhat stretched for resources and time thanks to the latest incident. "Okay. Put Charlie Troop on finding the new arrivals. Best if Rolf's people stay on our hidden artificer before they try again, this time inside the station proper, killing the Almighty knows how many. I'm sure the bio and chem warheads alone are worth murdering every living being on Keros."

"Roger that, sir."

**

"We recovered enough scraps of the toolbox to analyze, Skipper."

Rolf Painter placed a transparent case on the command post table.

"Along with Ozzie's remains, may he rest in peace." A faint smile cracked Painter's usually inscrutable countenance. "The blast wasn't powerful enough to ding the tunnel walls, let alone collapse them. The rocks that put Salford and the rest in sickbay were from the pile used to hide the IED — the tunnel simply acted like a scattergun barrel. Based on trace evidence, the explosive used is commercial grade and likely came from Tyrell's stocks, but the logs show no one entered the explosives bunker in the last few weeks, nor do they show unauthorized withdrawals. It means whoever stole what we figure was about a kilo and a half hid their tracks.

"We found no fingerprints on the outside, but enough on the scraps of whatever was inside with the explosive to give us a sample. I've run them through Tyrell's files, and they match those of a pair of miners who've been on the Assenari payroll for almost ten years — Harry Zbotnicky and Joey Henkel. Both are under arrest and sitting in the brig right now, scared out of their wits. They deny any involvement, of course. I searched their quarters and found a rather large amount of cash, cunningly hidden, and minute traces of several illicit substances."

"What are you thinking?"

"They don't strike me as smart or capable enough of building an IED with an anti-lift device as a detonator and setting a trap. Besides, they work Shaft One, and there are no records of them entering Shaft Two."

"*Maskirovka*," First Sergeant Hak muttered, shaking his head. "Someone is messing with us, hoping we'll chase shadows while the actual operation happens."

"Without a doubt."

"Is anyone on our watch list a Shaft Two worker?"

Painter nodded. "Hallikonnoen, but we can't find evidence she made a stop on Level Five. She spent the last few shifts on Level Nine. But considering her ability to slip past surveillance undetected, that doesn't give her an alibi."

"Are the men in the brig connected with Hallikonnoen?"

"Not directly. They hang around mostly with their team boss, one Lyle Fournier, whose current whereabouts are unknown. We've seen Fournier talking with Hallikonnoen a few times by my people, but team bosses getting together is nothing unusual." Painter paused, eyes on Delgado. "May I interrogate Zbotnicky and Henkel using field methods? They're unlikely to be conditioned, and right now, they're our only solid link."

"Go ahead, though I doubt you'll find anything useful. Small-time criminals are unlikely to know much. Whoever set the IED is a pro."

"True." Painter inclined his head in acknowledgment. "But it's worth a try."

"Anything else?"

"No, sir." Painter stood. "With your permission."

"Dismissed."

**

First Sergeant Hak stuck his head into Delgado's cubicle shortly before supper, wearing a sober expression.

"Guys from Bravo Troop investigating an open access hatch in one of the mechanical modules next to the lift shafts found Lyle Fournier's body in the crawlspace, sir. I was in the command post when they reported."

Delgado tossed his reader aside.

"Crap. Any visible signs of death?"

"Based on the body's contortions, the traces of vomit, and the utter look of horror on Fournier's face, Moses Singh figures drug overdose. They're moving the body to the infirmary now — in a body bag. I figure we should keep this quiet for the moment. Ejaz will deal with Doc Blake and report back to you while the doc will let Engstrom and Movane know."

Delgado nodded. Letting Command Sergeant Ejaz Bassam, Bravo Troop's leader, run with the matter would keep it at a lower profile than if he and the first sergeant barged in. That way, everyone would think the Marine garrison didn't suspect foul play, even though Fournier's sudden death was convenient.

Within thirty minutes, Bassam called to confirm that Doctor Blake's initial findings clearly indicated a drug overdose from a substance produced in the Protectorate Zone and smuggled into the Commonwealth. Sergeant Painter's people found traces of the same hallucinogenic in Zbotnicky's cubicle earlier.

"Any signs whether it was accidental or forced?"

"Nothing the doc could detect, but he'll run a full autopsy later today."

"Time of death?"

"No more than two hours ago."

"Meaning just after shift change when that module would be empty. Thanks, Sergeant. Delgado, out."

He turned to Hak and exhaled.

"Someone is disrupting the chain of evidence, it seems. Both Zbotnicky and Henkel pointed their fingers at Fournier as the man who disposed of their stash before our search. Knowing Rolf's interrogation methods, there's no way they could lie about it."

"For sure." Hak nodded wisely. "But I doubt Fournier's our bomb maker."

"I wasn't even thinking of him as a possible culprit. No. Whoever made and set that IED is responsible for the man's death."

Hak scoffed. "More *maskirovka*, then."

"A good thing you told Ejaz to keep it quiet. I'd rather keep the opposition wondering whether they have us chasing our own tails. Let's see what Rolf and his people can tell us about Hallikonnoen's movements in the last few hours."

"You think she's responsible?"

"She's the only one who's attracted our attention by behaving abnormally for a mine worker. How many of them would engage in sex with a chief engineer, then skilfully interrogate him afterward without said engineer noticing?"

# — Twenty-Seven —

"Sorry, Skipper." Painter shook his head. "I don't think Hallikonnoen put Fournier through an involuntary drug overdose. She's been under almost constant observation for the last day and was nowhere near the maintenance compartment."

"Almost?" Delgado cocked an eyebrow.

"We didn't have eyes on her when she was in her cubicle or the sanitary facilities, and that's it."

"So, either she gave your people the slip, or there's someone else who hasn't popped up on our sensor screen yet. If it's not Fournier sampling too much of his own inventory, in which case his death is unrelated."

"Looks like it."

A frown creased Delgado's forehead as he parsed the known unknowns.

"I'm leaning toward the hypothesis Fournier was murdered, and I'll bet the guilty party is connected with the inscrutable Jannika Hallikonnoen."

"Ditto, Skipper. We won't let up our surveillance."

"Add finding another pro like her to your list."

Hak let out a soft grunt. "Something's about to happen. I can feel it in my bones."

**

Over the hours following the Assenari shuttles' arrival, Charlie Troop's Marines, guided by Sergeant Testo from the command post, slowly and quietly closed in on the new arrivals. They scanned them discreetly from a distance while Testo matched the readings with what Bravo Troop collected with their handheld devices after the station scanners failed.

As always, the *Reach*, crowded, dark, and noisy, provided the perfect meeting place for people who didn't wish to be seen together. And for people who wanted to observe without being conspicuous. That night, Jannika Hallikonnoen met several newly arrived acquaintances whose biometric details joined the rest of the data in the tactical AI's input feed. Was a team coalescing around her?

Testo gnawed on his lower lip, contemplating the ramifications, his nervous system supercharged by hours of creative computer work and liters of black coffee. Movement on a secondary screen caught his attention. Someone was using Engstrom's terminal and access codes to dig into the command post node.

This time, the hacker was searching for Major Delgado's contingency plans in case of attack from both outside and within. After letting the intruder work away for a few minutes, his face twisted into a feral smile. He'd learned to recognize Engstrom's hand at the console, his ways of navigating the network, but whoever was up there right now worked with a different rhythm, one that felt more tentative. Nonetheless, they eventually came across the bogus plans and downloaded a copy.

Testo called up the remote sensor monitoring the executive corridor to identify the intruder as he or she left Engstrom's office only to find it offline. The operations sergeant swore volubly below his breath, although Charlie Troop's Command Sergeant Isaac Dyas, standing night duty, noticed, and gave Testo a questioning glance. Before the latter replied, the hack vanished.

"Never mind. The sensor in the executive corridor is out, Isaac. If you can send someone to replace it at around oh-three-hundred, that would be great."

Dyas gave Testo thumbs up. "Will do. Now, how about you hit the sack, buddy? You've been putting in sixteen-hour days, and that'll dull the mind."

"Yep." Suppressing a yawn, he stood and stretched. "See you later."

Before exiting the command post, Testo glanced at the date-time readout on the primary display. November 30th, oh-two-hundred hours. At this rate, they'd most definitely be observing Farhaven Day in Tyrell, a somewhat fitting parallel.

\*\*

Suffering from a bout of insomnia, Engstrom walked to his office with the vague intention of finding a way out of his predicament. Two suspicious deaths in less than a week, an IED in the mine, and an out-of-control Marine Corps major, along with whatever the drone found in the hidden Second Migration War bunker that caused Fleet HQ to slam top secret special access on the find. It was no wonder stress had been getting the better of him. Too much going wrong in Tyrell, and he could kiss his promotion to commodore goodbye.

Engstrom didn't expect to find good news or a solution by sitting behind his desk. But he also didn't expect to find someone else there. He stopped beyond the threshold of the office door, letting it close behind him, and stood rooted to the spot.

"What the hell are *you* doing here? How did you get in?" Tyrell Station's commanding officer performed the unusual feat of sounding uneasy and outraged at the same time.

"I think Delgado's still lying to us. His overt disinterest in Fournier's death is just the latest manifestation. Since you won't dig deeper into his node and find the truth, I will, Nero."

The tone was so scornful Engstrom felt anger building as he strode over to the desk, intent on shutting off his workstation. Because of Delgado, he had already lost a measure of control over the station. He was damned if he would surrender his authority over one of his close advisers as well. When he rounded the desk, he saw schematics on the display unrelated to any criminal investigation such as Terry Evans' murder or Lyle Fournier's suspicious death, let alone the IED.

"What in Hades is that?" He leaned over. "Oh, by the sweet Almighty, what do you think you're doing, looking at Delgado's contingency plans? If he finds out we've accessed them without his authorization, they'll hear the uproar all the way at Fleet HQ."

"Give it a rest, Nero. Lately, you've been acting like those Marines are omniscient superior beings. They won't find a harmless little hack, and if they do, I bet they'll be embarrassed at their lax security and won't make an issue of it. Still, if you're that worried..." The screen went blank as the connection was cut.

"Worried? Of course, I'm worried. Because you're irresponsible."

"I have what I came for anyway." A data wafer vanished into a tunic pocket. "Try yoga. I hear it does wonders for the blood pressure. Good night, Nero."

And with that, Engstrom was alone in the silent office on a deserted level. He stared out the window at the bleak landscape beneath more stars than a human could count in ten lifetimes and wondered if he had any options left. That he was little more than a figurehead as station commander became painfully obvious, and he was a rather solitary figurehead at that, one without friends, let alone people he could trust.

**

Several modules below the rarefied executive levels, Command Sergeant Isaac Dyas and his winger were whiling away their shift in the command post by reading training manuals while Charlie Troop patrols crisscrossed Tyrell Station when the tactical AI chimed softly, announcing it detected what Testo called an incident. He'd programmed it to register and report any occurrence that deviated from the station's regular daily and hourly cycles.

For example, it would report airlocks and doors normally unused during a shift being opened, station personnel without proper authorization entering restricted compartments or using restricted equipment, and other such events. All, of course, without the station operations center knowledge. One of the occurrences it monitored was out and inbound communications.

Tyrell reported to Fleet HQ and Assenari Mining head office on a defined schedule, which meant any transmissions outside of those times which weren't directed at known starships in the Keros system were at once flagged by the AI. That particular trigger had never been activated until now.

Someone in Tyrell had sent a brief subspace message, a microburst, using the orbital relay, but didn't route it through the operations center or the Marine command post, the only two entities who could authorize communications. Dyas analyzed the message but could neither decipher it nor figure who the recipient might be. The only bit of evidence he deduced was that it had been sent at such low power, the recipient wasn't far away. Probably in the Keros system.

As per the standing operational procedures, Dyas called Testo, who appeared within minutes, looking refreshed after only a few hours' sleep. Testo repeated Dyas' analysis, then sat back, eyes on the primary display, which currently showed a view of Tyrell as seen by the geosynchronous orbital platform which served, among other functions, as a subspace relay.

"You pretty much nailed it, Isaac. The recipient of that transmission is close. No further than the heliopause, I should think. I doubt the operations center even noticed."

"Do I call the Skipper?"

"Oh, yes. This is the sort of incident that can't wait until morning."

# — Twenty-Eight —

"The timing is absolutely perfect." Delgado sat back in his chair at the command post table after examining the mysterious transmission. "*Thunder Bay* will be FTL in interstellar space by now, meaning there will be no other legitimate starship in this system for the next fourteen days. Unless the Navy sends an unannounced patrol frigate through."

"Or whoever they tasked to empty that bunker shows up," Hak added. "From our side, I mean."

"We still don't know what's behind these events." Delgado tapped his fingers on the edge of the tabletop. "Are they related to the Migration War munitions or to that mysterious door at the bottom of a lift which doesn't appear in Tyrell's specs? We were scrambled and sent here at a speed anyone outside Special Forces can only dream of once HQ received the report from the recon droid."

Hak shrugged. "It might be both, with the bio and chem payloads being targets of opportunity."

"Still, that transmission means someone unauthorized entered the Keros system. My guess is that things will happen soon after one of the daily situation reports. Fleet Operations will only get nervous once Tyrell misses two in a row, which gives an intruder forty-eight hours before the alarm sounds. Any way of tracking the clandestine sender?"

Testo shook his head. "Sorry, sir. I tried, but whoever it was knew how to vanish. If the tactical AI wasn't looking for unauthorized transmissions, no one would be the wiser."

Hak let out an amused snort. "We may feel a little hard done by at being sent here on a few hours' notice so we can play garrison police, but can you imagine how fat, dumb, and happy a regular Marine company would be right now?"

Delgado gave his first sergeant a wry grin. "The proverbial sitting ducks. I can't see anyone from a line regiment daring to hack a naval station's network and spy on everything and everyone. Which, of course, is why we're here at Admiral Talyn's orders."

"To stop bad guys no one but us and their advance party know are coming." Hak chuckled. "How much of this did the Admiral suspect ahead of time, I wonder?"

"Probably more than we might think." Delgado's eyes returned to the view of Tyrell Station as seen from orbit on the primary display. "Any way of telling how far the transmission's recipient might be based on the signal strength?"

Testo grimaced dubiously as he glanced at his workstation display. "The AI has been running probabilities while we were talking, and its best guess would be the system's outer asteroid belt where an entire fleet could hide with no one in Tyrell knowing. From there, it's about a five-hour jump at maximum in-system speed to Keros' hyperlimit."

"Which means we can expect visitors as soon as midday, which is a few hours after today's sitrep transmission to HQ. Or not. But that still doesn't tell us what's in store."

"Nope." Hak shook his head. "It sure doesn't. Will you warn HQ?"

"Not yet. We're still working with suppositions, gut feelings, and circumstantial evidence. Besides, I won't make the mistake of underestimating the opposition. If we send a message out of sequence with the regular sitrep, it might tip them off we uncovered more than they expected, and I'm not ready yet to trigger events. Not that HQ can help us in any case. If someone's already on the way, they won't arrive any faster. I'll update the Admiral on everything during the next scheduled transmission."

"Makes sense. What now?"

A shrug. "We wait, watch, and listen while the situation develops without giving away our state of heightened vigilance. There will be more indicators of something about to happen. And on that note, how are we doing with the new arrivals?"

"Eight of them met Hallikonnoen in the *Reach* last night. It could be nothing more sinister than old friends having a beer and catching up, but Rolf's people don't think so.

Based on observed behavior, they figure she was passing out orders."

"We're keeping those eight under surveillance, Sergeant?"

"Absolutely, Skipper, since around twenty-two-hundred hours yesterday. And we're still watching Hallikonnoen, Limix, Movane, and Engstrom. Which means someone else sent the subspace message."

"Or the culprit messed with the surveillance network again."

Testo nodded. "Sure, Top. But the AI couldn't find any evidence of tampering around the relevant time."

"Yet we are dealing with pros, no question about it. *Sécurité Spéciale?*"

"Or their zaibatsu mercenaries. Some of the corporate security and intelligence outfits are proving rather good, from what I read in the most recent intelligence digests."

Hak scoffed. "The ones whose ass we kicked during the last few missions weren't particularly impressive."

"Compared to us, no. But what if a regular rifle company was here instead of one from the 1st Special Forces Regiment? Because that's what they're no doubt counting on."

"Surprise, surprise, surprise." Testo chuckled.

"My favorite principle of war, Sergeant." A pause. "Once the last patrol comes up from the mine, we're done underground."

"Yes, sir."

**

The day seemed to drag on as tension rose by increments, or so it seemed to Delgado and his first sergeant. None of the people under surveillance made a single move that was out of line. Still, many struck Erinye Company's covert watchers — those patrolling in person and the Marines sitting in front of surveillance video feeds — as worried, preoccupied, or anxious.

Delgado did not try to speak with Engstrom or anybody else save for members of his unit. Nor did he activate any defensive measures beyond heightened vigilance. His Marines were under orders to make their activities appear normal.

However, he couldn't shake the feeling that a strange mood, an edginess that defied description, permeated Tyrell. It was as if, in some primal part of the soul, the inhabitants of the isolated station understood an ion storm would soon engulf Keros. Passing through the corridors on his way to supper with Hak, Delgado felt that he should order the crew to batten down the hatches, set the storm canvas, and rig extra tackles to the rudder.

When he mentioned his thoughts, the first sergeant gave him a curious look and chuckled.

"Rereading pre-spaceflight wet navy war books, sir?"

"I can't spend all of my time slogging through the twisted history of the Migration Wars despite Colonel Decker's recommended reading list, now can I."

The *Reach* was as busy as usual when Delgado and Hak slipped into a darkened corner booth for an after-dinner drink. They ordered whiskeys and, while waiting for their glasses, silently scanned the crowd. Hak spotted Jannika Hallikonnoen holding court by the bar, apparently enjoying herself, unconcerned and relaxed. None of the people around her bore any resemblance to the men and women she'd met the day before.

"Do you think Rolf is right, and she's the one?"

"How often has he been wrong, sir?"

"Rarely enough to let me sleep quietly tonight, Top." Delgado grimaced. "The next scheduled sitrep is in twelve hours. Since nothing happened after the one sent out this morning, my gut tells me tomorrow's the day. They're still getting organized but won't wait for long. If we're right."

"We are. I can smell trouble in the air, sir. And so can you."

Delgado's eyes were drawn to the pool of light at the long, crowded bar. Jannika Hallikonnoen had turned around and was staring him right in the eyes, as if unable to resist throwing a gauntlet, one she realized he must accept.

Delgado slowly raised his glass as if in salute, eyes never leaving Hallikonnoen's broad face. The team boss replied in kind. It was a strange ceremony as if two foes suddenly decided they would acknowledge their rivalry in the best traditions of chivalry, just before dropping the gloves and fighting dirty.

"Hallikonnoen seems pretty sure of herself," Hak remarked after watching the silent interplay.

"Let's hope it's because she swallowed the *dezinformatsiya* we seeded throughout the command post node and not because she has a fifth ace up her sleeve." Delgado chuckled. "Unless this brief exchange was just a bit of bravado between two egomaniacs."

**\*\***

Jannika Hallikonnoen watched the Marine officer and his first sergeant leave the *Reach*, presumably headed for the barracks and bed. She couldn't quite understand what possessed her to acknowledge Delgado's existence. If he suspected her of anything, then by returning his ironic salute, she'd pretty much confirmed those suspicions.

Not that he could do anything at this point. Her plan would unfold no matter what Delgado and his Marines tried. They simply weren't as lethal as her action team, made up of deadliest black ops agents money could buy, even though they outnumbered her people by a wide margin. This wasn't a battlefield for mere infantry like them but a complex, three-dimensional space where those with specialized training, no fear of death, and no rules of engagement would win. Especially after she gained control of Tyrell Station's systems, locking most Marines in their barracks. The rest would then be taken out patrol by patrol.

She drained her vodka tonic and ordered another before engaging one of the team bosses around her in conversation, oblivious to off-duty Marines in civilian clothes sitting just beyond the dance floor.

Despite her best efforts, Hallikonnoen couldn't know Erinye Company, Ghost Squadron, 1st Special Forces Regiment — and not H Company of the 42nd, as she believed — was ready as well. And though the Marines weren't fanatics who'd willingly die for their cause, they were practiced at improvising as situations unfolded. But then, the *Sécurité Spéciale* agent wasn't the first of her organization who underestimated them. Unfortunately for her, however, none of those who failed came back to tell a cautionary tale.

# — Twenty-Nine —

The next morning, when Delgado and Hak entered the command post after a less than restful night, Sergeant Testo spoke before either could ask the obvious question.

"Today's sitrep, along with your report to the Admiral, went out over the main subspace channel, right on schedule, Skipper. We also received an encrypted one-liner from her earlier — the cavalry is on its way."

"Then I'm starting the timer. Let the troop leaders know they're at thirty minutes to move, except for Delta Troop. They should head out as soon as possible."

Command Sergeant Saxer's Marines, armored and armed, would quietly slip out of Tyrell proper and occupy the large-bore plasma cannon emplacements on the heights. There, they would assume local control should the operations center lose contact, or worse, fall into enemy hands.

"Roger that." Testo nodded.

Thirty minutes to move meant no more alcohol, no more wearing civilian clothes, combat gear laid out and ready,

**228**

weapons loaded, and off-duty personnel to carry their personal communicators. Those who carried needlers with non-lethal loads as duty sidearms would swap them for blasters.

The patrols throughout Tyrell continued as before, except that the Marines on duty now carried full ammunition pouches on their tactical harnesses. The change was barely noticeable to casual observers.

"And now, we wait." Delgado dropped into his accustomed chair and ran his hand, fingers splayed, through his short red hair. "Oh, joy."

"Yep," Hak grunted. "And I so do love pretending I'm a sitting duck."

As the morning passed, the command post time display dragged out the minutes and then the hours while Tyrell buzzed around them, as it always did. By noon, Delgado was ready to give the whole thing up as a false alarm. After all, if the opposition planned a strike, they would find plenty of opportunities before the next ship arrived.

He rose, stretched, and announced, "I'm about ready for some grub. How about you, Top?"

"Sure." Hak climbed to his feet

But before they reached the door, Testo's clipped words arrested their movements.

"The AI reports an incident." His hands danced over his workstation. "Another unauthorized subspace message, same strength and duration as before. The sender hooked into Tyrell's communications network from a terminal in Module One, more precisely the personnel office." A pause, then a muffled curse. "Surveillance in Module One is off — no audio or video."

"Send a patrol up there right away."

"Roger, sir." Testo flicked over to the company frequency and quickly rapped out a series of orders. "On their way."

Another pause. "Crap. Someone's systematically taking control of Tyrell's vital functions and locking out the operations center."

"This is it." When Delgado glanced at Hak, he could have sworn he saw a pleased twinkle in the older man's eyes. "Not so long a wait."

"They've shut off access to the subspace array, airlocks, lifts, internal communications, and the primary nodes. Do you want me to override?"

"Can you regain control later?"

"Yes, sir."

"Hold off for now. I'd rather not show my hand until we see what's up. From where are they working?"

Testo queried the tactical AI, then looked at Delgado over his shoulder with an air of amusement.

"Engstrom's office."

Delgado and Hak exchanged looks.

"Shall we?" The former asked as he stood.

Hak climbed to his feet as well, then pulled out his sidearm, checked its power and ammunition indicators before nodding. He waited until Delgado did the same, then led the way out of the command post. Warned by Testo, a scattergun-armed, grim-faced Sergeant Kuzek caught up with them by the stairs. Based on the behavior of the workers they passed, no one as yet knew something was up, though seeing the Marine commanding officer along with his first sergeant and his winger rush by gave some of them pause.

They found the patrol dispatched by Testo in the empty antechamber — Engstrom's assistant being off duty — attempting to open the office door, but the call screen remained stubbornly blank.

"It's been disabled, and no one's answering, sir," Lance Corporal Drake, whose patrol it was, said. "Sergeant Testo can't open it via the station network either."

"Step back." First Sergeant Hak pulled out his blaster, took aim at the call screen, and fired once. Then, he produced a multi-tool from his pocket and tore the screen's remains from the wall, exposing the emergency release handle.

"I'm not sure shooting it was necessary," Delgado said in a conversational tone.

"Sure, sir. But I wanted to make sure one of us fired the first shot in the upcoming battle. Now how about everyone steps aside before I pull the release." He glanced at Sergeant Kuzek. "You and I will provide cover. Drake, you and your winger are taking point."

After everyone nodded in turn, Hak said, "Ready, set," and yanked on the mechanical release.

The door opened silently, Hak quickly peeked inside to make sure no one stood beyond the door taking aim, then barked, "GO!"

Drake and Maiikonnen, moving in a crouch, scatterguns at the ready, sped through the opening.

"Clear."

Kuzek entered the office ahead of Delgado and stepped to one side as the sickly sweet stench of violent death hit their nostrils. Nero Engstrom's dead body lay sprawled on the imitation Persian rug, the back of his head blown away.

"I'd stay right there if I were you, Major." Ed Limix's voice came from the open door to Engstrom's private bathroom. "There's an improvised claymore pointing right at you, and I'm holding a dead man switch in my hand. Thanks for giving me a few moments to move out of the way with your ham-fisted assault on the door lock."

Kuzek raised a hand and silently pointed at the bookcase to their left, where a well-worn red toolbox, just like the one used for the IED in the mine, sat incongruously among the printed tomes and decorations.

"Low explosive charge, but filled with lovely ball bearings," Limix continued. "It goes off, and the lot of you become colanders. Or at least your faces will since I suppose your battledress uniforms prevent punctures. Now put your weapons down."

"You realize my command post is seeing and hearing this, Ed. A dozen Marines are on their way, and more are no doubt even now preparing to cut through the bathroom's bulkhead from the other side. The only way it ends is with your surrender."

An amused chuckle echoed through the door. "Sorry to disappoint you, Major, but the station is ours. Your

Marines aren't coming here, nor are they going anywhere else."

"Why are you doing this, Ed? Money? Politics? Revenge?" Delgado asked, trying to gain time for his backup. "By the way, you fooled me until now, so kudos. So, what's your motivation?"

"Nice try, Delgado. Now drop your weapons."

"Money. That has to be it. You took the deal of a lifetime to betray this station, your employer, and your comrades, right? Enough to retire on and vanish." Delgado cracked a sardonic grin. "Unfortunately, as you'll find out shortly, you're what's known in the business as a loose end, Ed. The money they promised you? It isn't coming. And you aren't leaving Tyrell alive."

He took a calculated stab at the answer.

"Come on, Ed. Jannika Hallikonnoen and the operatives who arrived aboard *Thunder Bay* are pros who work for a federal government agency that doesn't officially exist. They're the sort who plan on a clean escape with no chance of word getting out either now or in ten years. Surrender, and we'll keep you safe. Help us, and I'll put in a word with the judge advocate general, so you won't end up doing life on Parth."

"For the last time, lower your weapons. Jannika has this place sewn up."

To Delgado's finely tuned ears, Limix's tone was losing its earlier certainty, a good sign the miner wasn't a *Sécurité Spéciale* operative.

"Whatever Hallikonnoen is planning, it won't succeed, Ed. There's a reason we took over the garrison duties before the previous bunch finished their tour. Fleet HQ knew what was coming and sent us to stop them." He paused for a few heartbeats. "We're not from the 42nd Marines. My unit belongs to Special Operations Command and if you think Hallikonnoen can take control of Tyrell because she knows our plans, then think again. Everything you and Nero Engstrom pulled from our node was planted specifically as disinformation. We detected your hacks from the start and fed you fiction. We're very good at *dezinformatsiya* and *maskirovka* in SOCOM. Better than anyone else in the entire Commonwealth."

Limix didn't immediately reply, though they could hear him move in the bathroom's shadows.

"You're done for, Ed. Save what you can. When this is over, Hallikonnoen and her merry band will be dead. You can still live."

While he spoke, Delgado made subtle signals with his right hand, knowing the other four would watch him as he negotiated. And those signals were telling them to fall back. One step at a time.

"Nah. She's got your number, Delgado." Limix sounded even less confident than before. "I don't believe your Special Forces garbage."

"That's your choice. You know what's funny? I always figured Movane was the one up to no good."

"Ha." Limix scoffed, not noticing that Delgado and his Marines were now closer to the corridor than the IED. "That old sourpuss? She's as honest as her face is long."

"I'm sure Movane has her own thing, which neither you nor Engstrom knew about. No one who gets that high in the Assenari hierarchy is honest."

"You're telling me."

"Why did you kill Engstrom?"

"That was his fault. He tried to resist and gave me no choice. If he'd cooperated, that old fool would still be alive."

Hak slipped through the door, stepped aside, and grabbed the emergency handle. Kuzek followed him a fraction of a second later and ducked behind the wall on the other side, blaster aimed at the IED in the bookcase, leaving Delgado, Lance Corporal Drake, and Lance Corporal Maiikonnen. Delgado gestured at Drake, and both Marines stepped backward into the corridor.

"Last chance, Ed."

"Wait a minute. What the hell is happening. Where did your people go?"

Delgado fell back with alacrity and cleared the door. Hak pulled it shut, and just as the last sliver of the opening was about to vanish, Kuzek fired three rounds at the toolbox, destroying its core and the detonator.

It didn't blow.

When Hak opened the door again, they saw a disconsolate Limix standing in the middle of the office, a civilian pattern mining detonator dangling from his right hand.

"It's over, Ed."

Limix nodded once and dropped the detonator.

# — Thirty —

Delgado turned to Drake and gestured at Limix. "Take him to the brig. He remains in solitary, with no visitors until further notice. Put a bag over his head and take the back passages. I'd rather word of his arrest doesn't spread just yet."

"Yes, sir." Drake pulled a set of wrist restraints from his tactical harness and, with Maiikonnen's help, shackled the bewildered shop steward, who shuffled off between them, looking like a lost soul.

"I'll head for the infirmary and see that they pick up Engstrom's body," Hak said. He glanced at Kuzek. "You stick with the Skipper."

When Hak was gone, Delgado fought the irresistible urge to commit an act of vandalism and lost. He pulled out his blaster and walked over to the late station commander's desk. The weapon coughed once, punching a hole in the embedded terminal and rendering it incapable of connecting with any of Tyrell's nodes. It was a useless gesture, but he felt a small measure of satisfaction nonetheless.

He checked the improvised explosive device and made sure it was out of action, though part of him regretted not being able to reset it and catch the opposition flat-footed when they checked in on Limix. Then a thought struck him, and he opened a frequency with the command post.

"Zero, this is Niner."

"Zero."

"What is Romana Movane's last known location?"

"Wait one." Then, "Her office."

"Thank you. Ready to assume management?"

"Affirmative."

"Execute. Niner, out."

And with that, Major Curtis Delgado's command post supplanted both the station's operations center and whoever took over via Limix's treachery. He was now not just Tyrell's commanding officer by dint of rank, but because he controlled it.

"Let's see what Chief Administrator Movane says about this."

They found her office door unlocked, though she didn't respond to the call panel. Delgado opened it and found her lying on the floor, ankles, and wrists restrained with the sort of quick ties miners used. She stared at them with wide eyes, though she couldn't speak with the rag stuffed in her mouth.

Delgado knelt beside her and removed the piece of cloth. "Are you okay?"

"Limix. He did it," she croaked.

"Figures. He killed Engstrom." Delgado worked the quick ties and released her.

"I heard a scuffle next door." Movane sat up and massaged her wrists one at a time. "Who'd figure on Ed turning rogue?"

"It's called greed, Chief Administrator." Delgado stood, held out his hand, and helped Movane up. "A team of hostile operatives is attempting to seize Tyrell at this moment, and Limix was their inside man. He's headed for the brig, but the damage is done."

"What hostiles?" She frowned.

"I assume it's related to the hidden artifact, with the Second Migration War ammunition bunker thrown in as a last-minute bonus."

Movane appeared to chew on her words for a moment. "How did you find out?"

"About the artifact? We kept exploring abandoned galleries, looking for whatever it was so many people were attempting to hide by distracting us."

Her scowl deepened. "And the bunker?"

"That's why Fleet HQ sent us here in the first place. When the mining droid reported the find as per protocol, analysis of the visual record established the bunker was filled with biological and chemical warheads. Forbidden weapons, which, in the wrong hands, could kill millions. My primary job is ensuring no one tries to retrieve the warheads until specialists arrive. It was to proceed in secret, but since you, and by that, I mean Tyrell's leadership, were also hiding secrets — well, both secrecy streams intersected and created a mess."

"Who are you really, Major? You're certainly not the usual sort of Marine we see here."

"My unit and I belong to Special Operations Command. With Engstrom dead, I'm now also Tyrell's commanding officer, and we're in the middle of a crisis. I'll need your full cooperation so we can make sure no one other than the enemy dies today. But you'll be working from my command post until this is over." When she bristled, Delgado raised a restraining hand. "It's for your own safety and that of Tyrell. And refusal is not an option."

As he led her out into the corridor, the lift opened, disgorging Doctor Blake and two medics with a floating stretcher.

"Major. Your first sergeant said Captain Engstrom was murdered?" Blake seemed aghast at the idea.

"Sadly, yes." He jerked a thumb over his shoulder at the open door to Engstrom's office. "And I've placed Ed Limix under arrest."

Blake's eyes widened. "I beg your pardon? Ed Limix? What in the name of all that's holy is happening around here?"

Delgado shrugged. "Someone is working on a hostile takeover of Tyrell. Not that they'll succeed."

At that moment, his communicator chimed. He tapped the earpiece.

"Niner."

"Zero. We just detected another unauthorized attempt at using the subspace transmitter. The AI shut it off immediately."

"Good. I'm on my way. Niner, out."

Blake gave Delgado a grim look. "Shall I break out more body bags?"

The Marine slapped him on the shoulder as he walked past. "I'll try my best to make sure Engstrom is the only casualty from our side today. The enemy? Well, for them, you won't need body bags, just a convenient airlock."

"And tomorrow?"

"If this goes the way I intend," Delgado said over his shoulder, "the problem will be sorted by tomorrow. Come on, Chief Administrator. We have a mining station to save."

**

Jannika Hallikonnoen felt the icy hand of fear squeeze her guts for the first time since arriving on Tyrell as she forced herself to walk calmly down the corridor. Events were spinning out of control twelve hours ahead of schedule, which meant the entire operation was in jeopardy.

She knew Limix had failed when she lost access to the reactor controls from her hidden panel in Engineering Module Two, at the bottom of the base. Somehow, the Marines had found the tap and shut it off completely. While her action team was preparing to gain control of Tyrell and open it up wide for the coming raid, Delgado was laughing at their efforts. And for that, his death would be painful and prolonged.

But she still held one last card, a backup only she knew about. Limix did not possess the skills to manipulate the security programming by himself. No, he'd merely provided easy access to a workstation from which the security files could be modified. She had given him a data wafer containing instructions that would transfer sole control of vital functions to her.

However, those instructions also contained a subroutine by which she would secure a back door entrance into the system from any workstation in the operations center. Limix hadn't known about it, so even if the Marines traced his actions, they'd never find her insurance. No Marine could be that good a hacker. Not even one of Delgado's people.

As she rounded a corner, she glimpsed a by now well-known face beneath a rakishly angled blue beret — Command Sergeant Rolf Painter moving through a cluster of off-duty miners.

He was following her, that she was sure, and she mentally swore as a surge of hatred for the taciturn Marine noncom welled up her throat. She shoved a pair of protesting miners aside in her haste to break away from Painter and missed the two Marines stepping out of a darkened maintenance alcove.

They openly followed the *Sécurité Spéciale* agent to the clear tube connecting the Recreation Module to Administration Module Three, as if they didn't have a single care in the universe. Hallikonnoen took one glance over her shoulder and muttered a string of curses in her native Finnish, heart beating faster as she felt an invisible net tightening around her.

In Admin Three, traffic was much lighter. Greaves and Ng, closely followed by Painter, had no problems keeping Hallikonnoen in sight. She turned into a small corridor off the central passageway and slapped the access panel beside the door leading to the operations center. It slid open with a faint hiss, and she entered. The door closed behind her before the Marines reached the side passage.

Four pairs of astonished eyes looked up at her from the various workstations as she pulled a large-bore blaster from beneath her loose jacket.

"All right, my friends, raise your hands and place them on your heads." When they'd done so, she studied them with soulless eyes. "Cooperate, and you'll live. Annoy me, and you'll get a nice round hole in the forehead."

She indicated the spare parts closet. "In there, quick, before my patience vanishes."

They obeyed with alacrity. After locking the door, she took the duty manager's console and used its master controls to ensure no one could enter the operations center short of cutting a hole with a mining laser.

Out in the corridor, Painter caught up with Greaves and Ng.

"She locked herself in with the local override," Greaves reported.

"As expected. Zero, this is One-One. Hallikonnoen is in the operations center."

"Roger that. We're picking her up via the station net." Testo paused. "She gave herself a back door into the system and is attempting to lock up the module."

"You'd think the opposition's field agents are smarter than that."

"Niner here," Delgado's voice came over the company net. "They suffer from overconfidence, not lack of smarts. Let's let her roam the network and believe she can still win. At least until we've rounded up her team. That way, she won't try pulling a terminal gambit, like threatening to blow us into the Infinite Void."

"Understood," Testo replied. "But there's a limit to how long we can play this game before she either twigs or finds a way past our virtual walls."

"Understood. Niner, out."

Painter turned to Greaves and said, "Call the rest of your section up here, Lanny. When Niner gives the execute, blow your way into the ops center and neutralize Hallikonnoen. Don't bother trying to take her alive. She won't be of any use as a prisoner."

"Wilco, Sarge."

"I'm heading back to the CP."

\*\*

Delgado, also on his way to the command post with Kuzek and Movane, was standing by the lift doors when they heard a dull thud accompanied by a shock wave that coursed through Tyrell. Around them, workers stopped moving as they put on alarmed expressions. When no sirens sounded, the workers clustered into small groups and murmured among themselves.

The Marine tapped his communicator. "Zero, this is Niner. What was that?"

"Zero here, wait one. Contact report inbound." A few seconds passed, then Testo spoke again. "An explosion destroyed the communications module, including the subspace array. We've lost outward comms."

"What?"

Instead of answering his commanding officer, Testo said, "Go ahead with the sitrep, One-Two-Charlie."

"Roger that," Sergeant Moses Singh replied. "We were following one of the new arrivals up to the subspace array module. She caught sight of us and vanished into a maintenance crawlspace. From there, she somehow gained access to the transmission room and locked herself in. I tried to override the lock with our code, but it didn't work, so I used detcord to disable it." Delgado winced at the statement but remained silent. If the company's override didn't work locally, Testo couldn't do so from the command post either.

"With the lock blown, we pushed the door halfway open and were greeted by blaster fire. I tossed in a concussion grenade. It blew, triggering another explosion that ruptured the module's outer envelope because the door slammed shut when it sensed a loss of pressure. We pulled back to the next airlock and secured it."

Delgado nodded to himself. "The intruder had an explosive charge, perhaps with a kill switch that was triggered by the concussion grenade."

"Could be. She was carrying a miner's tool satchel. Sorry about that."

"No need to apologize. The rest of Tyrell retains structural integrity, and that's what really counts. We were going to lose the subspace array no matter what, especially if the intruder was on a one-way mission. Besides, once we miss the second sitrep in a row, HQ will send help."

Delgado paused, wishing reality was as simple as that. Unfortunately, his gut told him they would face an attack from above in the coming hours, and their only protection was four antiquated battlecruiser guns sitting on the high cliffs around Tyrell.

"Zero, round up the remaining targets. We are weapons-free. All callsigns may shoot to kill if necessary. We can live without the subspace array, but we can't without the fusion plant, the environmental system, or hydroponics."

Delgado and Kuzek stepped into the waiting lift, ignoring the appalled looks of workers who'd overheard the former's part of the conversation. When they stepped off on the lower level, he absently listened to the various patrols answer while he and Kuzek made their way to the command post.

He hoped no innocent miners would be caught in the crossfire, but by now, the base would be as stirred up as it had ever been, and the corridors would be thick with gossiping civilians, exchanging rumors.

Unfortunately, the order to round up the *Sécurité Spéciale* operatives came too late for at least one high-value target. Four explosions in quick succession sent shock waves through the station's structure.

"Niner, this is Zero. Those were the four control nodes for the big guns."

"That's what I figured. Thank the Almighty for contingency planning."

Despite the gravity of the situation, Delgado allowed himself a faint smile. He'd fooled the opposition with his fake plans, and thus, they didn't realize the control nodes were redundant. He always intended on having the guns crewed and served *in situ* by Marines whose training included the use of heavy direct fire support weapons in an anti-ship role, in other words, naval gunnery.

"Zero, this is One-Three," Command Sergeant Isaac Dyas' voice interrupted Delgado's thoughts. "We slagged the rats responsible for those last fireworks."

"Zero, well done."

Delgado and Kuzek reached the command post without further incident, dodging the questions of worried mine workers along the way. However, the Marine knew they would present another difficult situation sooner rather than later.

Testo turned around as soon as he sensed his commanding officer.

"One of Rolf's patrols stopped two *Sécurité Spéciale* operatives just outside the power plant module. Both are dead, but they clipped Reg Harris. Nothing fatal, although he's out of action and headed for the infirmary. And that makes ten enemy agents, not counting Hallikonnoen."

Delgado dropped into his usual chair and tapped his chin with the fingers of his right hand.

"We counted twelve new arrivals who were suspect. Where are the other two? Assuming our count is right in the first place."

"I'm afraid we lost them a few minutes ago, Skipper."

After a few more taps, Delgado's eyes narrowed. "Did the patrols pick up anyone near or in Hydroponics Module Three?"

"No."

"Then that's it. Send the nearest team."

# — Thirty-One —

"Hey, what are you two doing here? This is a restricted area. Station engineering personnel only."

Tyrell's junior environmental engineer stepped between the tiers of hydroponics beds, hands on his hips, and looked at the two intruders with a suspicion deepened by the five mysterious explosions which sent his precious plants swaying. Like everyone in engineering, he was frantically surveying vital systems for potentially life-threatening damage.

One man produced a blaster and pointed it at the engineer's head.

"This is my authorization. Take us to the hidden elevator shaft."

"I'm sure I don't know what you're talking about." Worry spread across the grizzled engineer's face, and he wished for a few of the steely-eyed Marines who'd replaced the previous garrison.

"This says you do." The agent pointed his blaster at the older man's forehead.

"And I say you don't." A hard voice erupted from the open stairwell door, behind and to the intruders' left. "Put your weapons on the ground real slowly."

In a fluid motion worthy of a pro, the first operative spun around, fell into a crouch, and fired three rounds through the open door, while the other stepped behind a plant tray as he pulled out his own weapon.

The engineer stood rooted to the spot for a few seconds, then turned and ran toward the main airlock as the thud of a scattergun filled the air, pellets ripping through tender lettuce leaves and peppering the intruder facing the stairwell. His face instantly turned into a horrid red mask, and an unearthly howl filled the hydroponics module.

Moments after the engineer passed through the airlock, three Marines entered, scatterguns at the ready, in a single file. Yet instead of firing on them, the so-far unhurt operative executed his backup orders and reached into the miner's satchel he carried slung over one shoulder.

"Drop it!" Sergeant First Class Rankin shouted from the stairwell.

The man gave him a sick grin and tossed the satchel into one of the lettuce trays. He then grabbed his partner's and reached inside again with a speed that left the Marines momentarily at a loss. Then Rankin twigged, and he shot the man where he stood.

"Everyone get out. Evac. This place is about to blow."

He pulled the stairwell door shut while the three Marines at the module's far end backed out at double speed. They barely had time to close the airlock when the first charge exploded, shredding Hydroponics Three's interior. The second charge went off moments later, and the main airlock buckled, sending the Marines in the access tube running for the far end.

\*\*

"What the hell was that?" Delgado exclaimed as he jumped up to peer over Testo's shoulder. Hak, who'd been monitoring the station's vitals, replied instead.

"Hydroponics Three. A pair of explosive charges, no doubt. Its upper level is essentially gone. The main airlock looks like it's failing, but the one on the access tube's far end is fine." Hak studied his display. "The lower level seems to have weathered the explosions."

Before anyone else could speak, the radio came to life with Rankin's voice.

"Zero, this is One-One-Minor reporting from Hydroponics Three." His tone was that of a man who'd just cheated death. "The missing tangos are dead, but so are the vegetables for the next few weeks. I'm in the lower level with One-One-Charlie. No casualties. So far, integrity is holding, but I'll evacuate in a moment. The personnel who were entering via the upper airlock made it out as well."

Delgado turned to his operations sergeant. "There's no longer any reason to let Hallikonnoen think she still has a chance. Isolate the operations center and tell the troops to move in."

Movane, who'd taken over a workstation and was running through her emergency checklist to deal with two blown modules, glanced over her shoulder.

"Jannika Hallikonnoen? She's one of them?"

Delgado nodded. "Hallikonnoen works for a shadowy intelligence agency which doesn't officially exist and whose director reports to the Secretary General himself. It's called the *Sécurité Spéciale*. The Fleet has been at war with it for a long time. Her team, or former team, since they're dead now, were likely mercenaries hired by the *Sécurité Spéciale*. Considering how easily some of them sacrificed their lives by blowing themselves up, I suspect they belonged to one of the more extreme religious sects whose adherents seek death in the name of their faith and hire themselves out so they can find it."

Movane shook her head in disbelief. "Two branches of the federal government fighting each other. No wonder the Commonwealth is heading straight to hell. So, once you round up Hallikonnoen, it's over?"

"No. I'm expecting one or more hostile starships to arrive in the next few hours. Hallikonnoen and her people were merely the door kickers whose job was seizing Tyrell's control nodes until the raiders arrive. And her plan would have worked against the usual garrison. But we've dealt with her sort many times before."

Movane's normally stoic expression cracked for a moment. "Then we're screwed, wouldn't you say so, Major? They destroyed the control nodes for the guns. We can't use them against those starships."

A pleased grin lit up Delgado's features. "The nodes are gone, but not the guns, and each of them has a trained crew onsite, ready to fire. I sent them out earlier today in the expectation that something would happen."

"SOCOM, eh?" Movane cocked an eyebrow at him. "Lucky for us you're here."

"Luck has nothing to do with it. Naval Intelligence, on the other hand…"

"Did they know about Hallikonnoen and the attempted takeover?"

Delgado gave her a noncommittal grimace. "Possibly. Perhaps probably. But they never tell us grunts, even if we're from SOCOM."

"I guess that would explain why they sent you instead of a warship squadron. Although if you're right, we sure could use one at the moment — a warship, I mean."

"And there might be a frigate or two inbound by now. Again, they don't tell us everything so that none of us can give away the entire plan. But keep in mind if the opposition is here for the artifact, they won't damage Tyrell itself lest they lose easy access. Whoever is coming will know that they face a limited window during which they can operate with impunity."

She nodded. "I see."

"Now that you know about us, when my people finish dealing with Hallikonnoen and we control the entirety of Tyrell once more, you will tell me what's down there that has the *Sécurité Spéciale* conducting a major direct action against a Fleet installation. You'll also tell me why Fleet

HQ doesn't know about it." Delgado saw Hak raise a hand. "Ah, here we go."

**

"Nooo!" Jannika Hallikonnoen screamed in rage as she saw her control over Tyrell change from all to nothing, and she knew victory had slipped through her fingers.

As she stared at the operation center's primary display, scarcely believing that a motley collection of misfit Marines had beaten the cream of the *Sécurité Spéciale* and its fanatical hirelings, Delgado's face appeared. He winked at her, then vanished, replaced by images of the dead operatives. At least those whose bodies weren't spaced by explosive decompression.

Hallikonnoen pounded the workstation console, fury making her want to reach into the station's network and rip Delgado's throat out. Moments later, a dull thump sounded behind her. She swirled around and saw the door being opened manually, its lock destroyed. She reached for her blaster, but in vain. A Marine scattergun coughed once, peppering her with dozens of tiny pellets that punctured her skin's exposed parts, killing her almost instantly.

The last emotion Jannika Hallikonnoen felt was regret, but not at having failed. She felt regret at never seeing her hometown again. Then, the last of the *Sécurité Spéciale* operatives in Tyrell was dead.

Several modules away, in the command post, Romana Movane stared at the image on the primary display with a sort of sick fascination.

"Wouldn't it be better if you'd captured and questioned her?" She asked in a strangled tone.

"No." Delgado shook his head. "They condition her sort against interrogation. She'd be dead the moment we tried. Besides, alive, she would remain a risk, no matter how small. We learned over the years it's best if we don't underestimate *Sécurité Spéciale* agents. Their top operatives are as resourceful and dangerous as ours, and I've worked with many of them. Now, tell me about the artifact."

"Ever heard of the L'Taung civilization, the proto-Shrehari who lived around a hundred thousand years ago?"

"Sure. They left traces all over this part of the galaxy, though the present-day Shrehari consider them a myth. So that's a L'Taung stash." Delgado nodded slowly. "Pretty much what we figured."

"Mind you, we've not found any unimpeachable proof, but what evidence there is corresponds with artifacts found in other star systems."

"Anyone make it past the slick doorway?"

"Yes, although it took a while. Assenari surveyors found it around two years ago before the Fleet bought Tyrell. Corporate HQ decreed the find a commercial secret and imposed a blackout on any mention of it. They ordered the hidden lift installed and sent a research team masquerading as engineers. Said research has been going on secretly ever since."

"Yet someone leaked information to the *Sécurité Spéciale.*"

Movane shrugged. "Corporate espionage is pervasive, even in the mining industry. Assenari has its own service. Not as big as those of the major zaibatsus, but still."

"What is behind that door?"

"Considering this planet once had an atmosphere and a thriving ecosystem before it was destroyed by an ancient cataclysm, which our geologists place at about a hundred thousand years ago, how about a L'Taung knowledge vault? Something to help rebuild their civilization once it recovers from whatever wiped most of them out."

"Except they never did. At least anywhere other than on Shrehari Prime, and it took them a heck of a long time." Delgado gave Movane a knowing look. "Whatever is behind that door could be worth an incredible fortune."

"Or it could be junk."

"That as well." Delgado stood. "Okay, people, now that we eliminated the internal threat, let's get into position. Chief Administrator, if you would suspend operations and evacuate the upper modules, we can start preparing Tyrell's entrances."

"What do you mean?" She gave Delgado a suspicious look. "You told me the guns are fully operational. Won't you strike while they're in orbit? Or do you intend on letting them enter Tyrell?"

He smiled at her. "If there's only one ship, I'll allow it to land and then seize it so we can find out who they are, where they come from, that sort of thing. If there's more than one and they leave some in orbit, then while I'm taking the ship that lands, I'll knock out the rest with the guns. Starships are vulnerable when they're sitting on the ground, and we're rather good at exploiting that vulnerability, especially since they won't expect us to board them while they try boarding us."

Her air of suspicion turned into one of astonishment. "That's just about the craziest thing I've ever heard, Major."

"The enemy will think the same thing as you and won't believe we'd ever try something of the sort. As my people will confirm, my favorite principle of war is surprise because it has won more battles than superior tactics, weaponry, or technology. Just wait and see. Meanwhile, please carry out my instructions."

"I guess it's your funeral as much as mine. I sincerely hope you know what you're doing. Do I still work from here?"

"Yes. But if you need to move about the station, please take one of our communicators. You and I should stay in constant contact until this is over." Delgado pointed at the spares sitting in a charging station near Testo's console. "And make sure everyone who has quarters in the upper modules moves to spare cubicles with the workers and us."

"They won't like that. There's a hierarchy here, with perks and privileges."

"Right now, the most important privilege is staying out of the line of fire, and the best place for that is with us unwashed proles. Oh, and I'd like everyone in pressure suits with helmets close at hand, just in case. We're armoring up as well. I'll also be barring the airlocks between modules at midnight."

Movane nodded once. "Understood. I'll see that the workforce is ready."

"Thank you."

# — Thirty-Two —

Shortly after midnight, First Sergeant Hak touched his workstation's display and called up a calendar. He then stood, adjusted his beret on his head, and came to attention.

"Major Delgado, sir, I wish to report," he intoned formally, surprising Movane, who so far found Delgado and his Marines surprisingly informal, "that another year has passed. It is now December 2$^{nd}$ on Farhaven, two-hundred and eighty-five years precisely since the 3$^{rd}$ Marine Regiment died at Fort Wagner."

Everyone in the command post rose, put on their berets, and came to attention. Uncomprehending but realizing this was important to the Marines, Movane also stood and adopted a sober expression.

"Thank you, First Sergeant," Delgado replied with equal formality. "Operations Sergeant, another year has passed. Please open a company-wide frequency."

"Aye, aye, sir," Testo replied. "Erinye Company is listening."

"Marines of the Erinye Company, another year has passed," Major Curtis Delgado started, "and it is now December 2nd on Farhaven, two-hundred and eighty-five years after the 3rd Marine Regiment's last stand at Fort Wagner."

Delgado took a deep breath.

"On December 1st of that year, the colony Farhaven was in full revolt against the government of humanity's first interstellar federation. It was the time of the First Migration War, which birthed a new compact between Earth and its soon-to-be sovereign colonies. The Marines of the 3rd Regiment, sent to quell the bloody uprising on Farhaven and protect colonists loyal to the government, had been fighting with increasing desperation for over six weeks, cut off from reinforcements and resupply, harried by the rebels at every turn and with no safe harbor. The countryside had turned against them, and a rebel army of fifteen thousand strong was hunting them down. In those six weeks, the regiment lost nearly half its strength to rebel ambushes and raids. They had no means of dealing with the wounded, and those who fell into rebel hands died a horrible death.

"Shortly before noon on December 1st, the Regiment's rearguard finally broke contact with the rebel army's lead elements and the survivors of a desperate retreat, protecting over four thousand loyalists, men, women, and children, streamed into Fort Wagner, the last government stronghold on the planet. Bereft of artillery, armored vehicles, and every other tool of modern warfare, they carried only small arms and crew-served portable weapons. At two in the afternoon, the gates of Fort Wagner slammed shut, and the overlapping rings of mines, obstacles, and compacted earth berms were closed. The long retreat was over because the 3rd Marines had no other place to go. Fort Wagner would be their last stand."

Romana Movane felt a shiver go up her spine as Major Delgado's hypnotic voice made the desperate scene so vivid.

"Shortly after eighteen hundred hours, the rebel army, counting on the momentum of their headlong pursuit, attacked Fort Wagner with little preparation. The garrison, every Marine who could shoot along with armed colonists, repulsed them easily. The rebels withdrew, leaving hundreds of dead and wounded lying on the grassy slopes beneath the fort. At midnight, a second attack, as badly planned and executed, also broke against the 3rd Regiment's fierce determination. But ammunition stocks were dropping fast, and the defenders' numbers slowly dwindled because of casualties. By now, the Marines knew it was only a matter of time. Twelve thousand against less than fifteen hundred, odds of ten to one, would overwhelm them."

Movane tried but failed to suppress a feeling of incredible sadness that overcame her as she listened to Delgado's words.

"Two hours after the second attack, a party of rebels, under a flag of truce, came to offer Colonel Greeson, commanding officer of the 3rd Marines, terms of surrender.

The Regiment would be permitted to march out of the fort with their weapons and baggage and occupy the nearby Tranto spaceport unmolested so that they may await transport off-planet. They made no mention of the four thousand loyalists, survivors of rebel massacres, and other atrocities. Unwilling to condemn his men one way or the other, Colonel Greeson took the unusual step of holding a Regimental Council.

"At oh-four-hundred, the surviving company and battalion commanders, first sergeants and sergeants major, as well as the regimental staff and regimental sergeant major, assembled in a large underground bunker. There, Colonel Greeson presented the rebel offer. He did not state his own preference but instead called upon each of the assembled Marines to vote in turn, from the most junior to the most senior. Command Sergeant Yolanda Turnik was the first. Before saying yea or nay, she asked Colonel Greeson what would happen to the loyalists if the 3rd Marines surrendered. When Colonel Greeson didn't reply, Sergeant Turnik said, 'If we abandon the loyalists to save our skins, we break our oath and sully our honor. I would rather die. We stay.' One after the other, the members of the Regimental Council echoed Sergeant Turnik's sentiments. When Colonel Greeson, as the most senior, cast the final vote, it was unanimous. The 3rd Marine Regiment would not leave without the loyalists. That decision was presented to the loyalist leaders, as was a bald estimate of their survival chances, which were nil."

Looking around at the solemn Marines in the command post, Movane could almost visualize the grim, exhausted Regimental Council, and she did not doubt these modern descendants of those long dead Marines would be as implacable, and as willing to die so they could keep their honor intact.

"At daybreak, Colonel Greeson met with the rebels and rejected the terms, as they didn't include the loyalists. When the Colonel and his party entered the fort again, they knew it was for the last time. Three hours later, Fort Wagner was subjected to a murderous assault which the defenders, reinforced by volunteers among the loyalists, repulsed at substantial cost. Sporadic bombardment and sniping continued as the sun rose in the sky, revealing a scene of death and desolation around the fort. Rebel bodies were piled up by the hundreds on the slopes and along the tree line beyond. But inside the fort, the situation was just as bad, and Colonel Greeson knew the end was near."

"At fifteen-hundred hours on the afternoon of December 2nd, the surviving Marines assembled for the last time as a regiment in the fort's courtyard. There, under the watchful gaze of his troops, Colonel Greeson burned the regiment's colors so they would not fall into rebel hands. He placed the ashes in a steel case along with the unit's war diary and buried them at the foot of the flagpole. Then Colonel Greeson ordered the regiment's battle flag nailed to the mast. It would not come down until the 3rd Marine Regiment was either victorious or wiped out."

Movane shivered again. She could almost hear trumpets sounding the last post while drums beat defiantly. What kind of mad courage impelled those men and women, she wondered.

"At five o'clock, as the sun kissed the horizon, the rebels launched a massive assault on Fort Wagner with every available soldier. Their casualties were beyond anything previously experienced on Farhaven, yet they finally broke through by sheer weight of numbers. Valiantly, the surviving Marines fought on, some with nothing more than the bayonet at the tip of their rifles. Slowly but surely, the regiment died, each trooper taking three rebels before succumbing, defiance still echoing loud around the central courtyard. The last platoon, ten Marines under the command of Second-Lieutenant Rudy Westphalen, held the entrance to the underground complex where the remaining thirty-five hundred loyalists, mostly children, the elderly, and the wounded, sought refuge. For nearly half an hour, the last platoon kept the rebels at bay, turning the courtyard into a charnel house."

Now Movane, to her own surprise, felt tears form in the corners of her eyes. She blinked them away and surreptitiously glanced around at the Marines. It did not surprise her to see the emotion mirrored in their faces. Here and there, a tear ran down a craggy cheek.

"Soon, however, Lieutenant Westphalen's little command numbered five troopers, himself, and no more ammunition. In an act of desperate courage that will live forever, Lieutenant Westphalen ordered his men to fix bayonets. Then, shouting the regiment's battle cry, *Faugh a Ballagh*, the last survivors of the 3rd Marine Regiment charged the astonished rebels. They died in a hail of bullets at twenty minutes past six in the evening. What followed will be remembered as one of the darkest acts of savagery committed since humanity spread across the stars. The rebels slaughtered each and every loyalist, turning the underground bunkers into immense mass graves."

Delgado took a breath as he struggled with his own emotions, though his voice had remained steady throughout.

"The men and women of the 3rd Marine Regiment died rather than break their oath and stain their honor forever. We will not forget their courage. We will always live up to their example. At the going down of the sun and in the morning, on this day, as on every other day of our lives, we will remember them."

In the command post and across Tyrell Station, every Marine replied somberly, "We will remember them."

For reasons she could not explain, Romana Movane knew it was more than just a ritualistic response. It was a promise, an oath, and Major Delgado's Marines would stand and die, if necessary, as the 3rd Marines had done. She shivered again at the power, the conviction, and the determination that filled the atmosphere, electrified it.

"Number One Company, A Squadron, 1st Special Forces Regiment, atten-SHUN." Curtis Delgado snapped out the order.

The haunting sounds of the last post echoed through the base, and the Marines in the command post raised their right hands to their brows in a formal salute.

After the last post, a minute of silence left them to contemplate the heritage their spiritual ancestors willed them, a difficult heritage, yet one which could not be ignored. The sound of the pipes playing *Amazing Grace* broke the deep stillness, and Movane felt another surge of emotion. When the last strains died away, Delgado spoke again.

"Three days after the rebels took Fort Wagner, losing over four thousand troops in the effort, a relief column of two full regiments landed on Farhaven. The rebels, drained and bruised by the stubborn 3rd Regiment, were quickly defeated. When the full extent of the massacre at Fort Wagner became known, the commander of the 4th Marine Division ordered every rebel soldier tried and executed for war crimes, smashing the rebellion on Farhaven forever. The 3rd Marines and the loyalists were avenged. To this day, at Fort Wagner, their memory lives on, and it will do so for as long as there are Marines to remember. Delgado, out."

Testo cut the transmission, and they slumped into their seats.

"You know, sir," Hak's hoarse voice finally broke the silence, "I was just thinking..."

"I know, Top," Delgado replied in a soft tone. "That we would face our own test on the anniversary date is mere coincidence, not some joke of the Almighty. We're not up against twelve thousand rebels, and our unit is not about to join the supplementary order of battle."

"Yeah."

After a few moments of silence, Movane turned toward the first sergeant and quietly asked, "What is the supplementary order of battle?"

"When a unit is wiped out in combat, killed to the last trooper, that unit is never restored. The Corps places it on the supplementary order of battle to be remembered and honored. The unit's name, insignia, everything about it enters the annals of history and will never be used by another. But if even one single Marine survives, the unit is reconstituted because a link to the past exists."

"Are there many units on that order of battle?"

"No. The 3rd Marine Regiment was the first. In the following centuries," Delgado replied, "despite the example of Fort Wagner, only three other units joined it. The 36th Marines after the battle of Leitfonten during the Second Migration War, the 78th Defense Battalion on Mission Colony during last century's Shrehari War, and the 144th Pathfinder Squadron at Port-Gentil, during the Hispaniola insurrection." After a brief pause, he continued, determination hardening his features. "I do not intend on joining them, Chief Administrator. You can be sure of that."

"What happened to Fort Wagner?" she finally asked.

"When the First Migration War ended, Earth withdrew federal armed forces from Farhaven at the inhabitants' request, as a condition for integrating the Commonwealth peacefully. The retribution meted out by the 4ᵗʰ Division permanently poisoned the colonists against the Corps, and there were no surviving loyalists who might oppose them. Earth agreed to the condition under the proviso Fort Wagner and the surrounding area be ceded in perpetuity to the federal government as sovereign territory. The Farhaveners objected, of course, but since the 4ᵗʰ Division garrisoned Fort Wagner once the rebellion ended, they had to either accept or re-fight the battle.

"Fort Wagner is now a memorial, the holiest of holies of the Commonwealth Marine Corps. The defenders are buried on the slopes under well-tended grass and bronze plaques. The fort itself was repaired and restored. A monument now stands at the site where Colonel Greeson buried the ashes of the regiment's colors. It is inscribed with the names of the Marines of the 3ʳᵈ who died on Farhaven and the names of the loyalists who were slaughtered in the fort. A reproduction of the 3ʳᵈ's battle flag flies day and night over the fort, illuminated by the eternal flame in front of the monument."

"You've been there?" Movane asked, touched by the intensity in Delgado's eyes.

"Yes. All Marines are encouraged to make a pilgrimage once in their life."

"It shows. What keeps the Farhaveners from retaking the fort? I assume the 4ᵗʰ Division is no longer in residence."

"At any given time, a rifle company from one of the OutWorld regiments occupies Fort Wagner on a six-month tour. They maintain the premises, tend the graves, and conduct a retreat ceremony every evening. But they are combat-ready, with heavy weapons, artillery, missiles, and plenty of ammunition. If the Farhaveners ever want a rematch, they'll face a brutal fight. The garrison company conducts battle readiness exercises regularly, just to hammer home the point. No, the Farhaveners will never again take Fort Wagner from the Commonwealth Marine Corps."

"Just as our unknown enemies will not take Tyrell Base from your company?" Movane asked in a subdued tone. Delgado nodded. "Then it is fitting they should try on the anniversary of the battle, I think."

Delgado was about to say more when Testo cut short all conversation.

"Contact, three ships approaching Keros and decelerating for an orbital injection." Though he sounded as calm as ever, Delgado picked up an undercurrent of anticipation.

"Tracking. One ship has fired." Then, "The geosynchronous orbital platform is gone."

"Call the stand to, Sergeant."

"Aye, aye, sir."

A lugubrious siren sounded throughout the station as the Marines put their helmets on and grabbed their weapons to the sergeants' calls of "Lock and load."

The ultimate battle for Tyrell was about to begin.

# — Thirty-Three —

"Geosynchronous orbital platform destroyed, sir," *Harfang*'s gunnery officer reported. "No other artificial satellites found."

Captain Junius Pellea, a wiry, olive-skinned man in his fifties, grunted in acknowledgment as he stroked his short salt and pepper beard. Like the rest of his crew, mercenaries working for a shadowy private military corporation based in the Protectorate Zone, he wore an unadorned black battledress uniform and carried a blaster on his hip.

However, unlike them and the crews of *Harfang*'s sister ships *Faucon* and *Busard*, Pellea was an undercover *Sécurité Spéciale* operative, one of several who'd infiltrated the Nexcoyotl PMC and turned it into one of the agency's unwitting black ops arms. He always led the missions carried out on the *Sécurité Spéciale*'s behalf, but this one left him somewhat uneasy. PMCs usually avoided contracts that would see them go up against the Commonwealth Armed Forces because losing meant death. Sometimes, even victory might see the offenders hunted by undercover naval units if word got out.

And Tyrell was not only a Fleet installation. It also housed a Marine unit. Of course, his colleagues should be in control by now, and the Marine threat neutralized. He also enjoyed an overwhelming advantage in numbers compared to a small, dismounted rifle company and had surprise on his side.

"Signals, any contact from the surface," Pellea finally asked, turning to look at the communications alcove behind him.

"No, sir. Nothing on subspace, not even a carrier wave, let alone normal radio. The place is pretty much dead for coherent EM emissions."

Pellea stroked his beard again. There could be many explanations for Tyrell's silence. The plan included seizing the transmission facilities or, failing that, destroying them. Perhaps they hit a snag during the seizure operation, and Tyrell's communications were rendered inoperative. He shrugged. Anything could have happened.

"You may scan the surface using active means now."

"Aye, aye, Captain."

On either flank of *Harfang*, a few kilometers away, *Faucon* and *Busard* mirrored Pellea's movements. Though not Sécurité Spéciale operatives, their captains were former Navy officers whose careers didn't progress as they wanted.

"The base's four main guns appear unpowered. They are in the rest position and cold, barely warmer than the surrounding rock. Life signs are clustered in the lower modules."

Pellea frowned. Shouldn't the life signs be more dispersed?

"Scan the surrounding area for emissions, life forms, or anything that shouldn't be hiding on the surface of Keros beyond Tyrell's perimeter," he ordered, suspicion raising its ugly head. Paranoia was a necessary survival trait in the Protectorate. "And search the high orbitals, especially the Lagrangians, for any ships running silent."

"Scanning." A few minutes passed in silence, then, "We're alone out here, sir. No indications of ships hiding in the Lagrangians or running silent in high orbit. Nothing beyond Tyrell itself that shouldn't be there."

Pellea felt a twinge of unease, his instincts telling him something wasn't quite right. But he suppressed his nascent misgivings. After all, what could a mere company of Marines do against the cream of the Nexcoyotl PMC assisted on the ground by the finest undercover operatives money could buy, fanatics who'd rather die than fail?

"Send to *Faucon* and *Busard*, begin the descent."

\*\*

"Come to papa, little mercenaries," Testo softly muttered, smiling, as he watched the three needle-shaped sloops. "I got yours right here."

He opened a frequency on the company net.

"Niner, this is Zero. Three targets coming down. They appear sloop-sized, and I estimate a hundred and fifty crew per ship, two hundred tops. The odds are heavily in our favor. Any bets?"

"Niner here. Is there anyone crazy enough to bet against us?"

"I can always ask those jokers when they land. We may earn some easy money for the company fund."

"Let's stick to looting their ships after we seize them."

"Roger that."

"Niner, out."

Sitting behind the polarized transparent aluminum window of the landing pad control center, Delgado searched the star-spangled black sky for signs of the oncoming sloops. The easy banter with Sergeant Testo belied his growing tension as pre-battle jitters tried to take hold, making him question his plan and its chances of success even though it was far too late for last-minute changes. But he knew the moment the enemy appeared, all that would vanish, leaving nothing but a cold clarity of purpose.

Standing by the door, darkened visor masking his impassive face, Kuzek held a plasma carbine loosely in his hands, muzzle pointing downwards. Unflappable as only those with a phlegmatic temperament could be, he simply waited, ready to cover his commanding officer when the action started.

Beside Delgado, Hak sat unmoving, his face also hidden by a helmet visor. He, too, held a loaded carbine. If

Delgado didn't know better, he'd suspect the first sergeant of taking a quick nap. But then he spoke.

"I figure this will be the biggest ambush we've ever set. Hell, maybe even the biggest in the regiment's annals since the Shrehari War. Making history, we are, sir."

"Only if we succeed. Remember, winners write the history."

"And that'll be us. Dumb bastards won't know what hit them." Hak sounded supremely confident. "They're expecting friendlies in control of Tyrell's systems and a garrison of mutts from a line regiment."

He paused for a few heartbeats. "Contact, sir. I make three moving shadows occluding the stars a hand-span above the triple peak straight ahead of us."

Delgado searched for them, then, "Seen."

The company net came to life at that moment. "All call signs, this is Zero, three contacts on final approach to the north-west, altitude two thousand."

One after the other, the four troop leaders replied to confirm, including Command Sergeant Saxer from gun emplacement number one.

\*\*

After what seemed an agonizingly long descent, two of the three sleek, mercenary ships lit vertical thrusters and slowly descended toward the pad on piercingly bright columns of energy, heavy landing struts fully extended. The third, *Busard*, remained at altitude and began flying a figure-eight pattern above Tyrell. A last-minute change in plans, but one that Pellea's gut insisted on.

His mercenaries were now dressed in nondescript, pressurized battle armor of a type legally available on the Commonwealth arms markets. Not as good as what Marines wore, but still better than unarmored suits. Their ordnance was a more eclectic mix — Shrehari small arms and Fleet-issue long arms stolen from weapons depots, along with a variety of non-lethal antipersonnel grenades such as flash-bangs, vomiting agents, and knockouts.

*Harfang* landed by the retractable gangway next to the hangar entrance while *Faucon* set down near the smelter's cargo doors. As Jannika Hallikonnoen promised in her last transmission, the gangway snaked out and latched onto the ship's main upper airlock. Only, it wasn't Hallikonnoen or any of her agents at the controls.

Inner and outer pressures equalized, and the raiders opened the heavy door sealing off their ship. At the other end of the tube, a figure dressed in civilian coveralls waved and smiled, signaling they should follow him. Then he turned on his heels and walked through the inner airlock and into a long and cold passage. Sixty mercenaries in pressurized armor under the command of *Harfang*'s second officer, thinking he was one of Hallikonnoen's men, made their way along the tube toward the reception area.

Below, the ship's belly ramp dropped open, and another sixty mercenaries under Pellea's command warily walked out in a single file. Pellea felt more unease. None of Hallikonnoen's agents came to greet them or even tried contacting them over short-range radio. Yet if the Marine garrison still held the base, why let them land? Once inside, the raiders could wreak havoc. No, Jannika and her operatives were there, working the controls and opening the way. Something must have gone wrong with the communications.

An airlock, set beside the huge hangar doors, swung open as the raiders approached, and an anonymous figure wearing a miner's pressure suit leaned out. He waved at the raiders, making impatient come-on signals. Equally impatient to enter, Pellea crammed his people into the airlock. It cycled, and when it was fully pressurized, the inner door swung easily on its hinges, revealing an immense, brightly lit space, empty but for old commercial shuttles and tired ground vehicles on the far side.

Their guide walked rapidly toward the left-hand portal leading into the station proper. Behind him, the raiders fanned out into two groups, one following the pressure-suited man, the other heading for the right-hand portal connecting the hangar with the smelter.

Upstairs, the first group of raiders reached the empty reception area, but their guide had long since vanished, causing puzzlement among the mercs. As one wag in the advance guard commented nervously, the lights were on, but nobody was home. Pellea's second officer looked around with growing unease.

A former Pacifican National Guard officer, she once pursued a group of terrorists into an abandoned factory with a so-called informant guiding her through the maze.

The factory covered several square kilometers and was a favorite hiding spot for subversives who opposed Pacifica's ruling oligarchs. The informant, a rebel posing as a loyalist, disappeared, and they ambushed her company. She lost a third of her troops before the terrorists fled. Needless to say, she didn't pursue.

Right now, *Harfang*'s second officer, who'd left the Guard in disgrace because of the incident, was overcome by an all too familiar sensation and didn't enjoy it one bit. Still, she had her orders, and her assault group moved deeper into the base, following the directions on their maps that would take them to Hydroponics Module Three.

But the corridors remained empty, and their handheld battlefield sensors, also stolen from Fleet supply depots, showed no nearby life signs. She succumbed to her need for increased caution and flicked on her radio.

"Take it easy, people. We have lots of time." Still, she wondered why the agent who'd guided them earlier didn't wait.

"No sweat, boss," *Harfang*'s senior bosun's mate and her landing party's point man replied. "Marines can't hold a place like this against us, not if they want to protect civilians. Especially with our insiders screwing them around."

"Don't underestimate them. Just be careful where you step. Falling into an ambush can really ruin your day."

Something in the second officer's tone, rather than her words, kept the bosun from replying, and he turned his eyes back to the sensor in his hand. He stepped through the bulkhead separating the arrivals area from the cargo handling section. On the far side of that underground maze lay the first of the modules.

The eerie stillness of the base and the absence of even a hostile face gave more than just the second officer an uneasy feeling. By now, everyone was wondering what happened to the man who'd waved at them from the station end of the gangway.

Meanwhile, Pellea's two-pronged assault group neared the pair of large, armored doors leading out of the hangar, and his disquiet grew. He looked around the large space, glancing up at the ceiling for the first time. Abruptly, he stopped and scrutinized the metal canopy above. A jolt of fear ran up his spine when he recognized the shapes of command-detonated anti-armor mines stuck to the roof of the hangar, cunningly camouflaged but just visible at this angle.

The left-hand door whooshed open, and their guide, who was ten paces ahead of the raiders walking point, stepped through.

Up in the hangar control room, invisible behind polarized transparent aluminum windows, Command Sergeant Dyas witnessed Pellea's frantic gestures toward the ceiling and knew it was time to trigger his part of the ambush. With his man safely out of harm's way after the door slammed shut, he picked up the detonator control tablet.

Across the landing strip, the assault group from the *Faucon*, one hundred and twenty strong, had split into four groups, each aimed at one of the smelter's four massive loading dock airlocks. Besides preparing the smelter for destruction, their mission was to backstop Pellea's strike groups and pin down any defenders pushed out of the upper modules.

As they neared, the outer doors slid open, in keeping with the plan, and the raiders entered. Once all were inside, the exterior doors slid shut, and the airlocks were quickly repressurized. Then, the inner doors opened, and *Faucon*'s captain realized they'd just made a massive mistake.

In the nearby hangar, Pellea opened his mouth to warn his people when a frantic message crackled over the raiders' frequency.

"Take cover. It's a trap!"

Pellea barely had time to recognize the voice of *Faucon*'s captain before she screamed once and fell silent. Then, the mines attached to the hangar ceiling exploded, showering him and his mercenaries with high-velocity shrapnel that punctured their pressure suits' vulnerable joints.

# — Thirty-Four —

The flash-bangs from the blasts in the shuttle hangar were barely subsiding when the two inner doors opened without warning, and a squad of Marines came through each of them, firing at point-blank into the reeling mass of Pellea's raiders with plasma weapons. After three volleys, they withdrew, and the inner doors slammed shut.

A few seconds later, the hangar space doors opened without a force field to keep the atmosphere contained, leading to uncontrolled catastrophic decompression. In a matter of moments, everything not secured to the floor or a bulkhead was sucked out, along with almost a hundred thousand cubic meters of air and sixty raiders, dead or alive.

Of those who'd entered, only a few, not including Pellea, survived the mines, the heavy weapons fire, and the explosive decompression, but not for long. Sergeant Dyas' Marines re-appeared through what were now inner airlocks and quickly crossed the hangar floor, firing at anything that moved outside, intent on boarding *Harfang*, whose belly

**280**

ramp was still grounded, before the skeleton crew aboard recovered from their surprise.

Inside the passenger reception area, *Harfang*'s second officer had stopped dead in her tracks when she heard the warning, but it was too late. Airlocks slammed shut ahead of and behind her landing party, sealing all but a few in the corridor. Those who were on point found themselves locked in the junction tube leading to Administration Module Two.

Before they could recover from the momentary confusion, Sergeant Testo's voice resonated through the corridor and tube.

"You're nicked, with no chance of escaping. The people sent to prepare the way for you are dead, meaning you've walked into an ambush. There are only two ways out now. Surrender or die. If you don't surrender, we will open fire with hidden remote weapon stations to puncture your suits, then decompress the area. Once that process begins, it cannot be stopped. I'm giving you ten seconds to place your weapons on the floor, remove your helmets, and place your hands on your head. Ten, nine, eight, seven..."

The first few intruders, understanding there was no other choice, complied. The rest followed before Testo's countdown reached zero. As Delgado told Movane earlier, true mercenaries — not Hallikonnoen's fanatics — fought solely for pay. Dying wasn't part of the deal.

"Good choice. The other half of your landing party didn't make it, by the way. They're dead, so now would be a good time to thank the Almighty you're not among them.

Mind you, from this point on, the slightest bit of resistance will ensure every last one of you joins them, so keep an eye on each other and stop stupidity before it starts. I can vent your compartment in a matter of seconds, should the need arise. Now please sit with your backs against the nearest bulkhead and wait."

Across the tarmac, *Faucon*'s four assault teams had blundered into a maze of booby traps whose invisible trigger beams and transparent wires crisscrossed the floor of the docking bays. When the first improvised explosive devices blew, killing the mercs walking point, Command Sergeant Bassam calmly gave his troop the order to open fire.

The raiders, cornered like rats, fired back, but their aim was relatively poor. Furthermore, the Marines were well hidden and made challenging targets. To say that the violence of the defense stunned *Faucon*'s landing party would be an understatement. Nothing had prepared them for the sheer brutality of the Marines' response, and that, more than the casualties and booby traps, made them lose heart. The first mercenaries surrendered less than two minutes after they entered the smelter. The rest followed moments later.

Leaving half of Bravo Troop to secure the prisoners, Bassam led the rest onto the tarmac where *Faucon* sat, belly ramp open.

Up in the landing strip control room, Delgado and Hak exchanged glances.

"So far, so good," the latter said. "I figure it's time we splash the vulture circling up there, sir."

"Yep." Delgado switched to the company network. "Four, this is Niner."

"Four," Command Sergeant Saxer, who'd been watching his fellow troop leaders hit the mercenaries hard over the command net's video feed, replied.

"You're weapons-free on the tango circling overhead."

"Acknowledge weapons-free."

"Make sure he doesn't crash into Tyrell."

"Wilco."

"Niner, out."

Hak let out a soft grunt. "I'd love to be on the bridge of that ship when they realize they're being pinged by the targeting sensors of four double-barreled battleship guns. At this range, even if Delta Troop is blind drunk, they can't miss."

"Now, where is that tango?" Delgado stared up at the starlit, airless sky.

Several seconds passed, then streaks of plasma reached for the heavens, meeting a mere thousand meters above the station where they struck the raider's belly shield.

"There you are."

A second salvo splashed, and Delgado saw the shield's color change from blue to deep purple before collapsing under the onslaught, all in a fraction of a second. The third salvo struck the ship's hull on the starboard side and damaged the starboard hyperdrive nacelle strut, sending it into a corkscrew spin as its thrusters fought to regain control.

It passed over Tyrell, shield after shield collapsing, and began shedding sparks of super-heated metal as the guns kept firing. The last they saw of the sloop was a blur vanishing behind the jagged peaks to the north. Less than a minute later, a new and very short-lived sun rose over the horizon, signs the sloop had crashed and suffered an uncontrolled antimatter fuel discharge.

"Wow." Hak glanced at Delgado again. "Imagine if that thing struck, say, a few kilometers from here. Or right on top of us."

"I'm trying hard not to, Top. But if it started firing on Tyrell, we'd be just as dead as if it crashed on our heads."

Hak allowed himself a grim chuckle. "Let me know what the Colonel and the Admiral say when they critique your after-action report, sir."

"It'll probably be something like well done, Curtis. You judged the risks appropriately."

A snort. "Keep telling yourself that, sir."

"This isn't quite over yet." Delgado pointed at the ships sitting on the tarmac. "One gone, two left."

He flicked on the company net again. "Zero, this is Niner. Call the bridges of those two grounded sloops on the common emergency frequency."

"Wait one." Then, "I'm not getting a response, but I can patch you in anyway."

"Please do."

A few seconds passed. "Go ahead, Niner. You're on."

"Grounded mercenary ships, this is Major Curtis Delgado, Commonwealth Marine Corps, and Tyrell Station's commanding officer. I know you're listening because you realize your raid failed in the most spectacular manner possible by now. Your advance team infiltrators are dead, as are half of your landing party members. The rest are prisoners, and you surely noticed the ship flying cover overhead just gave Keros a brand new crater. My guns can depress enough to engage and destroy you where you sit, or if you manage a liftoff, to shoot you down. Surrender or die."

He let that sink in for a moment.

"Right now, boarding parties are coming up your belly ramps. You will let them in and hand over control of your ships. Don't resist because, under the conditions, we will shoot to kill without a shred of compunction. We already terminated half of your complement."

An unknown voice cut through Delgado's next pause. "How about we shoot up your damn station, Major? It's kind of lonely out here, with help days away. A few salvos to destroy your structural integrity, and then we can lift while you fight for your lives."

"That won't stop my main guns. They're independent of Tyrell and controlled from a separate location. You're not going anywhere other than my stockade or into the Infinite Void, but you can choose the destination."

The man scoffed. "I doubt you have enough left. Let us lift unmolested, and we won't open fire."

"Just think about this, friend. I stopped your landing parties cold before they could enter Tyrell proper and destroyed one of your three ships. Do you truly believe I don't have enough strength to finish this? It's over. Surrender and let my boarding parties in. Depending on how the Fleet prosecutes you for attacking a government installation, you might even pick up your mercenary career again after a stay on Parth as a guest of the Commonwealth."

This time, the man didn't respond for what seemed like an eternity.

Finally, "You guarantee our lives?"

"So long as you cooperate fully. The Marine Corps does not abuse prisoners, let alone slaughter them unless they resume hostilities."

Delgado hoped the remaining crews weren't of the same zealous persuasion as Hallikonnoen's infiltrators who died rather than surrender. Two ships blowing their antimatter fuel tanks this close to Tyrell's spiderweb of modules would utterly destroy the station.

"We surrender."

After waiting for the two troop leaders to report the ships secure, Hak climbed to his feet.

"And now the arduous work begins — securing and feeding those prisoners until the Fleet figures out something's wrong and sends help."

\*\*

"Sergeant Testo?" Movane swiveled around to face the operations noncom.

"What's up, Ma'am?"

"Someone is attempting to access the main reactor module."

"Crap." Testo looked up from his workstation. "We probably have one last *Sécurité Spéciale* sleeper who plans on blowing us up now that they've lost."

He turned to the command post radio. "One-One, this is Zero."

Command Sergeant Painter replied almost immediately. "One-One."

"A tango is attempting to enter the reactor module. Send a team. Same rules of engagement as before. If he or she doesn't surrender, shoot."

"Roger. One-One-Alpha, you heard that? Execute."

"Wilco," Sergeant Greaves replied. "On our way."

Delgado, who'd overheard, merely said, "Niner acknowledges."

His attention was entirely focused on Bravo and Charlie Troops securing the two grounded sloops. At the same time, Hak worked on concentrating the prisoners in the main hangar until they figured out a longer-term solution to hold them pending the next starship's arrival.

Finally, "Zero, this is One-Two, ship secure. It's called *Faucon*, by the way. Remaining crew numbers fifteen. They're locked in one of the cargo holds."

"Zero, acknowledged. You heard that, Niner?"

Before Delgado could confirm, Dyas reported.

"Zero, this is One-Three. Ship by the name *Harfang* is secure. All fourteen crew aboard are locked away in a cargo hold as well. Apparently, the one we shot was called *Busard*."

"Zero, acknowledged."

"Niner, acknowledged."

Delgado felt the urge to board *Harfang* via the passenger tube but knew he should rejoin Testo in the command post. There would be time enough for tourism once Tyrell was back to normal. Or at least as normal as things would be until someone came for the prisoners and sloops.

One thing bothered him, however. This raid seemed aimed at seizing the artifact beneath the surface. Were they even aware of the Second Migration War biological and chemical warhead depot a few dozen kilometers west of here, at the bottom of the canyon? Or was that phase two once they took care of Tyrell? Hallikonnoen surely knew of the location, even if she wasn't aware of the contents.

Suddenly, Delgado felt a shard of ice pierce his gut as instinct gave him a potential answer. But before he could order his thoughts, the rumble of an explosion in one of the lower modules punched through Tyrell's contained atmosphere, sending a wave of deadly vibrations coursing across its assemblage of interconnected parts.

# — Thirty-Five —

The lights flickered for a moment, then the mournful howl of an alarm siren filled Tyrell.

"Zero, this is Niner. What was that?"

"Wait one, please."

Delgado increased his strides as a sudden foreboding drove out all other thoughts.

"Zero, this is One-One-Alpha." Sergeant Greaves' voice held the unmistakable edge of a man whose adrenaline was spiking. "That was a self-detonating tango just now. He got into the reactor module ahead of us, and when he spotted my point men, he blew his IED. Ng and Romero took the brunt of it, but they were still at a good distance. They're knocked out, probably concussed, though their suits retain integrity. Half of my section, me included, is stuck in the reactor module after the access tube doors automatically shut because of catastrophic decompression."

"Acknowledged. Sit tight. We'll see you back in a pressurized compartment shortly."

As Delgado entered the command post a few minutes later, he asked, "How's the retrieval effort?"

Testo pointed at Movane. "The chief administrator is putting an override on the access tube doors and turning the tube itself into an airlock. Apparently, they were designed to function as such in an emergency. Rolf is standing by with one of his sections."

"Good. And the main reactor."

Movane glanced over her shoulder. "Not good. The reactor controls were damaged, and it turned off automatically, though the core seems more or less intact, so we need not worry about a catastrophic failure. Yet. Barring an onsite survey by qualified personnel, I can only relay what the remaining systems are reporting, and Sergeant Testo won't allow one unless you give the okay."

"If it's not critical, then I'd rather we wait until our current situation has stabilized. That being said, where are we getting our power from right now?"

"You may have noticed a brief light flicker — that was the automatic failover to the backup batteries."

"Can the reactor be fixed, and how long will the batteries last?"

Movane grimaced. "It's not meant to be fixed onsite, only replaced as a single unit. Besides, I have neither the specialists nor the spare parts. Thanks to the solar collectors, the batteries will be good for an extended period, barring any further nasty surprises. But they can only power the habitat modules, not the mine, the smelter, or the guns, which means operations are essentially shuttered until help arrives."

Delgado chewed on the inside of his lower lip, eyes staring at a schematic drawing of the station. Then he consulted the time display.

"Fleet HQ should have noticed something is wrong by now. We just missed the second daily sitrep in a row. Besides, our last communication from HQ mentioned help was dispatched to check on us after I told them I suspected something was about to happen. But its arrival will likely not be for a few days, and my gut tells me this isn't over yet."

"What?"

Testo turned toward them. "I think the Skipper figures on another visit by mercenaries shortly."

"Why?"

"Sergeant Testo is correct. This batch was after the artifact. It was clearly an operation planned some time ago. However, there's still the matter of the Second Migration War ammunition bunker the recon droid found three weeks ago. If these mercs also had the mission to seize it, they would have done so in tandem with their attack on Tyrell. I figure the opposition quickly scrambled more resources in an attempt to piggyback taking the ammo on top of the artifact when they heard about what the bunker contained. But those additional resources aren't here yet."

Movane stared at him for a few moments. "Why would someone go after old, obsolete munitions?"

"The warheads stored in that bunker contain some of the deadliest biological and chemical agents ever invented. If they fall into the wrong hands, they could cause incalculable casualties."

Movane's face lost color as she understood the implications of what Delgado was saying.

"It's a bit of a twisted story, Chief Administrator. We've known for a long time that not all weapons of mass destruction stockpiles were found after the war because they were established in great secrecy, and all sides lost a lot of records during the fighting. In recent times, the Fleet rediscovered incomplete records indicating a bunker's presence in this general area, exact location unknown. When the droid found it and registered the markings on the warhead crates, it executed its primary programming by sending an encrypted report to Fleet HQ and imposed a complete blackout on its findings where you and Engstrom were concerned."

"I did find the idea of an artificial intelligence swearing us to silence a tad strange, but Nero went along with it. Was he aware that they programmed the recon droid with these added classified protocols?"

Delgado shrugged. "I don't know. But I doubt it. HQ is terrified of WMDs finding their way into the hands of the people we've been fighting, so the less who know about it, the better. Still, the opposition found out, somehow. Hence quickly replacing the regular garrison with a company from Special Operations Command."

Movane took a deep breath, then slowly exhaled. "I still can't believe one branch of the government would fight another so openly and with such brutality."

"It's about power, Chief Administrator. Getting it and using it to accumulate wealth, status, and the perks that come with ruling over others. Look at any era in our history, and you'll find dark and dirty wars waged between opposing factions in the same government. Those WMD warheads would make a perfect way for that organization to exercise blackmail on those who would stop it and its political masters."

"And what is their goal?"

Delgado gave her a sad smile. "Turning the clock back to a time when Earth ruled humanity with an iron fist."

"Isn't that why both Migration Wars occurred?"

He nodded. "Yes. But like most who crave power, they always forget George Santayana's famous aphorism that those who cannot remember the past are condemned to repeat it."

She cocked an ironic eyebrow at Delgado and said, in a dry tone, "I didn't know Marine Corps officers were also students of philosophy?"

"Blame my commanding officer. He encourages us to read widely and can literally drop quotations and facts culled from the last thousand years of history into any conversation."

Testo, eyes on his workstation, raised both hands and gave Delgado thumbs up. "And that's a fact in itself. The

Colonel is also a fan of poetry, pre-diaspora music, and high explosives."

"He sounds like a rather accomplished polymath, something I wouldn't expect of a Marine officer. You certainly seem to respect him."

Delgado nodded again. "We all do. He's one of SOCOM's legends, the sort who'd love to be here with us right now, working out a plan to take on any further enemy incursions and complete our mission."

"Did he also teach you ways of making the impossible happen? Because without those big guns, we're a wide open target."

"Don't you worry, Chief Administrator," Testo said over his shoulder. "The Skipper's fast becoming SOCOM's next legend. There's a reason the Colonel gives us the toughest assignments."

Movane gave Delgado an appraising look. "For some reason, I believe you, Sergeant. Your Skipper had us all fooled until almost the very end."

"He also took full control of Tyrell, Ma'am."

"What?"

"Sergeant Testo means he hacked into your network at my orders and gave us back door entrances to every system, node, and process."

Movane shook her head. "Why am I not surprised? I should be mad, but I suppose your doing so saved our bacon in the last few hours."

"Pretty much."

"Did your colonel teach you to be so sneaky?"

Delgado grinned at her. "Yep."

"Ah." Testo swiveled his chair around. "I found the identity of our self-detonating tango. Not one of the new arrivals but a Valenti Nabakov, environmental engineering section, who's been here for several weeks."

Delgado, who was watching Movane, saw her blanch.

"The name means something, Chief Administrator?"

She looked at him, indecision writ large in her eyes. "Valenti is — was — from Assenari Enterprises' Security and Intelligence Division. The motherhouse, you understand, not the Assenari Mining subsidiary. His job was monitoring the artifact for head office and uncovering any threats."

"So, a spy."

"And an assassin." When Delgado stared at her in question, she said, "He killed Terry Evans. She was a ComCorp operative who'd been conditioned. Valenti tried interrogating her, but she died almost instantly. And no, it wasn't at my orders. He operated by his own rules, taking his cues from head office."

Movane's words came rushing out, and she sounded relieved at finally speaking the truth.

"Why would he try blowing up the reactor and killing everyone in Tyrell just as we won the battle?"

Movane shrugged. "I couldn't say, but Valenti struck me as a man without a soul. The intensity of his devotion to duty was sometimes frightening."

"Another fanatic." Delgado exhaled slowly. "There are a lot of them around these days, it seems. Would Assenari

Enterprises' CEO rather destroy Tyrell than let the artifact fall into non-Assenari hands?"

She thought about the question for a few moments, then slowly nodded. "In a heartbeat."

"I guess you won't nominate Assenari for the employer of the year award."

"If we survive, I'll be giving them my notice. I didn't sign up for this."

# — Thirty-Six —

"Sir, I think there might be a problem with one of the outposts."

The man to whom this was addressed, a balding, stout Marine wearing the three diamonds and oak leaf wreaths of a full colonel, finished stirring his coffee. Then, he walked over to the watchkeeping officer for the Rim Sector, a middle-aged, auburn-haired lieutenant commander, and leaned over her shoulder to look at her workstation's display.

"What's the problem, Fiona?"

"Tyrell Station, sir. They didn't send their daily status report for the second time in a row. I checked the log, and it's never happened before." She glanced up at him. "In fact, I've seen no one miss two consecutive reports in my time here."

Colonel Maartens, who prided himself on knowing just about every ship, regiment, or installation in the Fleet, couldn't think of a single fact about Tyrell Station.

"Call up the data on Tyrell, will you?"

As words appeared on Lieutenant Commander Fiona Morelli's display, Maartens let out a soft sigh. Any hope of a quiet, final overnight shift in the operations center before he retired from the Corps at the end of the week vanished. The readout was eloquent in its lack of information. Everything except the name was classified.

But even more ominous, the brief listing ended with a notation that the head of Naval Intelligence's Special Operations Division, Rear Admiral Hera Talyn, had redacted Tyrell Station's file. And nothing good ever came from problems involving her department.

Maartens suddenly found himself in the unenviable situation of having to wake one of the most feared flag officers in Fleet HQ at oh-dark-thirty. Every senior officer knew who Admiral Talyn was. However, few knew much about her, except that she was married to a Marine Corps Special Forces legend, Colonel Zachary Thomas Decker, the 1st Special Forces Regiment's commanding officer.

And wake her for what? He couldn't say. But his years in the operations center told him it was probably a glitch, nothing one should get excited about. Still, the procedures were clear — when a problem arose with a classified operation, the sponsor must be called.

"Query Tyrell with a priority message, Fiona. Ask them why they've not reported. In the meantime, I'll call Admiral Talyn, just in case this is something she should hear about now rather than during morning prayers. Then, pull up the last week's worth of log entries for Tyrell and track down any ship that called there recently."

"Aye, aye, sir."

Maartens returned to his glass-enclosed office on the mezzanine above the bullpen and opened a comlink with Admiral Talyn's quarters on flag officers' row. Only twenty seconds passed before the audio came on, and a sleep-filled voice answered.

"Talyn here."

"Sorry to wake you, sir. This is Colonel Maartens. I have the overnight operations center shift. There may be a problem involving your branch."

"Go ahead." Any hints of drowsiness vanished from her voice.

"Tyrell Station has missed two daily status reports in a row, something that's never happened. We're attempting to contact them, but it'll be a bit before we can expect a reply. It might be nothing. However, since information on Tyrell is classified at your orders, I can't make that judgment and figured you should be aware right away."

"That was the right decision, Colonel. I'll be there in twenty minutes."

**

Rear Admiral Hera Talyn, head of Naval Intelligence's Special Operations Division, swept into the Fleet operations center and made a beeline for Colonel Maartens, standing in front of the three-dimensional projection of human space occupying the circular center's heart. A mesmerizing sight at any time, it was doubly so during the hour of the wolf, long after midnight but still before sunrise over Sanctum, Caledonia's capital.

"Good morning, Colonel."

Maartens, coffee cup in hand, turned and immediately stiffened to attention.

"Good morning, Admiral." If he was surprised at seeing her in uniform, even though he'd roused her from a sound sleep no more than fifteen minutes earlier, he kept it well hidden. "Would you like to take my office?"

"Certainly, and thank you, Colonel. Please have someone connect me with Major General James Martinson, 1st Special Forces Division — he lives here in Sanctum — and Colonel Zachary Decker, 1st Special Forces Regiment, at Fort Arnhem. I need to inform them of the situation."

She headed for the senior watchkeeper's office without waiting for a reply and sat behind the uncluttered desk. A pair of familiar faces appeared on the office's primary display in under two minutes — James Martinson and her spouse, Zack Decker.

"Let me guess," the latter said before she could get a word in edge-wise, "Tyrell stopped talking with us. Or did another emergency creep up before you fine intelligence people sniffed it out?"

"Good morning, Zack, Jimmy. Sorry for pulling you out of bed a little early, though I suppose it'll give you time for a longer run before breakfast. The Almighty knows you Marines enjoy it. Yes, Tyrell missed the second daily sitrep. Curtis called it, which means they likely are or were under attack and lost subspace communications. The question is, did they lose Tyrell?"

Both Decker and Martinson shook their heads.

"Doubtful. Curtis Delgado is one of the sharpest company commanders in the entire Special Forces community," Martinson said. "He's quickly turning into a younger and better-looking version of your husband."

"Sneaky, ruthless, overly fond of explosives, high altitude jumps, and historical quotes?" Talyn gave Decker an amused look.

A smug expression crossed his face. "What can I say? Apparently, I'm an inspiration to the next generation of door kickers. But joking aside, his planning and preparation, at least what he shared with us, is top-notch. I couldn't do better under the circumstances. The bigger question is, when will the cavalry arrive?"

"In just under a day and a half. *Garibaldi*'s captain is pushing into the highest interstellar hyperspace bands, but she's not exactly fresh from the shipyard. Until then, Erinye Company is our very own version of Schrödinger's cat."

"While I have you," Martinson said, "anything more about the artifact Curtis' people found and why we didn't know about it until his report?"

Talyn shook her head. "Sorry, nothing new has come up. The Assenari Enterprises zaibatsu has a pretty good corporate intelligence and security branch, right up there with ComCorp's, so I'm not surprised they kept it from us. Besides, Assenari isn't high on our threat list. Its management generally stays away from politics, unlike their counterparts in the larger conglomerates."

"But not from the *Sécurité Spéciale*."

"Apparently. Provided Curtis is right, and they couldn't have prepared an operation to take the WMD depot faster than we could ship the Erinyes to Tyrell. Hallikonnoen has been there for weeks already, and her reinforcements wouldn't have had time to pass through the Assenari hiring system and climb aboard *Thunder Bay* so quickly."

A grim expression crossed Decker's square face.

"Then either Curtis faces protecting two separate high-value targets simultaneously or will fight two separate waves of *Sécurité Spéciale* mercenaries, the original for the artifact and a hastily arranged raid on the depot."

"Or *Garibaldi* will arrive before the second wave and destroy it."

"From your lips to the Almighty's ear, my dear Admiral."

# — Thirty-Seven —

"What if we hook *Harfang* and *Faucon* to the station's power system and use their reactors for the guns? Surely, Tyrell is equipped to accept external sources." Delgado, who'd been pacing around the command post, stopped and looked at Movane.

She grimaced. "A possibility. There are several outlets near both ships. But there's one minor problem. The guns are fed directly from the station's reactor via specially laid large conduits. The conduits for external sources are smaller. They couldn't take the level of throughput required. And before you ask, we don't have stocks of the large conduits. Besides, my people aren't capable of jury-rigging a connection from your ships to those power conduits."

"Which leaves the ships themselves as our defensive platforms."

First Sergeant Hak let out a soft grunt. "No crews."

"Not to lift off, no. Unless we can convince the mercs at gunpoint it would be in their best interests if they obeyed every order."

"I wouldn't bet my pension on that." Hak shook his head. "The pop guns on those sloops won't make the same impression as our big boys, and grounded, they can't deploy shields, which turns them into sitting targets. The sort that might just experience a catastrophic antimatter containment breach a few dozen meters from Tyrell."

Delgado nodded. "Right. If the station is destroyed, we'll have a heck of a time keeping tangos from raiding the ammunition bunker."

Movane gave him a hard look. "Never mind the civilian lives that depend on you, Major."

"I'm sorry, Chief Administrator, but keeping the tangos from seizing enough WMDs to murder millions is more important than the lives of everyone in here, ours included."

"The needs of the many," Testo said in a quiet, almost reverential tone.

"You'd sacrifice the lot of us?"

"If there's no other choice." He smacked his thighs with his open palms. "But we're far from being there yet. One thing I've learned serving in SOCOM is we're blessed with so many talented folks in our ranks that we never lack for innovative, workable ideas."

"And high explosives specialists," Hak grunted. "How about we booby trap the WMDs? If they go off on Keros, no harm done because it has no atmosphere. I'm sure HQ won't mind if that keeps them from falling into enemy hands."

"Then why," Movane asked, "didn't your superiors order you to destroy them the moment you arrived?"

Delgado shrugged. "No idea. They didn't tell me, and I didn't ask."

"Why not?"

"Because in our line of business, questions often go unanswered. It's called need to know." He glanced at Testo. "Recall Delta Troop. There's no point in them sitting at guns we can't power."

"And put them aboard the sloops since they're now our most experienced gunners?" Hak suggested. "Not that I suggest they engage, but so you have the option, should something unexpected present itself."

"Actually…" Delgado tapped his chin with an extended index finger. "How about we booby trap the WMDs *and* pretend we're the mercs who landed aboard the sloops? A second wave will know about the first and expect to see allies."

"That'll only work if the second wave isn't from the same outfit. Otherwise, they'll know we're not mercs. I don't give Tyrell an ion's chance in a plasma salvo if that happens."

Movane looked at Hak and Delgado in turn. "But we can use our prisoners as hostages, can't we?"

The latter shook his head.

"No. Mercs, especially those from outfits operating in the Protectorate Zone, don't do the hostage game. They'll simply shoot Tyrell full of holes and let their former colleagues die with the rest of us. But if they can retrieve the ships without risking further casualties, they'll try. In any case, Delta Troop will split in half and act as gunnery crew aboard the sloops and while they're waiting for action, they can drain the computer cores of relevant intelligence. I'm sure HQ will be interested in finding out who they are and where they come from. The Admiral is big on retaliation strikes these days, *pour encourager les autres*, as they say. Who's best employed booby-trapping the ammo bunker?"

"You mean the bunker itself or the warhead crates?" Hak asked. "Because if you want to give them a delayed surprise so we can lay doggo and watch them go boom in orbit, then I'd look at doing the crates. Charlie Troop has a few more explosives wizards than Bravo Troop. I'm assuming you'll keep Rolf and his people patrolling Tyrell and quelling any uprisings."

"Charlie Troop it is. Chief Administrator, we'll need one of your shuttles to fly my people there."

"Do you even know the exact location? The recon droid made sure no one here found out."

A nod.

"Yes, we do. It's a bit far for a hike in armored pressure suits. Approximately two dozen kilometers west of here, at the bottom of the canyon."

Her eyes widened. "That close? And your superiors knew about it for over a year?"

"Yes. Just not exactly where until the recon droid found the hidden entrance. Now, about some transport?"

"I'll arrange it. Do you need a pilot?"

"I have a few flying sergeants in the company — an improvement instituted by my commanding officer a while back, so we wouldn't be dependent on outsiders. One of them will do. I'd rather not risk civilians seeing things they shouldn't."

"Very well. I'll make sure one is prepared." She turned around to pass on the necessary instructions.

"Another thing, Chief Administrator."

"Yes?" Movane said over her shoulder.

"We used up most of our Fleet-issue explosives stores stopping the first wave and need unrestricted access to Tyrell's holdings."

"I'll call up the chief artificer. He'll show you our depot."

\*\*

"Cheerful spot, ain't it, Sarge?" The shuttle's pilot, Sergeant Xavier Vennat, whose normal call sign was One-Three-Charlie, kept his eyes glued to the controls as he slowly maneuvered the Assenari Mining craft.

Occupying the jump seat behind him and connected to the cockpit intercom so they could talk without using the radio, Command Sergeant Isaac Dyas grunted in reply. The depths of the canyon lived in perpetual twilight, but it was still easy to see that it was formed by flowing water hundreds of thousands of years ago, before the cataclysm that stripped Keros of its atmosphere. Perhaps the river had even been navigable.

"Just concentrate on flying this ancient crate, Xav. I don't fancy a hike back to Tyrell, let alone a long climb out of this damned ditch."

"Getting a touch of the *cafard*?" Vennat asked in an amused tone to show he was kidding.

"The stuff in that ammo depot is a fracking horror show, so I'm not overly enthusiastic about messing with it even if we're in an airless environment and wearing combat-grade tin suits." Dyas paused, then, "Not to mention more mercs could show up unannounced and be on top of us before we know it. So yeah, I'm feeling a wee bite of the old bug after being cooped up in that damned mining station, Xav. But not to worry."

"I'm not." Vennat stared at the primary display, which provided a real-time view of what was ahead. "We're almost there. That faint hump to port, one kay from our current position — the entrance is beneath it. And there's a nice convenient open space where we can land."

They touched down a few minutes later, and Dyas realized the hump was an overhang, like so many others they'd seen along the way, a spot where the ancient river had undermined its banks. He aimed his handheld battlefield sensor at the dark space beneath the overhang, but as he expected, it picked up nothing of interest.

Since they'd flown suited up with the entire shuttle depressurized, getting Charlie Troop's demolition experts and their improvised explosive devices offloaded took only a few moments. As planned, two scouts entered the darkness ahead of the team, sensors in hand, looking for threats as well as the hidden door.

The space appeared vaster and deeper than Dyas expected, with enough room for a sizable cargo shuttle which, he supposed, would have been the point of choosing this spot in an area where the planet's crust was particularly rich in minerals that could stop orbital sensor scans from penetrating too deeply.

"Found what looks like a hole drilled by the recon droid's laser," one of the scouts announced as he reached a blank wall.

Dyas closed the remaining distance and examined the small, perfectly round opening. He reached inside with his hand.

"This must be part of the door. It opens up about twenty centimeters in."

"Stands to reason, Sarge. The recon droid would have been looking at density readings as part of its programming. Hidden chambers, that sort of thing."

"Then let's find the door handle. It'll be purely mechanical, perhaps not even locked."

"Done," the other scout said moments later. He waved them over to a spot three meters from the droid's borehole. "My sensor sees a perfectly vertical hairline crack in the wall. Can't make it out with my Mark One eyeballs, but it's there." A pause. "And it's picking up a mechanism of sorts under a veneer of probably fake stone. Metal only, nothing that looks like a depleted power source or explosive."

Dyas walked over and examined the spot indicated by the scout, then rapped it lightly. Nothing happened. He tapped it a little harder, and a thin pancake of stone flipped up, exposing a handle.

"That easy, eh?" The scout said.

"Whoever established this depot was counting on secrecy rather than fancy technology that might fail at the wrong moment. Besides, tech wasn't quite as fancy as ours back then, especially in the realm of sensors."

Dyas grabbed the handle and tested it by pulling up, then down, and then twisting each way. On his last try, it turned ninety degrees.

"Someone give me a rope. We'll yank the door open from outside the cave just in case there's a live claymore or any other nasty little surprise waiting for us."

But nothing happened as the three meters by four meters door swung aside on hidden hinges. Moments later, Dyas' point men cautiously entered.

"You gotta see this, Sarge."

# — Thirty-Eight —

"I estimate around five hundred warheads stored in hard cases," Dyas reported after walking around the depot. "Enough to wipe out the better part of four continents on your average human settled world. And that's the ones with chemical markings only. I couldn't begin to estimate the damage those biologicals would cause."

"More the reason for not letting any fall into hostile hands," Delgado replied. "What do you think is possible?"

Dyas didn't immediately reply, eyes panning the stacks of gray, oblong plastic cases about the size of an average coffin. Their yellow markings didn't indicate which side in the war stored them in an ancient river cave on an airless world for future use. Fortunately, that war ended before their owners could return and deploy them.

"To tell you the truth, I'm a little leery of prying those cases open. We don't know how the locking mechanisms work, what's inside, or even whether the warheads deteriorated to the point of leaking. Sure, there's no atmosphere to propagate chems or bios, but if we catch a

**311**

whiff, we'll be bringing it back to Tyrell, and we have no Class One decontamination facilities. Besides, I didn't bring enough explosives and detonators to rig more than a few dozen with movement-triggered timers, and I'm not even sure that of those will work properly. We're not exactly well equipped to build IEDs with complex detonators."

"So, what do you suggest?"

"Turn the movement-triggered timers into anti-handling devices by removing the timer module and slide them between the cases nearest to the door, then daisy-chain the rest of the IEDs along the stacks. That way, if they move one of them, everything goes."

Delgado didn't immediately reply, and Dyas guessed he was discussing the proposal with Hak and Testo.

"Won't they see the setup?"

"Depends on how sloppy they are. We'll make sure our presents are as well hidden as possible. But even if they spot one or two, that doesn't mean they'll have an easy time of it. Besides, I'll rig enough charges on the underside of the overhang to collapse it via remote detonation at your command. A reserved demolition if you like."

"Okay. Do it. Niner, out."

Dyas turned to his people. "You heard him. Let's rig this place for the best fireworks show within three parsecs."

**

"Rolf's people just broke up a fight in Habitat Module Three," First Sergeant Hak reported when Delgado returned from the heads, "and a few of the prisoners are getting a little antsy at being confined to a hangar we can space whenever it suits us."

"Tough. And no, I'm not reopening the *Reach*. If need be, I'll lock the habitat modules and let them indulge in free-form martial arts. We'll patch up the survivors when this is over. If there are any."

Movane let out a soft snort. "Getting a little tetchy, Major?"

"Someone has to, and as commanding officer, that responsibility rests with me." When she glanced over her shoulder, Delgado winked at her.

"Let me speak with the straw bosses among the workers, and I'll see they settle." She climbed to her feet and left the command post.

"It's a shame, you know, sir." Hak gave Delgado a wry smile.

"What is?"

"That Madame Movane will calm the restless spirits. I think Alpha Troop is enjoying a bit of physical activity slash head knocking."

A scoff. "I get it. Everyone is tense."

"We're past tense, sir. Ever read of a last stand in a place called Rorke's Drift back before spaceflight." Hak paused for a moment, searching his memory. "Late nineteenth century, or thereabouts. One of the Colonel's favorite leadership examples from the old days on Earth. Outnumbered troops holding the line against all odds."

"Vaguely? Why?"

"They fought off a few attacks before wondering whether the next one would be their last. That's pretty much where we are."

"We only fought off one."

"No, sir," Hak replied in a patient tone. "The first attack was internal — Hallikonnoen and her operatives. The mercs carried out the second."

Delgado studied his first sergeant, wondering what he was trying to say without saying it. "And?"

"Reading the account, something stuck in my memory. Back then, the highest award for valor in battle awarded by the nation defending Rorke's Drift — the British, as I recall — was called the Victoria Cross. They awarded eleven of them for that single engagement, seven of which were the most ever received in a single action by one regiment."

"I still don't understand your meaning."

"The recipients survived the battle, sir. No posthumous awards. They won against all odds. And so will we."

Delgado smiled at Hak. "I doubt any of us will earn a Commonwealth Medal of Honor here, Top."

"No, sir. But we will see this through to the Admiral's and the Colonel's satisfaction, and that's what counts. Medals, they can pin to the cushion carried by one of the mourners at your funeral. Being in the good graces of our superiors, that's as close to immortality as it gets because it delays mortality at their hands." Hak gave his commanding officer a knowing wink. Rear Admiral Talyn, who controlled most of Ghost Squadron's missions, wasn't the forgiving sort.

**

"Niner, this is Zero."

Sergeant Kuzek's voice in Delgado's earbud woke him with a start. After greeting Charlie Troop in the hangar and confirming the reserved demolition would work when the time came, he and Testo had crashed, leaving Kuzek to run the command post. Delgado sat up, instantly awake. He tapped his communicator.

"Niner."

"Contact, sir. Ground surveillance picked up two ships in orbit, sloops like the ones we captured. Neither is emitting radio waves, but we are being pinged by sensors. Looks like the second wave is here."

Delgado glanced at the clock. Only eighteen hours had passed since Dyas and his people finished booby-trapping the ammunition depot, which meant the arrival of a Navy ship might not occur for several more hours. They were truly on their own.

"Stand to. Everyone in pressure suits, ready to button up, civilians included."

Moments later, the alarm sounded throughout Tyrell, followed by First Sergeant Hak's voice announcing the unidentified ships in orbit and passing on Delgado's instructions.

Romana Movane showed up in the command post moments after Delgado and took her workstation to monitor Tyrell's infrastructure status.

After a few moments, she asked, "What's stopping the ships in orbit from dropping a few kinetic penetrator rods on us, Major? I'm under the impression we're not dealing with people who have consciences."

"Fear of retribution," Delgado absently replied, scrolling through the duty log as per his habit when taking the command post after spending a few hours of downtime. "Mass murderers are almost always hunted down by the Fleet nowadays, especially when Armed Forces personnel are among the victims, and the current Grand Admiral has been doing so with ruthless vigor. Every merc outfit in the known galaxy understands SOCOM units will prosecute them with extreme prejudice, even well beyond the Commonwealth sphere."

"Extreme prejudice?" She let out a humorless chuckle. "A euphemism for killing them, right?"

"Taking prisoners is not a major consideration. If they surrender, fine. Otherwise, they merge with the Infinite Void. Most of the blacker than black ops mercenaries — as opposed to the normal private military contractors like the ones we captured — prefer going out in a blaze of gunfire. They well know the only other choice is a slow, agonizing death on Parth's Desolation Island."

"You sound as if you speak from experience."

He gave her a crooked grin over his shoulder. "No comment, Chief Administrator."

"Don't you think booby-trapping the munitions depot might make them angry enough to contemplate retribution despite the risks?"

A shrug. "Perhaps. But if I deny them access to those WMDs, then I'll be doing my job. The rest is in the hands of the Almighty. Or if you don't subscribe to any religious faith, in the hands of fate. Besides, they might figure we're entirely ignorant of the Migration War ammunition depot. They wouldn't know about the garrison duties being taken by a SOCOM unit sent especially for this sort of contingency."

"Regular Marine units don't make IEDs?"

"They don't have nearly the same training and experience as we do, especially in adapting civilian material to military use."

"I see."

Movane fell silent, and they spent the next two hours monitoring the station, Erinye Company's dispositions, and the tangos in orbit until, finally, "Why didn't they launch shuttles yet?"

Delgado turned to his operations sergeant. "Good point. One orbit should be enough to take the lay of the land. I'll bet there are shuttles inbound as we speak but coming up on the depot flying nap of the earth, beyond Tyrell's line of sight."

"Which is pretty much how we operate." Hak nodded, eyes on the tactical projection. "Why wouldn't the buggers learn from us."

"Let's hope your theory is right, Top. Because it means they'll try to empty the depot without involving Tyrell."

"Until it goes boom. Then, they might give us the stink eye."

"Right. But we don't have a choice."

A few more minutes passed, then Testo said, "Contact. Four shuttles, civilian cargo pattern, just appeared over the western horizon, flying nap of the earth, pinging us hard with sensors."

The primary display shifted from tracking the ships in orbit to the approaching craft, which looked as innocuous as any in commercial use — boxy, inelegant, covered with black streaks from too many atmospheric re-entries. They did not, however, display any visible markings, and their position lights were off.

Delgado stared at them for a few heartbeats. "Can't see any weapon pods, but that doesn't mean they're not armed."

"We could ping them in return and find out," Testo suggested.

"Better not in case they're equipped with threat detectors. I'd rather they believe Tyrell is in mercenary hands."

Another few moments of silence, then, "They must know how low our guns can depress because they're actually flying lower than that, Skipper. Not that their sensors will pick up anything other than cold emplacements and dead power circuitry." Testo paused. "And they've slipped into the canyon."

He touched his workstation screen, and the primary display shifted to a view from the remote sensor Sergeant Dyas placed in a concealed spot across the canyon and a thousand meters to the east of the ammunition depot. It had a direct line of sight to Tyrell so it could transmit via laser and thus not be detected by the intruders.

At first, they couldn't see the approaching shuttles, but then Testo pointed at a slow-moving dot in the canyon's shadows.

"There's the lead."

One after the other, the remaining three came into sight, though it seemed as if they were barely moving forward.

"Could it be they don't have the precise coordinates?" Movane asked.

"Maybe, but if I were leading that raid, I'd be cautious on final approach no matter what," Delgado replied.

A few minutes later, Testo said, "They have the coordinates. That's exactly where Charlie Troop's shuttle landed yesterday."

"Here we go."

# — Thirty-Nine —

Commander Hari Zabala, captain of the patrol frigate *Garibaldi,* shook off the usual nausea he and ninety-nine percent of humans experienced when shifting between hyperspace and normal space and turned his eyes on the primary display. The combat information center's artificial intelligence, which didn't suffer from human weaknesses, had already called up a live view of Keros.

"CIC, this is the bridge. Systems are nominal. Sublight drives are firing to put us on a course for Keros orbit as fast as safety protocols allow."

Zabala glanced at the display embedded in his command chair and nodded at the officer of the watch.

"Thank you, bridge."

"Sir." The sensor chief raised his hand.

"Go ahead."

"The navigation instructions for this system mention a geosynchronous orbital platform above Tyrell Station, but I cannot find it. There are, however, two civilian sloops without ID beacons in low orbit. Their emissions do not show weapons powered or shields raised."

Zabala, a stout, dark-complexioned man in his early forties, sat back and rubbed his square jaw with a spade-like hand.

"Perhaps whatever made HQ send us here at maximum speed has already happened. Any sign of radio or subspace transmissions?"

"Negative, sir," the signals chief said. "Shall I hail those sloops?"

"No," Zabala replied after a brief moment of hesitation. "In fact, I believe we'll rig for silent running the moment we've reached our target velocity. Did you hear that, bridge?"

"Rig for silent running the moment we reach target velocity, aye, sir."

"And we'll clear for battle stations as we come into maximum effective engagement range of those sloops."

After a moment, the sensor chief raised his hand again. "I have a visual of Tyrell Station, sir. Looks like there are two sloops on the tarmac. Their configuration is similar to the ones in orbit."

The view on the primary display zoomed-in until Tyrell filled it.

"What's with the module on the upper left?" Zabala asked. "Looks like it suffered damage. And the one to the right."

"The first would be the communications module and the other a hydroponics module," the combat systems officer said after consulting a schematic of Tyrell. "Looks like they suffered from catastrophic decompression, perhaps because of an internal explosion."

"Pan the entire area at this resolution. Let's see if there's more visible damage."

"Yes, sir."

As the sensor slowly swept across the landing strip, Zabala raised a hand. "Stop. What are those speckles lying haphazardly all over the place? Can we zoom in even more?"

After a moment, the sensor chief said, "Looks like pressure suits, sir."

"With bodies in them, I presume, unless the Tyrell Marine garrison celebrated Farhaven Day in a novel fashion."

"They're scattered mostly in front of the shuttle hangar door, and if I'm not mistaken, those pressure suits appear to have small marks everywhere."

"Punctures? Are those sloops part of the enemy force they sent us to intercept, and those suits lying around the result of Tyrell's garrison stopping them in the shuttle hangar and initiating a catastrophic depressurization to clear them out?"

"Could be, sir. They don't look like standard issue Marine armor."

Zabala rubbed his chin. "What the name of all that's holy happened down there?"

"Couldn't say, sir, but we're picking up plenty of emissions and life signs, which would indicate the station is still pressurized and its denizens alive."

"Sir," the sensor chief glanced over his shoulder. "We just picked up a series of minor explosions at the bottom of the rift canyon running south of Tyrell, approximately twenty-five kilometers due west. Our angle doesn't allow us to see what's there, however."

"It won't be anything good. You can count on that."

\*\*

"Oh, crap." Hak exhaled slowly as a series of flashes lit up the darkness below the overhang, followed by a spray of shrapnel. "So much for the idea they might spot the anti-lift devices and back off until our help arrives. I wouldn't want to be in the vicinity right now, getting my suit covered in whatever nasties were released from the warheads."

"HQ won't be overjoyed," Testo said. "I'm sure of that."

"It's not the optimal outcome." Delgado allowed himself a soft sigh. "Sergeant Testo, please log my intention to detonate the reserved demolition as of this date and time. We might as well seal everything in."

"Let any live ones out first?" Hak asked.

"Sure. Let's give them a few minutes to deal with casualties."

They watched pressure-suited figures emerge from the shuttles and cautiously work their way under the overhang.

"I'd love to be on their radio frequency right now."

Movane turned to Delgado. "Major, out of curiosity, why wouldn't you seal the lot of them into that cave if they're as nasty as you've described?"

He gave her a faint smile. "Just because we're SOCOM doesn't mean we kill people indiscriminately. Their mission has failed, and that's enough for now. Subjecting them to a slow death by collapsing the entrance comes under the heading of cruel and unusual since they do not present an imminent threat."

Hak let out a grunt. "What the Skipper means is that it would be a war crime."

Movane's eyes widened. "Oh. I hadn't thought of it that way. I guess my ignorance of your rules is showing."

"Mercenaries are human too. Now, if they climb aboard those shuttles and come at Tyrell guns blazing to avenge themselves, my people crewing the weapons aboard the grounded sloops will take pleasure shooting them down, which, in this environment, means killing them outright."

Moments after entering the depot, the mercenaries came back out, dragging injured or dead comrades with them.

"By my count, everyone is out, sir," Testo said.

"Blow the reserved demolition."

Before the intruders even closed their aft ramps, let alone lifted off, another flash lit up the underside of the overhang, and it collapsed in what seemed like slow motion at first as the rock cracked, then all at once.

Testo whistled softly. "Nobody's going back in there without serious excavation gear."

"Yep. And now we wait for their reaction. Pass the word to close up pressure suits and hang tight. Delta Troop may power weapons but not targeting sensors yet."

\*\*

"Four shuttles lifted out of the canyon, sir, near where we picked up the explosions," *Garibaldi*'s sensor chief reported, "and the ships in orbit are powering weapons."

Zabala tapped his fingers on his command chair arm and nodded to himself. "Time we made our presence known. Bridge, up systems."

"Up systems, aye," the first officer responded.

"Guns, target the ships in orbit and those shuttles and ping them mercilessly. Let them feel our presence."

"Targeting, aye, sir."

"Communications, open the emergency radio frequency, and route to my chair."

"Opening emergency radio frequency, aye," the signals petty officer replied. Then, "You're on, sir."

"They noticed us, sir," the combat systems officer said. "Powering weapons and raising shields."

"Unknown vessels in orbit around Keros, this is the Commonwealth Navy frigate *Garibaldi*. Shut off your weapons and drop your shields. I will construe any attempt to fire at Commonwealth Armed Forces Station Tyrell as an act of war, and I will destroy you without offering quarter. The same goes for your shuttles, who are ordered to rejoin their ships without making a detour for Tyrell.

Your cooperation means you will live. Disobey my orders, and I will erase you from the universe. We will entertain terms once you've obeyed. Otherwise, there will be no point in discussing anything because you will be dead. *Garibaldi*, out."

A minute passed, and another, before a reply finally came.

"Frigate *Garibaldi*, this is the private military corporation ship *Utrecht*. We don't want any trouble and will power down weapons and shields. But so you understand, I have casualties aboard those shuttles stemming from illegally laid improvised explosive devices and suspect the guilty parties are in Tyrell Station."

"Perhaps you wandered into something you should have left alone. Such as a planet under Fleet control that's out-of-bounds to unauthorized traffic."

"We know nothing about that, *Garibaldi*. Our contract merely stipulates we were to retrieve items from an ancient, unclaimed supply depot at a given set of coordinates on Keros."

At that moment, a fresh voice broke in.

"*Garibaldi*, this is Tyrell Station. I'm the interim commanding officer. The ships in orbit are here to steal a cache of warheads belonging to the Fleet and know full well this planet is a military reservation. Because of circumstances, I will discuss later and not over an open channel, they forced me to deny them access using explosives. Word of warning, *Utrecht*, your people in the shuttles are covered in very nasty substances, which will activate the moment their pressure suits come into contact with a normal atmosphere. As in, they will kill everyone aboard your ships. Since you know what was in the munitions depot and that your people triggered anti-lift devices causing warheads to rupture, you will be aware of this. If you plan on recovering those shuttles and the crew aboard, you'll need to run them through a Class One decontamination protocol."

Zabala sat up. "What?"

"Sir, I'll explain later. Right now, the situation is a bit messy, especially for *Utrecht* and the other PMC sloop."

"Her name is *Anvers*," the merc captain said.

"Do you know how to set up a Class One decontamination protocol?" Zabala asked.

"I'll sort it out. Once I've done so, may we leave?"

"No. You'll stay in orbit until I confer with Tyrell's commanding officer."

"Understood. *Utrecht*, out."

Zabala turned to his communications chief. "Arrange a secure link with Tyrell."

"Aye, aye, sir."

# — Forty —

"My name is Major Curtis Delgado, sir. I command the Marine garrison. Captain Nero Engstrom, Commonwealth Navy, the station's commanding officer, was murdered three days ago, and I took over."

To say Zabala was examining Delgado with suspicion might be a bit strong, but he nonetheless felt under scrutiny by the naval officer.

"We were dispatched here at highest possible speed to help you with an unspoken threat under orders from Fleet HQ directly rather than via my chain of command, so please tell me what happened and how we can assist."

"Yes, sir. Thank you. I'll preface this by saying my people and I work for SOCOM." Zabala's eyebrows shot up at hearing the acronym, but he remained silent. "Rear Admiral Hera Talyn of Naval Intelligence is my mission controller — we're here at her behest — so you'll understand when I say I can't speak of certain matters."

"The plot thickens. Understood." Zabala nodded once. "I assume this is related to that WMD warhead depot you spoke about earlier."

"Yes, sir. It was discovered a few weeks ago, and we relieved the regular garrison because intelligence realized unfriendly interests knew about the find and were keen to seize the weapons, which date back to the Second Migration War."

Zabala grimaced. "Ugh. I can only imagine what horrors are down there."

"We were attacked by a first wave of mercenaries — three ships, two of which landed to seize Tyrell but were seized by us instead, and one which we killed with the station's guns. You'll find the wreckage and an impact crater close to our location."

"Really? Well done, Major. I'm impressed."

"Both ships on the ground are undamaged, but we killed about half of the crews when they forced their way into Tyrell. The rest, over a hundred, are being held in the shuttle hangar as prisoners of the Fleet."

"So those are bodies we see scattered on the tarmac."

"Yes, sir. The mercs had an advance team on the inside, though we neutralized them before their arrival and led the raiders into a prepared ambush. Unfortunately, that advance team destroyed the communications module, one of the hydroponics modules, and damaged the reactor module. As my first sergeant put it, these were self-detonating tangos, likely from one of the religious sects which consider suicide in the service of their deity a blessing and hire themselves out to organizations conducting black ops."

Zabala raised a hand. "Hang on. They damaged the reactor module?"

Delgado nodded. "We've been running on battery power since then. Fortunately, with no atmosphere to block the sun's rays, they're kept topped up during daylight hours. But the entire module will need replacing before the mine can go back into operation. Until then, the several hundred civilian personnel here are idle. Which brings me to the list of things for which I need your help."

"Go ahead."

"First, could you send a subspace message to whoever signed the orders sending you here, asking for an Assenari Mining Corporation ship to pick up the civilians as quickly as possible? This place will probably be out of business for a few weeks, if not a few months, and the workers aren't exactly cheerful people."

Zabala glanced away for a few seconds, and Delgado saw his lips move but heard no sounds. He turned back to the Marine.

"It's going out in the next minute or so."

"Thank you. Next, can I turn the sloops we captured and their surviving crews over to you? Since there's no prize money involved and SOCOM is tight-lipped about our operations, they're yours along with the honors involved."

"Done. I'll send prize crews within the hour. Make sure the prisoners are loaded aboard, suitably detained, but with access to sanitary facilities, water, and food."

"Yes, sir. We've done this before, so you'll find the sloops ready to lift the moment your people are aboard."

A faint smile briefly relaxed Zabala's serious countenance. "No doubt."

"And I must send a full report to Admiral Talyn if you won't mind transmitting it as an operational urgent. It'll be encrypted."

"Certainly. If I may ask, why didn't you use the subspace transmitters in those mercenary ships to call home?"

Delgado let out a grim chuckle.

"We tried, but the relay in this system refused to recognize them as legitimate, and I couldn't find anything resembling an authorization or override code. Of course, it would accept a distress call, but a general broadcast when I figured there were still more tangos inbound didn't seem prudent, and I was right. My best gamble was seeing if the second wave believed their earlier comrades took possession of Tyrell. And I was right."

"Anything else we can do, Major?"

Delgado shook his head. "That'll take care of the immediate issues. Once my report reaches HQ, I expect a flurry of orders to help us sort this out so we can go our separate ways."

"In that case, *Garibaldi*, out."

Once Zabala's face vanished from the command post's primary display, Hak gave his commanding officer a sardonic look.

"Flurry of orders? Doesn't sound like the Admiral, sir. A single, all-encompassing directive is more her style."

Delgado grinned at him. "But the good commander doesn't need to know that."

"True." Hak stood. "I'll go organize loading the prisoners aboard the sloops. Or rather, make that singular if we can fit every last one of them aboard *Harfang*. Otherwise, the prize crews will be stuck moving it from the passenger gangway to make room for *Faucon*."

Before Delgado replied, Testo let out a stream of invective.

"What?"

"The sloops in orbit just destroyed their shuttles with anti-missile calliopes as they were on final approach, sir."

Delgado and Hak exchanged glances.

"I guess they couldn't manage a Class One decontamination process after all," the latter said.

"Live by taking bad contracts, die by taking bad contracts. If ever I find myself beached, the last thing I'll do is sign up as a private military contractor."

"Amen, Skipper."

"Aw, for frack's sake." Testo slumped in his chair. "The tangos in orbit blew themselves up."

"More death worshiping zealots, I guess," Hak said in a resigned tone. "I think we won't like where this could go if the opposition keeps arming, equipping, and employing them. At least regular mercenaries and organized criminals know when it's time to quit."

Delgado allowed himself a brief grimace. "Which is precisely why they started using the self-detonators."

"Captain Zabala's calling again, Skipper. Coming up on the primary."

"Did you catch that, Major? The ships in orbit self-destructed." Zabala seemed like a man in disbelief.

"Yes, sir. We did."

"Who kills themselves instead of surrendering?"

Delgado chewed on the inside of his lower lip for a few moments, wondering how much he should reveal, then decided information about this new threat would percolate through the Fleet soon enough.

"What follows is top secret, sir. Something I'd rather you didn't discuss with your crew."

"Understood. I'm in my day cabin, alone."

"Ever heard of the Hashashin, sir? An ancient sect from which we derived the Anglic word assassin?"

Zabala shrugged. "Vaguely."

"They were religious fanatics who'd give their lives to accomplish a mission and would rather die than be captured. The Hashashin vanished around the late thirteenth century, though fanatical fighters willing to die for their faith and cause never really disappeared. They just keep mutating from one era to the next, sometimes disappearing from the sensor screen for generations, only to reappear in a novel form. Well, they're back once more. In the last year or so, someone weaponized the latest incarnation of these eternally present holy warriors, formed them into private military corporations as a cover, and sent them on one-way black ops missions, just like the Hashashin of old."

"So, the crews aboard those ships were your Hashashin?"

Delgado nodded. "At least that's my theory. They and the infiltration team that blew up three modules, killing themselves in the process before we stopped them. My people took care of the rest, thankfully, before they accomplished their mission. I've never encountered suicidal mercenaries before. The regular sort is in it for pay, not a holy death. By the way, we don't know what they call themselves. Naval Intelligence named them Hashashin for lack of anything better."

"And what god or gods do they worship?"

"Again, we don't know. As I said, they emerged from the shadows so recently, we're only now aware of their existence, though I suppose they were perhaps responsible for targeted assassinations or other small-scale black ops in recent times, incidents for which we never found the culprits."

"I see." Zabala rubbed his chin. "Does that mean the ones you took prisoner aren't Hashashin?"

"No. They belong to a known PMC headquartered in the Protectorate Zone, one loosely affiliated with a large, diffuse organized crime group."

"How did you tell the difference?"

A predatory smile lit up Delgado's face. "They surrendered meekly after we bloodied their noses."

# — Forty-One —

Rear Admiral Hera Talyn allowed herself a pleased smile when Colonel Zack Decker's and Major General Jimmy Martinson's faces appeared on her office display.

"Gentlemen, you'll be pleased to hear that Erinye Company is battered, bruised, stirred, and shaken, with severely depleted ammunition stocks and short several serviceable pressurized armor suits, but otherwise in good health. All Marines stood roll call this morning. I can't say the same about Tyrell Station. Three of its modules are damaged beyond repair, including the reactor, and several adjoining ones suffered collateral damage. Operations are essentially at a standstill until we replace those modules. There were, thankfully, no casualties among legitimate employees. An Assenari ship is on the way to deliver a repair team and remove the workers. It'll be a few weeks, maybe even a few months before Tyrell is back up and running."

She went on to relay Delgado's report, which arrived less than thirty minutes earlier, transmitted via *Garibaldi*.

When she fell silent, Decker frowned. "Hashashin? Is Curtis sure?"

"What he describes bears the hallmarks of previously identified Hashashin attacks."

"Not that we've identified many," Martinson said.

Talyn inclined her head. "Granted, but I agree with his assessment. It confirms information obtained by our sources on Earth. The *Sécurité Spéciale* is upping the ante by using fanatics about whom we know little now that we're effectively neutralizing their usual assets through direct action and intimidation."

Decker let out a grunt.

"I guess it was inevitable they'd go for the unspeakable after we put the fear of the Almighty into most organized crime groups and mercenary organizations. That'll bring our dirty little war to a new level. But well done Curtis. Seizing two ships and downing a third, along with taking over a hundred prisoners — he'll be in my chair before long at this rate." He gave Talyn a suspicious look. "Unless someone with more stars on the collar than you takes umbrage at his burying the munitions depot beneath a few hundred tons of rock."

She shook her head. "He did precisely the right thing under the circumstances. While Assenari repairs Tyrell, it wouldn't surprise me if a recovery team with remotely operated heavy excavation machinery digs the depot out, perhaps only to make sure Curtis' people rendered the warheads completely inoperable. And if they didn't, then an injection of a stable polymer to fill the cavern will do the same thing. As of now, it's been designated one of the most dangerous toxic waste dumps in the known galaxy. I'm briefing the Grand Admiral in two hours on the matter, and I'll find out what he thinks at that time. Keep in mind he considers Curtis a splendid officer after the recent trip to Earth."

"When is Erinye Company coming home?"

"They and *Garibaldi* will stay at least until the workers are evacuated, and a replacement garrison arrives to guard Tyrell during the reconstruction. How and when that'll happen isn't clear yet, but Curtis is loading the prisoners into a single sloop that will head straight for Parth as soon as possible with a prize crew from *Garibaldi* and a contingent of her Marines. The other sloop will stay to transport the Erinyes home, also with a prize crew from *Garibaldi*."

Decker nodded once. "Makes sense. And what about the artifact in the basement?"

"Oh, dear." She gave her partner an amused smile. "That won't go over well with the Grand Admiral, I'm afraid. The late Nero Engstrom's predecessor will face troubling questions once things settle, as will Assenari Mining's chief executive officer and his boss, the CEO of Assenari Enterprises. Oh, and by the way, Terry Evans, the woman who died soon after Curtis arrived, remember her? She was a ComCorp operative, killed by an Assenari Enterprises operative, who then tried to destroy Tyrell by blowing up its reactor. Curtis figures he was a sort of organic dead man's switch tasked with denying the artifact should it be endangered."

"If Assenari can't keep it, no one can?"

"Perhaps not so much that but something based on the logic that only Assenari knew the exact location, and once Tyrell was gone, the thread liking it with the artifact was broken."

"Nasty. You figure he was a Hashashin as well?"

Talyn made a vague hand gesture. "Could be. Perhaps from a different faction or clan. In any case, my people will be delivering pointed messages to Assenari's top leadership. After all, their hireling tried to destroy a Fleet-owned installation."

\*\*

Curtis Delgado, First Sergeant Hak, and Romana Movane, sitting in the landing strip control room, watched *Harfang* lift off with its cargo of captured mercenaries. It would head directly for Parth, where the Commonwealth's long-term prisoners were housed in a vast network of institutions. There, they would be put on trial and, if found guilty, sentenced to hard time for attacking Tyrell, though Delgado doubted any of them faced permanent exile on Desolation Island. He didn't wish that on anyone but the worst criminals, not after hearing Colonel Decker describe his experience there during a mission that saw him play a condemned prisoner a few years ago.

"I wonder if we'll see any of those buggers wearing Marine black and working with us in a few years," Hak said as his eyes traced the sloop's ascent.

Movane gave him a sharp glance. "How's that, First Sergeant?"

"Ever heard of the Marine Light Infantry?"

She shook her head. "Can't say that I have."

"The regiment recruits from the Parth prison system — condemned men and women with military experience who are unlikely to re-offend after a basic training regimen that essentially reprograms their personalities. Much of its cadre are volunteers from elsewhere in the Marine Corps and the Army, mostly people looking for a new life or a fresh start without leaving the service. Call it a human recycling program."

"Interesting."

"And successful," Delgado said. "They're considered by many of us as the finest light troops in the Corps, tough, capable, tireless, willing to take risks that would make regular Marines think twice, and capable of absorbing casualties without breaking stride. The MLI belongs to SOCOM these days, so it's entirely possible that some of the mercenaries aboard *Harfang* might cross paths with us, albeit under a different identity. And now, Chief Administrator, I believe you and I have an appointment with the artifact in the mine. I trust the secret lift still works?"

"Yes, it does. Although my superiors won't be happy if I took you for a visit."

Delgado snorted with amusement. "That'll be nothing compared to my superiors' unhappiness at your bosses keeping it from them. I expect Assenari Enterprises' CEO to receive a very pointed rocket from the Grand Admiral shortly. Had the Fleet known about something that might attract the wrong sort of attention, Tyrell would likely not be in its current state, facing millions of creds in repairs and with production suspended for months. Never mind the fact that if it weren't for us replacing the regular garrison because of the Second Migration War ammo dump, the mercenaries would likely have seized Tyrell and endangered the lives of everyone here, yours included."

Movane's face hardened. "It wasn't my decision, Major."

"No, I'm sure it wasn't. But you were involved with the matter of Fleet-appointed commanding officers not reporting the artifact."

"I was only following orders."

"An excuse which hasn't worked since the mid-twentieth century. That being said, you'll show me everything now, so I can complete my report."

**

"What do you know about the L'Taung, Major?" Romana Movane asked after sealing her pressure suit. They were in the hydroponics module's mechanical compartment, which had survived the bombs on the upper level, preparing to take the lift to the artifact.

"About as much as most people know. So, is that it? A L'Taung artifact?"

"Yes. Or at least we're as certain as can be, all things considered."

"We suspected as much."

"You've encountered L'Taung artifacts before?"

"Out in the Protectorate Zone. Not that you ever heard me say so, since the Treaty of Ulufan forbids military operations there. But simply based on their architecture and the materials they used, the L'Taung were a tad more advanced than any current civilization in the known galaxy, ours included."

"Good. Then I won't spend an hour explaining things." She turned toward the lift door, summoning the cab.

A few moments later, the door slid open, revealing an unadorned but brilliantly lit car. Delgado and Movane stepped in and grabbed the rookie bar attached to the walls at waist level. She stroked the black control pad, and the doors closed. A second or so later, the lift depressurized, and its floor dropped out from under their feet as they sped to an airless chamber deep below the surface.

After what seemed like an eternity to Delgado's protesting stomach, the lift slowed and, moments later, stopped. Without further commands, the door opened, revealing the same impossible section of tunnel that puzzled the Marines a few days earlier.

Wordlessly, Movane led the way to the slick doorway. She touched a wall section beside it, uncovering a large knob that she pushed inward. The outline of a smaller door appeared around the knob, and she gave it a shove. The door swung aside effortlessly, and Movane stepped through after indicating Delgado should follow her.

"Welcome to the ultimate mystery, Major."

As the door opened, lights of human manufacture came on, revealing a large cave whose walls vanished into the distance. Unknown forces had smoothed them and the cathedral ceiling. Large doors set at regular intervals pierced both sides for as far as the eye could see.

Shiny gray crates, marked with glyphs that bore more than a passing resemblance to modern written Shrehari, sat in neat rows on one side of the cavern while hulking metallic constructs, machinery perhaps, Delgado figured, filled the other. A few of the crates were open, and he walked over to one of them.

"You've checked the contents?"

"Yes. Feel free to look."

He lifted the lid and peered inside.

"What are those? Crystals?"

Glassy blocks engraved with glyphs, each the size of a human adult head, were nestled inside individual compartments. Judging by the height of the crate, there were at least four layers of them.

"Assenari's research and development scientists believe those are memory crystals — data storage."

"How many are there?"

"Well over a hundred thousand, possibly the entire accumulated knowledge of a civilization vanished so long ago, its descendants consider it a myth."

"You figure this is a knowledge vault, then. I read about the theories behind such things."

She raised both hands, encompassing the cavern. "What else could it be?"

"I gather your R&D people didn't yet crack the code?"

"No. One of my predecessors as chief admin sent an entire crate to headquarters shortly after we gained entry into this place, but nothing so far."

Delgado turned to face Movane. "And Assenari decided it would rather keep this find a secret instead of harnessing the power of an entire species to decode these crystals. How short-sighted."

"As you said earlier, Major, knowledge is power. If Assenari discovers a way of accessing the data inside those crystals, who can tell what potential they unleash? It might become the most powerful zaibatsu in history, eclipsing even the mighty ComCorp."

"Not anymore."

"No, I guess not. When the Fleet forced Assenari to sell Tyrell, there was panic in the C-suite back home. But as it turned out, the secret remained inviolate."

"Until recently. Whoever hired those mercenaries certainly found out. Was Engstrom aware of this?" He gestured at the endless row of crates.

"Yes. He was a smart man, but not a particularly honest one. He wanted his name associated with the find once it became public and wasn't averse to a generous payoff for keeping it secret in the interim." She paused for a few heartbeats. "Although after what happened, I figure either

Valenti Nabakov or one of his colleagues would have ensured Engstrom died in an accident once his tour here ended."

Delgado stepped over to the row of machinery. "And this?"

"Not a clue. There's no power source that we can detect, and before you ask, we didn't try shipping one home for analysis. The researchers here — three of them also masquerading as environmental engineers — are still working on identifying their functions."

He studied the first few examples, then wandered over to the nearest side door.

"What's behind these?"

"Thousands and thousands of smaller items, most of which remain a mystery. We sent specimens back to head office." A pause. "How where the mercenaries going to load all of this?"

"Perhaps they didn't know how much there was. Or they planned on taking control of Tyrell so cargo ships could land at leisure. We'll likely never find out. Any obvious weaponry."

"Yes, and we shipped exemplars of those as well." She reached past him and pushed on a knob just like the one on the outer door. It, too, swung aside without requiring more than a light touch. "Go in and see for yourself."

After inspecting half a dozen side rooms and taking readings of each with his battlefield sensor, Delgado made a record of the crystals and the machinery, then said, "I think we're done here, Chief Administrator. Just one more question, though. How did the L'Taung get this down here, and how did they intend to retrieve it?"

"Via what is now the Tyrell Mine. We found this shaft pretty much as it is today when operations were relocated from played-out ore veins a hundred kilometers east of here a few years ago. The L'Taung made sure it looked like a natural borehole, so we suspected nothing until we reached this level and removed a rockslide they purposely left to disguise the access tunnel." She paused as they passed through the door and closed it behind them. "Now I have a question for you. Did the Fleet really buy Tyrell because it wants control over raw material sources, or because it knew about the Second Migration War ammunition depot but not the exact location?"

"I'm sorry. That's a question I cannot answer."

She stared at him for a few moments. "Understood."

# — Forty-Two —

Andreas Bauchan, one of the Secretary General of the Commonwealth's most senior advisers and head of the secretive *Sécurité Spéciale,* raised his head when a tall, striking brunette swept into his formal office inside the ancient Palace of the Stars on the shores of Lake Geneva. She dropped into one of the chairs, stretched out her long legs, and crossed them at the ankle.

"How goes it?"

Warrant Officer Miko Steiger of Naval Intelligence's Special Operations Division, known on Earth as Britta Trulson of the Deep Space Foundation, smiled at Bauchan. They'd become close enough since their first meeting that she enjoyed unfettered access because of a carefully planned scheme to gain the *Sécurité Spéciale*'s confidence by feeding Bauchan verifiable intelligence. He now thought of the Deep Space Foundation as one of his private-sector assets, more reliable than the organized crime and military corporations he relied on to evade the Fleet's unwanted attentions.

The truth, however, was much different. Admiral Talyn had turned the Deep Space Foundation into an undercover Naval Intelligence branch by planting agents among the senior staff and co-opting its information gathering resources.

Rather than smile back as usual — after all, they were more than just business partners — Bauchan grimaced.

"I'm not having a good day, my dear. Two operations, or rather an operation in two parts, failed spectacularly a few days ago. News arrived this morning. We've lost a good agent along with hundreds of auxiliaries and five starships and nothing to show for it."

He tapped his desktop with his fingertips, a gesture Steiger had learned to recognize as a sign of growing irritation, and she remained silent.

"They should have succeeded against the forces in place. The plan was sound. The auxiliaries were among the best and the agent in charge, who vanished and is presumed dead, never failed us before. I can only conclude something critical changed between the time we launched and the actual clash, and that has Rear Admiral Hera Talyn's fingerprints all over it. Her direct action specialists have been a step ahead of us for quite some time. It almost makes one believe in prescience. If anyone has it, she does."

"I'm sorry to hear that. But yes, Talyn is a redoubtable foe, and she employs the best of the Special Forces community to good effect. Perhaps that's what she did in this failed operation — substitute the adversary you were expecting with her deadliest assets once it was too late for a change in plans."

Steiger figured Bauchan's operatives faced her Ghost Squadron friends head-on and lost. They were Talyn's go-to for short-fuse missions ever since Colonel Decker took command. But she couldn't afford the slightest hint of speculation on the matter since Britta Trulson wasn't privy to the inner workings of SOCOM's most dangerous elements.

Bauchan nodded absently, eyes on the antique clock adorning a sideboard, fingers stilled.

"Yes. That is her style. But I can't help wondering whether she's turned one or more of my people or embedded a few of hers in my organization. This latest failure simply adds fodder to the theory she's not just unbelievably fortunate." He turned his hard, soulless gaze on her. "Even a spymaster of Hera Talyn's caliber cannot score so many wins, one after the other, without help. I simply refuse to believe so."

Steiger bit her lower lip in an affected manner she knew he enjoyed. "If I understood more about this failure, perhaps I could find answers for you."

He studied her for a few heartbeats.

"Let us posit a Fleet installation on an airless world operated entirely by contracted civilians, with a Marine Corps company as security. We infiltrated an agent to prepare the way and sent a team of Holy Shadow Warriors to neutralize the defenses so that a three-ship PMC contingent from the Protectorate could seize it. A further two ships crewed by Holy Shadow Warriors were to arrive simultaneously or not long afterward for a separate mission next door to this installation. All failed. The Holy Warriors who didn't die in combat committed suicide as per their creed rather than surrender, while the PMC crews were either killed or surrendered. To a single Marine Corps company. What does that tell you?"

"My best guess is Talyn replaced the garrison with a contingent from the 1st Special Forces Regiment. Which means she had foreknowledge of something. Or perhaps merely a pricking in her thumbs."

Bauchan exhaled, tapping his fingers on the desktop again. "That was our assessment as well. Yet, it bothers me that Talyn knew when to put her pet killers across our path. That question urgently needs an answer."

She held his gaze for a few seconds. "I should think you sprung a leak, darling. Someone privy to your operations who plays for the other side. I'm afraid that sort will be found in any organization, even Talyn's. Perhaps a good house cleaning might be in order."

Steiger figured a useless snipe hunt after a failed operation was what the plan to destabilize the *Sécurité Spéciale* needed. But Bauchan's people getting even that much information on said mission's failure so quickly meant Admiral Talyn faced another round of internal investigations as well, which wasn't good news. However, from reading the files, she knew that the Black Sword purge a few years earlier didn't eliminate every last traitor in the Fleet's ranks.

"Yes." Bauchan looked away once more. "It's so hard to hire reliable help these days, isn't it?" A pause, then he turned his eyes on her again and frowned. "Is your visit purely social, or was there something that couldn't wait until tonight?"

A sudden chill ran up Steiger's spine. Did Bauchan suspect her? His tone and mannerisms were a little off, more than she could attribute to annoyance at the operational failure he mentioned.

"Social, nothing more. I met with the Education Secretary's staff on a Deep Space Foundation proposal for university research grants in psychohistory and thought I'd pop in and say hi before heading back to the office. We haven't seen each other in what? Five days? I simply missed you."

"I was a little preoccupied." He absently tapped his desktop again, eyes sliding back to the clock on the sideboard.

"And you obviously still are." She gave him a fond smile she hoped didn't look forced and stood. "So I'll leave you to it."

Steiger waited for a moment, but Bauchan remained seated instead of coming around the desk to give her the usual hug.

"Until tonight, then." She blew him a kiss, turned on her heels, and left.

As her taxi exited the Palace of the Stars and headed for downtown Geneva and the Deep Space Foundation's offices, she wondered whether Bauchan remembered mentioning an exciting development in the Rim Sector a few weeks ago while they lay in his bed, enjoying a little pillow talk. Though it was in passing, without further details, Steiger informed her Naval Intelligence superiors that something was afoot. Obviously, Admiral Talyn used her warning to good effect if Bauchan's operation failed. His Holy Shadow Warrior mercenaries had enjoyed a string of successes since the *Sécurité Spéciale* first harnessed their fanaticism, and this was, as far as she knew, their first defeat.

Then a thought struck her. Bauchan, like most of his sort, was a superb actor, even though he possessed nothing that might resemble a human soul. Perhaps he nurtured suspicions and was testing her to see if she would be spooked into blowing her cover, maybe via an unexpected recall to the Foundation's home office on Cimmeria. But she'd invested too much time and effort in her mission to run at the first sign of danger.

No, whatever may come, Miko Steiger would remain Britta Trulson, the Deep Space Foundation's liaison with the *Sécurité Spéciale* until the bitter end. Besides, she knew from studying the memorial wall outside the Chief of Naval Intelligence's office that undercover field agents operating alone, especially those who belonged to the Special Operations Division, faced a much higher casualty rate than any other branch of the service. And she'd made her peace with that the moment she signed on.

However, Steiger would embed the code word indicating her cover was potentially blown in her next routine report to the Foundation, from where it would be retransmitted to Fleet HQ by another undercover agent. Perhaps the Admiral might have other intentions for her. Even though Talyn and Bauchan were more alike than either would admit, at least she cared about the people under her command. Bauchan, on the other hand, probably never shed a tear for another human being in his entire life.

By the time she entered the offices she shared with two Foundation staffers from Cimmeria, neither of whom were even remotely connected to Naval Intelligence, and a locally engaged employee who Steiger knew was actually one of Bauchan's agents, she'd regained her equanimity. After all, what was the point in living dangerously if one didn't face the risk of capture and execution by the enemy? A senseless thrill ride?

# — Forty-Three —

"How's business?" Colonel Zachary Thomas Decker dropped into one of the chairs facing his spouse's desk and tossed his beret on the other.

"Booming." Rear Admiral Hera Talyn gave him a fond smile. "What brings you to Sanctum a day early?"

"Jimmy and Kal want to buy me a drink and pick my brains on solutions to certain hiccups they're encountering in building up the division. Throw in the fact I'll spend an extra night with you, and the offer was irresistible. Besides, I think Josh enjoys having me away so he can correct what he believes are my lacuna as a commanding officer."

"He'll get his chance in the hot seat soon enough, honey."

Decker made a face at her. "Already scheming to take the regiment away from me?"

"And what are you doing these days, other than planning and administering with the occasional foray into recreational demolitions on the Fort Arnhem range thrown in?"

Decker sighed. "Nothing exciting. I truly miss the days when you and I were crisscrossing the Commonwealth, sowing terror among our enemies, and taking a righteous sword to those who soiled humanity by their presence."

She chuckled. "How lyrical. But remember, for everything there is a season, and a time for every purpose under heaven."

As she spoke, his eyebrows crept up in genuine surprise. When she finished, he said, "Ecclesiastes. I guess I *have* been rubbing off on you in more than the biblical sense. Nicely done."

She inclined her head. "Why, thank you, my good colonel. I expect the usual reward for diligence when we're in our quarters tonight."

"That's a promise. So, what's new?"

"The prize ship *Harfang* landed the Nexcoyotl PMC prisoners on Parth and is headed for the nearest starbase to be sold, and its crew returned to *Garibaldi*. The prize ship *Faucon* is on its way to rendezvous with *Mikado,* which will take Erinye Company aboard for a new mission." When Decker frowned and gave her a questioning look, she smiled. "No rest for the wicked. They're not coming home just yet, in large part because time and distance make them the best choice rather than send another of your available units."

"Not that there are any idlers at Fort Arnhem these days, but fine. And you would have told me when?"

"Tomorrow. I just received approval from the CNI for a retaliatory strike on the Nexcoyotl principal base of operations in the Protectorate Zone. Best we teach every PMC an object lesson by destroying Nexcoyotl. Otherwise, they might think we're losing our edge."

Decker let out a soft grunt. "I'd be happier if we found out where those Hashashin are hiding. Normal PMCs can be cowed with a few slaps across the head. It's the zealots who scare me. One of these days, they'll be told to crash a starship into an OutWorld capital and kill millions."

"We're working on it, and their time will also come. We do face more immediate problems, however."

"Such as?"

"Miko figures Bauchan is onto her, probably because we foiled his plans so comprehensively. Concurrently, we could also have a mole somewhere around here if Bauchan found out about the ammunition depot not long after we did."

"You're leaving her on Earth?"

Talyn nodded. "There's no other choice at the moment. If she climbs aboard a starship, Bauchan will take her in and see if they can interrogate her despite the fact she's conditioned. They may share a bed from time to time, and Bauchan may even be inadvertently feeding her real intel during their post-coital moments of bliss, but he's as incapable of sentiment as any good spymaster."

"Then we should be on the lookout for false intel designed to blow Miko's cover."

She nodded again. "That's already being taken into consideration. And keep in mind, Miko is just as expendable as we were in the day."

"I know. And so does Miko, but no one wants to see a comrade die in a fetid dungeon from a drug-induced cardiac arrest, her body tossed in an incinerator and her ashes thrown out with the garbage. We Marines can be quite sentimental about proper burials with military honors." He glanced at the clock on Talyn's desk. "And that being said, how about you buy me lunch at the Officer's Mess? I'm not due to meet with Jimmy and Kal until fourteen hundred."

"You just enjoy making heads turn when the most infamous married couple in Sanctum enters."

He gave her a broad grin. "Yep."

**

"Well, well, well. Guess what just showed up on my hangar deck — reams of ragged refugees from a backwater outpost." The Q ship *Mikado*'s captain, Commander Sandor Piech, a compact, square-faced officer with gray hair and a gray beard, stuck out his hand after returning Delgado's salute and granting permission for Erinye Company to come aboard. "How are you doing, Curtis?"

"Same old, same old, sir. I gather you received new mission orders for me?"

"Indeed. And from our beloved black ops employer. We're headed for our favorite hunting grounds in the Protectorate again to terminate a mercenary outfit called Nexcoyotl whose HQ is on Galadiman."

A lazy grin lit up Delgado's features. "What a coincidence. We took three sloops and inflicted a few hundred casualties on a Nexcoyotl raiding force recently. I guess HQ wants us to finish the job as an example of why PMCs should never accept contracts putting them in direct conflict with the Fleet."

"Sounds like you enjoyed good times wherever that was."

"Buy me a coffee, and I'll fill you in once we're FTL."

"Deal."

"I hope you're stocked up on my kind of ammo because we pretty much used up our first line."

"Ammo, dropships, rations, rods from God, you name it, we carry it. They keep us ready for your lot at all times nowadays. Another innovation that no doubt comes from our favorite employer. I trust you remember where the barracks are and don't need hand-holding?"

"Sure." Delgado glanced at Hak, who was mustering the company in front of *Mikado*'s shuttles and made the go-ahead hand signal.

"Then I'll see us off. Come to my day cabin after we jump."

**

"Sir?"

Andreas Bauchan, who'd been staring out at a leaden Lake Geneva beneath a dull, gray carpet of cloud obscuring the surrounding mountain peaks, turned away from the window.

"What is it?" Bauchan gestured at his chief of staff to take a seat.

"We received a message from our station chief on Galadiman just now, sir. I'm afraid it's not good news. Approximately thirty-six hours ago, an unknown military force raided the Nexcoyotl PMC headquarters. They destroyed four sloops on the ground, a dozen armed shuttles, and the company's armory. As well, they ransacked the offices, took any documentation and computer cores they could find, and the funds and precious metals stored in the vault. Since the raid occurred during the middle of the night, Nexcoyotl suffered few casualties, but it is effectively finished as a PMC."

"How many ships were on various contracts when this happened?"

"Three, but they no longer have a home base nor money to pay for supplies, fuel, parts, and salaries. Although we don't know yet, I'm sure we'll find Nexcoyotl's various bank accounts drained by unknown parties, but probably Naval Intelligence."

Bauchan carefully took his chair and sat back, schooling himself to seem unworried as he gazed at his chief of staff.

"Then we shall strike Nexcoyotl from our list of assets and engage a suitable replacement."

"Yes, sir." A pause. "It was the Fleet, of course, using a Q ship and Special Forces operators. We've seen this pattern before."

"Without a doubt — retribution for Tyrell. Was there anything else?"

The chief of staff shook his head. "No."

"Thank you."

When he was alone once more, Bauchan turned his chair to face the window and stared back out at the lake. He wasn't the sort who'd wonder whether he overreached, whether the dual operation, one long in planning, the second hastily added on top, should never have been attempted. Nor, to his surprise, did he feel any genuine anger.

The raid on Nexcoyotl was obviously a warning from Hera Talyn, aimed at him and the PMC community in general. It would make hiring ordinary mercenaries for operations that might anger the Fleet more difficult. Fortunately, the Holy Shadow Warriors — he privately thought it a ridiculous name, and much preferred what the fleet called them, Hashashin — were coming into their own, now that he'd arranged for steady funding to buy ships and weapons. Even recruitment seemed amazingly good, despite the fact those who signed up knew they would probably die in the service of their deity sooner rather than later. Perhaps he should see about sending their best assassins to kill Talyn. However, Bauchan understood that in doing so, he would likely sign his own death warrant, and one day face her husband, the redoubtable Colonel Zachary Thomas Decker.

And that left Britta Trulson as the only remaining question mark. Since the beginning, his closest advisers had been leery about her, one of them even quoting Virgil, *timeo Danaos et dona ferentes* — fear the Danaans even when bearing gifts. Or, in this case, the Deep Space Foundation's envoy to Earth. Yet so far, she'd given them nothing but solid intelligence and advice, and she'd passed every test he set her since news of the Tyrell disaster reached his ears.

Bauchan glanced at the antique clock on the sideboard and stood, adjusting his hand-tailored jacket. It was almost time for his weekly briefing to the Secretary General of the Commonwealth, a man increasingly nervous about unrest in the OutWorlds and colonies and the Fleet's growing resistance to direction from Earth. Telling him of this latest outrage would only make the man more desperate for a solution to regain control, even as it inexorably slipped through his fingers.

Perhaps he would search for a way of terminating Hera Talyn after all with, as she liked to say, extreme prejudice. She, Larsson, and every other senior officer were in contempt of the Commonwealth government. A purge. Yes. Bauchan smiled at his reflection in the mirror above the fireplace, then strode out of his office with the confidence of a man determined he would triumph over his enemies and not, as they no doubt wished, die like the rest.

# About the Author

Eric Thomson is the pen name of a retired Canadian soldier who spent more time in uniform than he expected, both in the Regular Army and the Army Reserve. He spent his Regular Army career in the Infantry and his Reserve service in the Armoured Corps.

Eric has been a voracious reader of science fiction, military fiction, and history all his life. Several years ago, he put fingers to keyboard and started writing his own military sci-fi, with a definite space opera slant, using many of his own experiences as a soldier for inspiration.

When he's not writing fiction, Eric indulges in his other passions: photography, hiking, and scuba diving, all of which he shares with his wife.

Join Eric Thomson at http://www.thomsonfiction.ca/
Where you'll find news about upcoming books and more information about the universe in which his heroes fight for humanity's survival.

Read his blog at https://ericthomsonblog.wordpress.com

If you enjoyed this book, please consider leaving a review with your favorite online retailer to help others discover it.

# Also by Eric Thomson

## Siobhan Dunmoore
No Honor in Death (Siobhan Dunmoore Book 1)
The Path of Duty (Siobhan Dunmoore Book 2)
Like Stars in Heaven (Siobhan Dunmoore Book 3)
Victory's Bright Dawn (Siobhan Dunmoore Book 4)
Without Mercy (Siobhan Dunmoore Book 5)
When the Guns Roar (Siobhan Dunmoore Book 6)
A Dark and Dirty War (Siobhan Dunmoore Book 7)

## Decker's War
Death Comes But Once (Decker's War Book 1)
Cold Comfort (Decker's War Book 2)
Fatal Blade (Decker's War Book 3)
Howling Stars (Decker's War Book 4)
Black Sword (Decker's War Book 5)
No Remorse (Decker's War Book 6)
Hard Strike (Decker's War Book 7)

## Constabulary Casefiles
The Warrior's Knife
A Colonial Murder

## Ashes of Empire
Imperial Sunset (Ashes of Empire 1)
Imperial Twilight (Ashes of Empire 2)
Imperial Night (Ashes of Empire 3)
Imperial Echoes (Ashes of Empire 4)

## Ghost Squadron
We Dare - Ghost Squadron No. 1
Deadly Intent - Ghost Squadron No. 2
Die Like the Rest – Ghost Squadron No. 3

CPSIA information can be obtained
at www.ICGtesting.com
Printed in the USA
BVHW020150250723
667765BV00003B/28

9 781989 314432